CW00972050

In a World of Lies, I Fell into an Unforgettable Love

Misaki Ichijo

In a World of Lies, I Fell into an Unforgettable Love

Misaki Ichijo

Translation by Yui Kajita
Cover photo by Koichi

Yen On
150 West 30th Street, 19th Floor
New York, NY 10001

Visit us at yenpress.com • facebook.com/yenpress • twitter.com/yenpress
yenpress.tumblr.com • instagram.com/yenpress

First Yen On Edition: November 2024
Edited by Yen On Editorial: Christopher Fox, Anna Powers
Designed by Yen Press Design: Wendy Chan

Yen On is an imprint of Yen Press, LLC.
The Yen On name and logo are trademarks of Yen Press, LLC.

Library of Congress Cataloging-in-Publication Data
Names: Ichijo, Misaki, author. | Kajita, Yui, translator.
Title: In a world of lies, i fell into an unforgettable love / Misaki Ichijo ; translation by Yui Kajita.
Other titles: Uso no sekai de, wasurerarenai koi o shita. English
Description: First Yen On edition. | New York, NY : Yen On, 2024.
Identifiers: LCCN 2024033361 | ISBN 9798855400373 (hardcover)
Subjects: CYAC: Terminally ill—Fiction. | Love—Fiction. | Friendship—Fiction. | High schools—Fiction. | Schools—Fiction. | Clubs—Fiction. | LCGFT: Romance fiction. | Light novels.
Classification: LCC PZ7.1.I15 In 2024 | DDC [Fic]—dc23
LC record available at https://lccn.loc.gov/2024033361

ISBNs: 979-8-8554-0037-3 (hardcover)
979-8-8554-0038-0 (ebook)

10 9 8 7 6 5 4 3 2 1

LSC-C

Printed in the United States of America

CONTENTS

Scene 1. Makoto Tsukishima 001

Scene 2. Aoi Hayami 087

Scene 3. Tsubasa Minami 127

Scene 4. You Don't Know How Much Time I Have Left to Live 173

Scene 5. I Don't Know How Much Time You Have Left to Live 211

Scene 6. A Light from the Past 249

There are 365 days in a year—8,760 hours.

It sounds like a lot, but I can't really picture it. Those numbers feel too distant for me to wrap my head around, like death or love. I guess breaking things down doesn't always make them easier to understand.

Still, I can't help myself, so I try converting it into seconds.

31,536,000 seconds. Now the time really does lose all meaning, too abstract to make any sense of.

Yet this is the amount of time I've been given. The measure of my life.

What should I do with the time I have left? What *can* I do?

I probably won't be able to use it for anything; I've got nothing I want to achieve, nothing to overcome.

All I have is a wish. I might not even have a full year left to live—but I at least want to tell the person I like how I feel about her.

Scene 1.

Makoto Tsukishima

1

It was March, the end of my first year in senior high school, when I found out how long I had left to live. Winter was just giving way to spring, and even the earliest cherry blossoms had barely taken their first peek at the sky.

I used to get sick all the time when I was little; that was just the way I was born. My fever would shoot right up, and even on the days I was well enough to go to elementary school, I'd often end up at the nurse's office. Then, a little while after starting junior high school, my condition started to improve. I still got a fever sometimes, but even I was surprised at how normal I felt. My body was finally mine.

In my first year of senior high school, my health stayed stable, and my bouts of illness were gradually becoming a thing of the past. I was just starting to hope that I might be able to keep my health up the following year and maybe even further down the line—but then I got a call from the hospital. I'd gotten a checkup there in addition to the health checks they do at school, and they wanted to talk to me about the results. I hadn't noticed anything wrong in particular, but I'd come down with a few colds over the winter, so I'd been worried my immune system was getting weaker.

The doctor asked my parents to come with me to the hospital. Dad's tall, and he's the most cheerful guy you'll ever meet—a stark contrast to me, who's average height and something of an introvert. While we were sitting in the waiting room, he tried to lift my spirits, saying things like "Don't worry, buddy. I'm sure it's nothing serious." Mom chimed in encouragingly, too.

Dad's good cheer and Mom's kindness had gotten me through rough water countless times in the past, so I was convinced I'd find a way to get through whatever the issue here might be. I tried being optimistic, telling myself that just getting a call from the hospital wasn't a big deal.

But things weren't so simple.

"With this disease, it's best to assume that you have one year left to live."

That was what the doctor told us in the consultation room after a complicated explanation about my test results.

"Oh..." I didn't feel even a tiny bit sad—mostly just shocked and confused. My parents were, too. They hadn't seen this coming any more than I had.

My doctor went on with a grave expression. We wouldn't have to worry about things like medical bills, because what I had was one of the rare diseases recognized by the government as a subject of special research. It was also a rule that doctors who detected this illness were required to notify their patients as early as possible, which is why she was telling us this now. She informed us about lots of other things, like how the disease would progress and how costs would be covered by insurance, and asked my parents to set up another appointment in the near future to go over it in more detail. She also promised to do everything in her power to prolong my lifespan.

Even though I was at the center of this, I felt like I was listening to a story about some stranger. My mind was completely blank from the shock, and I struggled to connect their conversation to myself.

I guess I wasn't the only one feeling this way. When I glanced at Dad, he looked dazed, and Mom was staring mutely at the floor. None of us could either comprehend or accept the reality. Once the doctor had finished her explanation, she asked me to wait outside while she spoke to my parents. After a little while, Mom and Dad came out, too. We paid the bill at reception, then walked back to the car without uttering a word.

Numb silence filled the car. I don't know how long it lasted before Dad eventually spoke.

"I was thinking...why don't we go see another doctor?"

"Huh?" I blurted out in surprise.

"Yes," Mom agreed. "We need a second opinion—otherwise, we can't be sure."

I was shy to tell them to their faces, but I really respected my parents. They've always cared for me, put me and my illness first, and made sure I had everything I could ever need. They're both kind people, and even though they can sometimes be *too* kind, I admire them both from the bottom of my heart. But right now, even my gentle parents were refusing to accept the reality of the situation and were trying to fight back against it.

After some discussion, we decided to ignore what we'd just been told and consult a specialist. It was possible there had been some kind of mistake. It could be something less serious.

"All right, now that we've got a plan, let's go have a treat for lunch," Dad said as he started the car, putting on a brave face. If I were him, my voice might've trembled, but Dad wasn't like that. He drove out of the hospital parking lot.

Even at that point, though, I think we all knew deep down that it hadn't been a misdiagnosis. We were just desperate to look away from the truth, at least for the time being.

On another day, we went to a different hospital. After a long examination, they gave me the same diagnosis.

Mom and Dad still didn't give up. And neither did I.

We went to yet another hospital. Same result. Apparently, it was a difficult disease to treat with current medical care. They said once I reached the halfway stage, I would start losing consciousness with increasing frequency, and that it would eventually end in death.

Back then, when we were going around from one hospital to another for more tests, it was hard on all of us. On Dad, with his trademark high spirits, and on Mom, with her wisdom and kindness. We experienced grief, despair, and a whole range of other emotions. Each of us had a silent lake of loneliness seeping into our hearts. And the source of that lake was me—the fact that I might have a disease that gave me only one more year to live. We wept, we laughed, we screamed; there was so much going on back then.

But in the midst of all that confusion, we managed to settle on a few things:

We would accept the reality of the disease. We wouldn't force ourselves to act cheerful, but we wouldn't suppress our joy, either; we'd laugh when we wanted to laugh and cry when we wanted to cry. And we'd never lose hope.

Once we agreed on that, we went back to the first hospital. We talked to the same doctor, and since she assured us that should anything happen, they would do their utmost to take care of us, we decided to cooperate with their research of the disease as well.

Nearly a whole month had slipped away by that time, and spring break was just around the corner.

I'd developed two new habits by then. One was writing in my "dark notebook"—a place for me to spew out my sadness and struggles and everything else I couldn't possibly share with anyone. What I wrote in there was top secret.

The other was a bit more upbeat: keeping track of all the things I wanted to do in a "bucket list notebook." I'd seen people make lists like this in movies and books, but I'd never thought that I might write one myself. It was useful for organizing my thoughts, though, so I used it to write down everything I wanted to do, assuming that I really did have only one year left. And my plan was to put it into action, starting from spring break.

For the first time in my life, I went on a solo trip. Being away from my family made me realize all over again just how important they were to me, and looking at the sights I'd gone all that way to see, I learned something new about myself: that simply looking at scenery didn't impress me so much.

I went around by myself, calmly ticking items off my list one by one at my own pace. I went to a neighboring town to eat ramen that was expensive for a high schooler; I took out my savings and bought a whole set of manga; I bought the cool sneakers I'd had my eyes on.

You'd think there's no limit to human desire, but there is. If you rule out the craziest ideas and the ones that are obviously impossible, you eventually hit a wall.

There was one thing I'd written down early on, but I still hadn't mustered up the courage to do it:

Tell Tsubasa Minami how I feel

By now, it was already mid-May. Spring break was over, my second year of senior high had begun, and the Golden Week holiday had whizzed by.

I was never the type to have a huge number of friends, but I did have some. I distanced myself from them in the new school year, though, since I didn't want to drag them into inevitable misery when my life ended. I didn't make new friends, either, just kept to myself.

Nevertheless, that crucial wish on my bucket list remained: *Tell Tsubasa Minami how I feel.*

Minami and I had been in the same class in first year, which was how I'd met her. She always had a smile on her face and was bubbling with energy—to me, she was dazzling, brimming with life itself. Her entire being seemed effused with a healthy, wholesome glow.

I guess I admired her partly because she had something I didn't. Come to think of it, I'd always liked people who were the complete opposite of me—healthy and bright—ever since I was in elementary school.

It wasn't like I wanted to go out with Minami, though. That was too much to hope for. Besides, I was trying to stay away from people as much as possible. My wish had nothing to do with having a relationship with her. I just wanted to tell her how I felt—that was all.

I had to avoid making it feel too formal; I didn't want to write her a letter or ask her to come meet me somewhere. I had to tell her in a more casual, everyday setting.

One day, after school, I was standing in the hallway pondering over how to go about it when Minami herself called out to me.

"Hi, Tsukishima. Haven't seen you in a while. What're you staring at the sky for?"

"Huh?" I was shocked. We hadn't said a word to one another since we got split into different classes for second year, yet here she was, just as I was trying to figure out how to tell her how I felt. "Oh, uh... Hey. It's been a while. No reason in particular."

"Oh yeah? Anyway, it really has been ages. How've you been?" she said with a smile. She was nice to everyone. Her short hair swayed a little as she tilted her head; it was a great style for her.

Luckily for me, there was no one around. I hadn't planned on it at all, but this was definitely my chance. I tried my best to keep my cool and sound as casual as possible. "Uh, pretty good. What about you?"

"I guess I'm good, except for my scores on those mini exams we did. I was just staying behind after class going over stuff, but I keep getting stuck on math."

She was the kind of person who could strike up a conversation with anyone, so it wasn't hard to keep the ball rolling. Eventually, the discussion turned to how we had ended up in different classes this year, and we filled each other in on what we'd been up to lately.

Should I tell her now? What should I say exactly?

I almost got cold feet, but I psyched myself up. Even if you hesitate, the world moves on. That was especially true for me, since my time was likely a lot more limited than most people's. As I spurred myself on with these thoughts, I concentrated on what I was going to say and was so preoccupied that I'd completely lost track of the conversation.

"Oh, speaking of," Minami was saying, "I started a club for movies—"

"Hey, so…," I cut in. It was abrupt, but I wasn't going to get a better chance than this.

"Hmm?"

I put on an awkward smile so I wouldn't sound too serious. "To tell you the truth, I like you, Minami. Uh, but it's not like I want to go out with you—more like I'm a fan… Um, like, that time in first year…" I'd mentally prepared myself for this, but I just couldn't seem to find the words. I wish I'd been able to explain exactly what it was that attracted me to her.

"What? Really?" she asked, taken aback.

"Y-yeah."

"But you don't want to go out with me? How come?" She looked genuinely curious. And no wonder—whether or not she had any feelings for me, it was a puzzling thing to hear after a confession.

"Oh, well, you know… I'm happy enough just seeing you from afar." I bumbled through an excuse since I couldn't say anything about my illness.

Minami let out a *pfft*, then burst out laughing. "Like watching a rare bird?"

"No, not like that."

"Sorry, just kidding. I mean, it's pretty rare to have someone tell you to your face that they like you, so I guess you caught me off guard... But I don't know, it really made me happy. Thank you."

Minami's smile lit up with a soft glow. I thought it had been worth mustering up my courage just to see that expression. I wanted to stay with her a bit longer, but it felt awkward standing around after what I'd told her. So instead I said, "Well, um, see you later," and took off.

"Oh, yeah. See you," she replied, waving to me.

My confession had come out of the blue, and I hadn't been able to explain the whole of it, like how much I liked her personality. But it would have been weird to go back and tell her all over again, and I didn't want to bother her. What I'd said wasn't perfect, but it was good enough...

2

I still felt a twinge of regret the next morning, but I went about the school day as usual, looking out for things I wanted to do. While changing classrooms, I saw Minami walking with her good friend Hayami. Minami's eyes met mine. She smiled and raised a hand, and I returned her greeting in surprise.

"Who's that?" Hayami asked her.

"Tsukishima—we were in the same class last year."

Though I was close enough to hear them, I didn't go over to talk. We were headed in different directions, so we just kept going.

The two of them were walking down a path bathed in sunlight; I was going down a path in the shadows. I'd been looking for more things I wanted to do, but I was almost out of ideas. My only remaining wish was to be as kind to others as possible and to live peacefully until my fate caught up with me. And with the way things were, keeping my distance was the best way I knew to be kind to those around me.

Still, there were some people I saw at least a little: one of them was the school nurse. My parents and I had informed the school about my illness at the beginning of this school year. We asked them not to let any of the students know, and they respected our choice. I met with her to talk over it, too, just in case something happened while I was at school.

She was in her late twenties and somewhat eccentric. She said she used to be in the drama club back when she was in school. Frank but reliable, she looked out for me, and at her request, I stopped by her office at least once a week after school to chat about all sorts of stuff.

"So, how are things lately? Anything new?" the nurse asked. She'd made me a cup of coffee, and it was nice to feel the warmth coming through the mug.

"Nothing much. Just the usual," I said.

"Are you still trying to stay away from everyone?"

"Well, yeah. Pretty much."

"Because you don't want to make anyone sad?"

"It sounds corny and cheesy when you say that out loud, so could you please give it a rest already?" I said with a wry smile.

It didn't really bother me, though, and the nurse gave a chuckle. It had already been more than a month since we'd started our weekly meetings.

"Okay, then. Do you want to hear something else that's corny and cheesy?" she asked.

"As long as it's not something else I've said in the past."

"'I don't think you'll find what you're looking for in solitude.'"

I looked up at her, startled. After a moment's hesitation, I asked, "What do you mean by that?"

"It's a line from a play I did when I was an undergrad."

"Huh. What was it about?"

"A young boy who chose to cut himself off from others ends up finding love."

"Sounds dramatic."

"You think so? I thought it was a pretty ordinary, run-of-the-mill story."

I could sense that she was trying to tell me something, but I just stared at the mug in my hand. My face was reflected in the coffee.

"I respect how you choose to live your life, Tsukishima, but I don't think you have to go out of your way to avoid people."

"Okay."

"Are you listening to me?"

"Sort of."

"You think I'm a pesky, preachy auntie, don't you?"

"More like a nice, preachy sister."

The nurse shot me a skeptical look, then let out a sigh. "You're better off dishing out those sorts of compliments to a cute girl in your class instead. Don't you have a crush on anyone?"

"I dunno..."

Minami's face flashed in my head, but I'd completely given up hope of ever having a relationship with her. Maybe what I felt was less resignation than a sense of having accomplished my mission already. My feelings were settled, and nothing was going to change that. Or, at least, that was what I'd told myself.

I spent that weekend alone, as usual, not having found anything to add to my bucket list.

I bought a new video game and tried it out, but I stopped playing midway through, wondering whether this was what I really wanted to do.

Monday came around, and I passed my time at school as I always did.

It might sound silly, but I looked forward to the time in between classes when I would walk from one classroom to another; there was always a chance I might run into Minami somewhere. Just as I was thinking about her, I spotted her near the library. Hayami was with her, too, along with two other girls I didn't know, and the four of them were discussing something with worried looks across their faces.

This time, I didn't catch Minami's eye. I didn't approach her, either.

...When did this start? When did I become so acutely aware of her presence? This new part of me had appeared without warning. Whenever I saw Minami, something squeezed my heart tight, and I would see a glow in the air around her. Everything about her felt special to me.

After school that day, I dropped by the nurse's office; there was no set rule about which days of the week I went to see her. She made me a cup of coffee, just like she always did. Though she made it from a bag of ground coffee rather than beans, she brewed it with care, and it gave off a pleasant aroma.

"So, have you found a crush yet?" she teased, handing me a cup.

"Please, give me a break."

She laughed. Then her expression changed, as though she'd noticed something. "You look even more lifeless than usual. What's up?"

"You don't have to say 'even more than usual.'"

"Sorry." She smiled.

Of course, I knew she didn't mean any harm; she wasn't the kind of person who would hurt someone with thoughtless comments. She never said anything just for the sake of talking, and she always cared about the feelings of the person she was speaking to. I had the same respect for her as I did for my parents. Maybe that was why I found it so easy to reveal my innermost feelings to her.

"Actually…I've pretty much run out of things I want to do."

"You mean that list you were telling me about?"

"Yeah. I managed to do the thing I thought was going to be the hardest…and now I'm wondering what else to do."

"How about falling in love?"

"Uh…don't you think that's kinda girly?"

"Being in love is one of the best ways to connect with people."

I had no idea how to respond to that.

"This might sound a little selfish…," the nurse went on. "But even if you stick to your wish, you still have time, you know. Enough time to get close to someone, and also to distance yourself from them."

I stared at her in surprise. I hadn't thought about it like that.

"It's a bit of a backward way of going about things," she said with a grin. "But you can decide when to end it yourself. So why not take the leap if there's something, or someone, you want to pursue?"

Minami's dazzling presence crossed my mind. I longed to know more about her, to talk to her, to laugh with her while we looked into each other's eyes... Embarrassed, I looked away from the nurse, focusing on the door of the office instead—but just then, it opened.

Life can be really cruel sometimes. I say this from experience.

But at the same time...

Life can also take you by surprise in a good way.

"Hi, is anyone here?"

I caught my breath. By some twist of fate, it was Minami who'd come into the office.

School is a mysterious place. Your crush is there, somewhere, and when you happen to catch sight of them, you feel a sweet tug at your heart.

"Huh? Tsukishima?" Minami said, clearly surprised to see me.

"Uh, hi," I replied.

"Oh, you're drinking coffee? Nice. Did the nurse make it for you?"

"Yeah. Something like that." Inside, I was flustered by Minami's sudden appearance, but I somehow managed to sound normal.

The nurse turned to Minami, all gravity in her voice from our earlier conversation gone. "What is it, Minami? Did someone get hurt?"

"Oh, no, everything's fine. I just wanted to ask you if you could put this up on the notice board here," Minami said, holding up a sheet of paper. It had a quirky advert printed on it in large letters: WANTED: AN ORDINARY MALE.

Apparently, the nurse knew what it meant. "Let me guess: for your filmmaking club?"

"Exactly," Minami said. "Aoi drove away the guy who was going to play the leading role, so we're looking for someone else."

"Aoi—you mean Hayami, your vice president? What happened? He didn't try to do anything weird to her, did he?" the nurse asked.

"Well, no… She just thought he was an insincere, immoral kind of person…"

"Immoral?"

"And she said his acting was over-the-top, even though he's in the drama club."

"Whew, she doesn't hold back, does she? But, well, I guess you've got to be like that if you're serious about making films."

The conversation seemed to make perfect sense to Minami and the nurse, but I had no clue what was going on. Hayami was the girl I saw walking with Minami the other day who was in the same class as her. Hayami was a bit of a celebrity among students in our year—known for her beautiful looks and elegant, sylphlike eyes—but since she exuded a *don't-talk-to-me* aura, most people didn't talk to her. But she and Minami seemed to be close.

Noticing my confusion, the nurse said, "Ah, that's right. It didn't exist back when they did the school club intros at the start of spring, so I guess you haven't heard about it. Minami and her childhood friend Hayami started a filmmaking club last month. Didn't you say you have four members so far, including the first-years? All girls, right?"

"Yep, that's right. The four of us used to make films together in junior high, too."

"Ah, I saw the one you made," the nurse said. "All the teachers were talking about it. It won some kind of award, didn't it? I remember the vice principal getting really excited—he thought it'd be great press for the school."

"He asked us to make a promo for the school last month."

"I heard. He was happy with how it turned out. Thanks to that, the school approved your new club without a fuss, so it was worth it in the end, right? You're lucky they allocated club funds *and* a clubroom for you when you've only just started."

"I think so, too. It's a big help," Minami said.

In first year, Minami hadn't belonged to any after-school club, just like me. I had no idea she'd started one herself this year—and a club for *making films*, on top of that. I was impressed.

"Hmm." Minami turned to look at me. "Didn't I tell you about the club the other day, Tsukishima?"

"You did?" I mumbled.

"Um, you know. That time after school, in the hallway."

"In the hallway… Ah, sorry about that. I guess I was too focused on other things and missed what you were saying."

"Well, you did look super nervous." We both smiled weakly, recalling the scene.

The nurse was watching us with an eyebrow raised, and

when my eyes met hers, she flashed me a cheeky grin. She saw right through me. I don't know if it was because she had a lot of life experience, but she was really good at noticing things like that.

"So, Minami, what was it you asked about for the film club?" The nurse jumped in, her voice deliberately upbeat. "You wanted to put up a poster?"

"Ah, yes, please. This is it; I thought it needed to make a strong impact, since we're looking for the lead actor. Can I put it up here?"

"Sure. By the way, what kind of guy are you looking for? Someone 'ordinary'?"

"That's right. We want to submit our work for a summer film festival, so we're hoping to start filming straightaway. There's not much to it—he just needs to be a normal guy. We don't want anyone who draws too much attention, since Aoi wouldn't like that, and preferably not someone already in another club. He doesn't have to have any acting experience, but ideally he'd be around five foot seven, on the paler side because it shows up well on-screen, and sincere..."

As she listed off the qualities she was looking for, Minami started staring at me as though something had just dawned on her. It wasn't just Minami; the nurse, too, was looking at me in surprise. The room fell silent. I didn't know what to do with all the attention.

"Uh, what is it? Um...why are you both staring at me...?"

The nurse gave me a pat on the shoulder.

"Go for it. Then, it's settled." There was something compelling about her grin that wouldn't take no for an answer.

3

"So, that's the story. Tsukishima's joining us with the nurse's recommendation. Let's welcome him with a round of applause!"

Only about fifteen minutes after our encounter at the nurse's office, I was standing in the classroom allocated to the film-making club on the third floor of the clubrooms building. With three girls sitting in front of me, my face was fixed in a nervous smile.

It was my first time seeing the headquarters of the filmmaking club. Tripods and other equipment were arranged neatly in the room, and a rack stood in one corner where smartphones and other electronics were charging. There was one desk with a laptop—presumably for editing footage—and four desks had been placed together in the center of the room, around which the three other club members were now seated.

No one clapped.

Hayami was eyeing me suspiciously. Something about it was extremely intimidating. One of the other club members, a smallish girl with the ribbon of a first-year student pinned to her uniform, was glancing around at everyone, startled by the news. I got the impression that she was a conscientious, good-natured kind of person. In contrast, the other first year with long hair was just watching me with what seemed like mild curiosity. Honestly, I couldn't really tell what was going through her head.

When the nurse had told me to "go for it," I'd tried to protest, not wanting to get involved in anything too complicated. "*Uh, what are you talking about?"* I'd asked. *"There's no way I can star in a movie."*

"It's not a good idea to make up your mind before you even try something. Don't you agree, Minami?"

Understandably, I'd assumed that Minami wouldn't want to make a movie with the guy who'd told her he had a crush on her just the other day. But to my surprise, she seemed to be seriously considering it.

After thinking for a while, Minami said, *"That might work, actually. Tsukishima has a sanitary feel about him."*

"What? Wait, what do you mean 'sanitary'? Like I'm clean and tidy?" I was totally out of my depth.

"You can act like you're the clean type, but you can't fake being sanitary—it's like when the way someone lives feels pure and honest. My favorite novelist, Keiko Nishikawa, says she keeps that in mind when she's writing."

"Sorry, but I don't really get it," I told her.

"That's exactly what I'm talking about. That regular-guy confusion," Minami said excitedly, as if it were already a done deal that I was going to be in the movie. *"Well, what are we waiting for? Let's go to the clubroom. Can I borrow Tsukishima, Teach?"*

"Go right ahead," the nurse replied. *"And feel free not to return him."*

"Hey, I'm not some rental DVD. Wait, are we really going?"

And just like that, Minami had half pushed me to the clubroom, where I'd found myself under Hayami's death stare like I was some shady intruder.

"Hey, Tsubasa, how about we make another movie with just the four of us?" Hayami suggested, addressing Minami. "I can rewrite the script."

"Remember what we all decided on?" Minami said. "We said we'd go with a straightforward concept so we can get an award at the indie film festival. You know we need a guy for that."

"We can still make it work if you play the lead, Tsubasa—you can be the director and act at the same time. It's not like we *need* a guy in it."

"So we're switching to a story about friendship between girls? That won't match the theme of this year's competition, though."

Minami and Hayami were having a serious debate, but they were still forgetting about one crucial detail: I was only there because Minami had dragged me along. I hadn't even agreed to act in their movie yet, but apparently, that didn't matter at all to them.

"Why are you so against bringing a guy in anyway?" Minami asked Hayami. "You were fine with it when you wrote the script."

"Well, I thought it might be a good idea at first, but then pretty much all the guys who volunteered were after you or Ena—not here for the movie. I'm just sick of it."

"Tsukishima isn't like that."

"Oh yeah? We'll see about that."

I wanted to jump in and clarify, even though it might have made me seem a bit ridiculous. However, before I could say that I never volunteered in the first place, Hayami turned her eyes back on me.

"Hey. What's your name again? Tsukishima?"

"Uh, yeah, that's right."

"Why are you so nervous?"

"I think it's pretty normal to be nervous when someone's glaring at you," I admitted honestly.

Hayami frowned and let out a deep sigh. "Look. I know this might be annoying, and it's rude of me to ask, but could you just tell me you're not here for Tsubasa Minami?"

"Um, what for?"

"Just say it."

"Uh… I'm not here for Tsubasa Minami."

"Do you really mean it?"

"Uh, well—"

"Answer me."

"It's true. I mean…it's not like I have a motive or anything." I was a bit confused by the whole situation, but it was fair to say that I had no ulterior motives.

Hayami stared at me, and after a little while, a look of mild surprise crossed her face. "Huh. You're actually…telling the truth?"

I didn't know what had convinced her, but I felt relieved. "Um, sorry. But I haven't even agreed to be in the movie yet."

"Huh? What's he talking about, Tsubasa?"

"Uhh, sorry. I forgot to fill you in on that part. I ran into Tsukishima when I went to ask the nurse for permission to put up the poster. I explained that we were looking for an actor, and the nurse suggested I take him with me."

"So you just dragged him over here? Poor guy. You should let him go back," Hayami said with a sigh. I remembered the nurse saying that the two of them had been friends since childhood, and I felt like I'd gotten a glimpse into their relationship: the happy-go-lucky, freewheeling Minami, who leaped into things on impulse and the reliable, levelheaded Hayami, who had to rein her in. I still wasn't sure what I should do, though.

"By the way, Tsukishima. What do you think of movies?" Minami asked.

"Uh, what do you mean...?"

"Like, are you interested in them?"

"Well...I like watching them as much as anyone else does, but I've never thought about being in one myself." Minami and I were standing side by side, our shoulders almost touching. My heart was racing, but when I averted my eyes, she placed a hand on my shoulder.

"Don't worry. Everyone gets nervous at first."

"Uh, but—"

"You'll get used to it in no time."

"No, I—"

"Once you get started, you'll see how much fun it is. You'll be totally hooked."

"Wait, what?"

"Tsubasa, let him go. I don't want to watch my childhood friend harass some guy," Hayami grumbled.

Both here and in the nurse's office, something about Minami seemed different. It was as if she was even more carefree than usual—maybe even a little *too* free...

"I can't quite put my finger on it, but has your personality changed a little?" I couldn't help but ask.

"Huh?" Minami's brows arched up in surprise. "Uhh, yeah, I guess you could say that. Aoi always calls me a film freak, you know. When it comes to movies, I get a bit—well, maybe *quite* a bit crazy."

"'Quite a bit'? You're a *lot* weirder than everyone thinks

you are," Hayami chipped in wearily, and Minami burst out laughing.

I'd been in the same class as Minami last year, but this was the first time I'd ever seen her like this. It made me want to see more sides to her that I'd never known about. Joining her filmmaking club was a whole different story, though; for one thing, I could never take on the leading role in a movie. It was just not possible. I knew I'd only mess things up.

Besides, if I got involved with someone, I would only end up making them sad with my eventual, likely inevitable death. Even if we weren't especially close, it would still be tough for them to lose someone in their life. That was why I had to distance myself from everyone as much as possible. I was convinced it was the right thing to do.

Unsure of what to say, I stayed silent for a little while.

"Could you just think about it and get back to me?" Minami asked, handing me a bound stack of papers, which she told me was the script. Refusing it outright would have made me feel bad, so I took it.

On the cover was a title: *The Girl Who Dies from a Rare Disease.* It was catchy in a way, and they told me that this was the movie they were planning to shoot.

After that, Minami gave me her number and I gave her mine, then I was allowed to leave. I left the clubrooms building and walked home by myself, watching the veil of twilight descend over the sky. On my way to the train station, I looked up and couldn't help but wish that my hold over my life wasn't so tenuous.

But when I stopped to think about it, I realized that even if you weren't suffering from an incurable disease, you never knew for sure how long you would live.

4

The next morning, I was lost in thought as I walked to school. I had been thinking vaguely about death ever since the night before.

Before I found out I was terminally ill, I used to assume that death was something that waited for you at the end of time. But I was wrong; we're all being handed over to death every minute, every second of every day, even now. It doesn't matter whether you're sick or not. No one can tell what's going to happen at any given moment.

Still, it was true that I had a clear time limit of one year. I sat through class, all the while mulling over questions like whether it was really a good idea to hang out with people. During recess, I gazed outside from my seat by the window. It probably had something to do with the fact that I was often sick growing up, but I'd picked up a certain skill: to be an inconspicuous wallflower in the classroom, neither fitting in nor becoming too isolated.

Eventually, it was time for lunch. After a moment's thought, I picked up my bento box and headed for the roof.

The flat rooftop was enclosed by a fence, but since it was still deemed dangerous, the school kept the door locked and students had to get special permission to go there. Thanks to the nurse, though, I had a secret spare key to get in.

I opened the door and walked out into to the middle of the roof. All alone, I gazed up at the sky.

Feeling the wind on my skin, I heard a variety of different sounds drifting up from the floors below. The muffled buzz of students all around the school reached my ears, carried on the breeze. Everyone was gathered in this one spot, living their lives alongside one another.

I was the only one standing in a different place. Ever since my childhood illnesses, I'd always been like this. I'd always been alone...

I heard the door open behind me and instinctively turned around. To my surprise, Minami was standing there, and she walked over to me with a sheepish smile on her face.

"Sorry," she said. "I followed you here. I thought we could eat lunch together, so I went over to your class, but then I saw you coming up to the roof... I wanted to talk to you about the movie and stuff."

I felt another sweet tug at my heart—the one person who was incredibly special to me had just appeared right in front of my eyes. Before I could respond, she'd already walked right up to me.

"I didn't expect you to just go and open the door to the rooftop," she said. "You have a key?"

"Oh, yeah. I hope you'll keep it a secret, but the nurse gave me a spare."

"Whoa, really? Lucky! Come to think of it, it looked like you and the nurse are pretty close."

"I don't know about that."

"That could mean all sorts of things. But I get it; she's pretty. Everyone likes her—she has that special charm, I guess."

"You're the only one I like, Minami," I told her, surprised to hear the words coming out of my mouth. I had no idea why it was so easy to say something like that, even considering I'd already confessed to her once before.

Minami looked at me round-eyed, just as surprised as I was. Then, with a soft smile, she said, "You're a lot more passionate than you look, Tsukishima."

"Oh, uh, no, I didn't—uh, it just slipped out… Um, so—"

"Your ears are bright red. How cute," she teased.

"Stop it. You're embarrassing me." Her remark had made me self-conscious, and I could feel the heat spreading even farther across my face. I thought she'd laugh seeing me like this, but her reaction was a little different; she was smiling, but for some reason, she looked lonely, too. All of a sudden, a sense of stillness settled inside me.

"Um…there's something I wanted to ask you," she said eventually. "Do you mind?"

"Huh? Sure, go ahead. What is it?"

"When were you struck by gentle lightning?"

"Huh? What's that?"

"Gentle lightning is like…" Minami looked up at the sky, then recited what sounded like a line from a movie: "'If you never fall in love, life has no meaning. Unless you care for someone and feel that stab of pain as sharp as death itself, there's no point in living. You have to make an effort to fall in love. You have to open your heart to someone else. Open your heart and live—then one day, someday, you'll be struck by gentle lightning.'"

The words made a strong impression, but I'd never heard them before. "Is that a line from something?" I asked, curious.

"It's from a movie I like. A grandpa says it to his granddaughter, telling her she should learn to fall in love." Minami smiled sadly again. "To tell you the truth, I'm not really sure what it's like to love someone, either."

"Oh, does that mean...you've never had a crush on anyone before? Not even once?" I was taken aback.

"Nope, never. Maybe it's because I've been obsessed with making movies since way back in elementary school. I feel like I'm missing out on something important, though... Sometimes I actually get worried about that."

If you get close enough, you see that everyone, no matter what kind of person they are, has a complex inner self. I realized it was the same for Minami, too. Now it made a bit more sense why she wasn't going out with anyone, even though she was popular at school.

"You were that small when you started making movies, huh? Well...I don't think that's something you should worry about too much. Come to think of it, what's your type—if you have one? What sort of person do you tend to like?"

"Aoi shakes her head whenever I say this 'cause I sound like a total film fanatic, but if I had to pick a type, I'd say it'd be like a movie protagonist. You know, someone with a dark side who's burdened by sadness but still fighting against something... Someone hiding a secret. You know what I mean?"

I almost let out a chuckle. My backstory was nothing like that kind of character's, but I couldn't help but notice the similarities.

"Hey, you laughed at me."

"No, I didn't— I wasn't making fun of you, I swear. But...those characters are so cool because the actors are good-looking."

"Looks don't come into it. It's *how they live* that I like. I don't really pay attention to their looks anyway."

"Good-looking people always say that." As soon as I said it,

I realized it was a blunder. But Minami just teased me with a playful grin.

"Hang on, are you talking about me? Well, then...was it my looks that made you fall for me?"

"...Not just that." If I only liked her for that, I wouldn't have felt the need to share my feelings with Minami. I was attracted to her because I knew she was a kindhearted person who wouldn't be mean to someone or treat them badly just because they were different. I hesitated for a moment, but I steeled myself to tell her everything—about the day when I was struck by gentle lightning.

"Everyone... They all act like they've forgotten all about it, like nothing ever happened, but you remember the girl in our class who was getting bullied last year, don't you? The one who transferred to a different school in second term?"

Minami's expression turned slightly somber.

"I stayed out of the bullying, but I couldn't help her, either," I admitted. "I thought of saying hi to her every morning, actually. I figured that something as small as a friendly word from someone might change how she felt. But...I know it's pathetic of me to say this, but I couldn't bring myself to do it in front of everyone. I just said hi and smiled at her every once in a while when no one was looking. That was all I could do."

It wasn't the entire class that had bullied her—only some of the girls. But everyone else had pretended not to see it was happening; we just ignored it in that particular way people do when someone's clearly a target. It was awful. By standing back and letting them bully her, we were just as much to blame.

But Minami was different. Even though she knew about the bullying, she had still gone over to talk to the girl. Minami would casually strike up a conversation with her, and if the girl was getting left out during class, Minami would invite her to join her own group.

In the end, the girl transferred to another school during summer break. The school found out what was happening and took stricter measures on bullying, and everyone in our class put the matter behind them.

Still, I knew the girl had been grateful for what Minami did. Every time Minami talked to her, this big smile would spread across her face.

I didn't go into all the details, but I told Minami that that was the first time I'd started noticing her in a special way. I was surprised at how smoothly and naturally I could tell her the truth. Her reaction was different from what I'd expected; she just stared at me, wide-eyed.

"Oh, but, um...I started talking to her because of you, Tsukishima."

I was too bewildered to say anything.

"I think I caught on to what was happening before you did," she went on. "But there's a chance the bullying will get even nastier if you just march right up to them and step in, so I didn't know what to do... Then I saw you saying hi to her and realized, 'Oh, right, a little thing like that could make a big difference.'"

"But...it's not like I talked to her every day, and I only did that when I thought no one was around."

"It's tricky, trying to help in a situation like that. But you were the reason I made up my mind to go talk to her. She's turned things around at her new school and is doing really well now, by the way. She still texts me sometimes; she told me she found a place where she belongs. I have a pic of her, too—wanna see?"

Minami showed me a photo on her phone: The girl who went away was beaming with other students, probably her friends, all wearing an unfamiliar school uniform. I'd felt sorry for her, imagining how she must have felt when she left our school, and wondered how she was doing. But now she'd found a place where she could keep smiling like that. I was surprised and relieved to see her looking happy with her new friends—it couldn't have been easy for her.

"I didn't know that. But…I'm glad to hear it," I murmured, looking up from the screen. Our eyes met, and Minami smiled. Just then, I heard a strange, high-pitched noise.

"Oops," said Minami, putting a hand to her stomach with a sheepish grin. "Sorry, that was me. Wanna have lunch? I'm starving." She held up her bag with her bento box.

We sat on the rooftop and ate our lunch. Though there was a bit of sun, it wouldn't bother us if we sat in the shade of the small shedlike structure that led to the stairs. We used our handkerchiefs to brush the dirt off the ground, then sat down with our backs against the wall. Each of us had a bento box in our lap, and we gratefully started eating.

"Ooh, your *tamagoyaki* looks really good, Tsukishima."

"Oh yeah, my dad loves cooking. Wanna try a bit?"

"Sure. I'll trade you one of mine."

It felt a bit surreal to be having lunch with Minami on the rooftop. And not just that—I'd even managed to tell her the whole story about my feelings for her, instead of leaving her with my half-baked confession from the other day.

I put down my chopsticks for a little while and gazed off into the distance. The invigorating blue of the sky stretched out around us. With the girl I liked sitting by my side, and no more regrets or desires to hold me back, I had a weird thought that now might be the perfect time to die.

But of course, life doesn't come to an end so easily. I was still gazing at the sky in silence when I felt Minami's eyes on me. As I turned to her, her face broke into a smile, and she held up her hands, making a little window frame with her thumbs and forefingers.

"What's up?" I asked. "Ah…did you get an idea for your movie or something?"

"How'd you guess? That melancholy look on your face just now would've made a great scene."

"Melancholy? I'm pretty sure I was just zoning out."

"Nope, it was better than that. What were you thinking about anyway?"

"Huh? Um…that it's a nice day."

"You're making that up, aren't you?"

Her guess was so spot-on that I burst out laughing, and she grinned and lowered her hands. I suddenly realized I wanted to ask her something.

"By the way, I never got around to asking—you're the director, right? Of that movie."

"Oh, I didn't tell you that? Yeah, I am. Aoi wrote the script, and I'm the director. I operate the camera, too—it's sort of a hobby of mine."

"What got you into making movies?"

"Hmm, it's pretty simple, actually. There's this movie I watched when I was little where the protagonist was shooting a film, and I wanted to take a shot at it. Aoi knew a lot about that stuff from back then, so she helped me out."

"Huh. That's pretty cool."

"The hard part is finding the time. There's so much I want to film and so many competitions I want to submit our work to. The indie film world has really been taking off lately, too. Like, just this summer—"

Minami looked so excited as she talked. I could tell that she was the kind of person who would keep on making new things, and that that would never change. I felt a tiny bit jealous.

Even so, I still hesitated about being part of her movie. I was scared that if a newbie like me tried to fill the leading role, I'd ruin the whole thing.

"Hey, Tsukishima. Do you wanna try making movies now?" Minami asked, leaning closer to me. I didn't think she'd noticed how I was feeling, but the question was still on point. I gave her a tight smile.

"Just a little bit. But…I have zero experience."

"That's totally okay. For the movies we make, you won't need any."

"Are there really movies like that?"

"Sure. Like, a *lot*. The important thing is that someone *feels* like the right fit for the character they're playing, not how good they are at acting. Some directors pick an amateur for the leading role on purpose, since their acting doesn't have any particular quirks—and those movies can win international awards, you know."

I'd glimpsed yet another facet of Minami. Her words were brimming with earnest fervor; she was clearly committed to the art of making films. She was having so much fun with it that she just couldn't get enough.

After a while, the school bell rang, so we packed up our bento boxes and left the rooftop.

"I'll be waiting for your text," Minami said. I gave a noncommittal grin.

We walked in opposite directions down the empty hallway toward our respective classrooms.

"Tsukishima!"

I turned around at Minami's voice. She had called out to me from a short way off and was grinning at me.

"Come join our crew, Tsukishima! Let's make a movie together!"

I gave her another evasive smile. "I'll let you know," I said. Minami nodded back.

Afternoon classes started, and time passed uneventfully, as it always did. There was the usual hustle and bustle among my classmates during our short break, but I was in a world of my own. The stillness in which I sat alone was no different than usual, yet somehow it felt unbearably quiet.

I told myself that this feeling wouldn't last. Come tomorrow, I wouldn't even notice the quiet. I'd go back to the calm that I'd come to expect of my life. That was what I preferred and how it should be. I'd keep looking for bucket list items that I could do on my own, and I'd check them off, silently and solemnly, until the day I died.

Or, at least, that was what I used to think. Now I didn't know what to make of myself.

When I got home, I took out my bucket list notebook and added something new to the list:

Try making a movie, even if I'm hopeless at it

* * *

I stared hard at the words in my notebook. If I wanted to be melodramatic, I would have said it was the decision of a lifetime. I had to choose what to do, what I wanted to do, in the little time I had left. I had to choose whether I wanted to spend time with people or not.

The minutes ticked by, but I still couldn't move away from my notebook. It was the first time I'd ever stayed still like this for such a long time just to think. Before I was aware of it, the room was already bathed in the orange glow of sunset.

The world kept spinning mercilessly. No matter what I did or didn't do, time kept moving forward. Each of us must decide how to be free in our own way in this unceasing world.

I made up my mind, reached for my phone, and tapped on the messaging app.

"Can I be part of the movie?"

Conscious of my racing heart, I stared at the message I'd typed. I sent it to Minami.

Since she might not reply immediately, I opened the script she'd given me, trying to distract myself by scanning the words. But her response was surprisingly quick.

"Thanks for messaging me! Of course you can. Come to the clubroom after school tomorrow. See you there, rookie!"

I wasn't sure why, but it felt like something had opened up inside of me. It had happened so slowly, but it was there.

I wrote back, "*You got it, Director.*"

I went back to reading the script, conscious of how I was choosing to spend the time I had left. I noticed that, for the first time in a long time, I was sitting in my room and smiling.

5

"It's the third week of May now, so we'll do our best to finish filming before July at the latest. Then we'll finish editing before we go into summer break and submit it to the indie film festival. That's the rough overview," Minami concluded.

The day after I'd made my decision, I headed to the filmmaking clubroom after school with butterflies in my stomach. Minami was already there to welcome me, and Hayami eyed me suspiciously. I sat down in a fifth chair they brought over for me.

As the leader of the club, Minami went over the schedule. We had about one month for filming and two weeks for editing. Even to a newbie like me, it sounded pretty tight. Minami introduced me properly to Hayami, the vice president of the club who acted as the assistant director and screenwriter. Minami and Hayami had been friends since preschool, and they'd started making movies together in elementary school.

"I guess you were too serious about Tsukishima to let him go, Tsubasa." Hayami sighed wearily. "I thought he'd never say yes to playing the lead."

"Of course I was," Minami said cheerfully. "He's perfect for the role, and I just really wanted him to be in our movie."

"Let me ask you one more time: You're sure you don't want to scrap the concept and start over?" Hayami asked.

"Yup. Sorry, but I'm positive about that. You said it yourself, Aoi—we should go with something that has mass appeal. We've all worked on this story since spring break, and we were all convinced it was going to work, so it'd be a shame to throw it away now. Besides, I want us to challenge ourselves."

The two of them discussed the film's direction in serious tones for a while longer, but eventually, Hayami backed down. With a deep sigh, she turned to me and asked, "Tsukishima, you got any acting experience?" She had a different vibe from other students: kind of listless in a grown-up, worldly way.

"Oh...um, not at all," I answered.

"You had school plays when you were little, right? What roles did you play in those?"

"I was a tree."

"A tree?"

"I played a sort of villager, too."

"A 'sort of' villager...? What does that mean?"

"Um, it was something like a villager, but I don't really remember... Maybe a townsman?"

Hayami seemed to be sizing me up. Since I'd often come down with a fever back then, I'd always had a filler role so that it didn't really make much difference whether I was there or not. I wondered if my lack of experience was too dismal even for an amateur.

"Well, I guess it's a good thing you're coming at this with a clean slate."

Apparently, I'd passed her test, and I let out a sigh of relief. It was only then that I noticed Minami was recording us on her phone. "Hm? Why are you filming?" I asked her.

"Just thought it was a good scene. The way the tension and relief showed on your face was so natural."

"As long as you're in our filmmaking club, Tsukishima, you

better get used to this," Hayami said. "Tsubasa's going to point her lens at you whenever she wants, and then she'll tell you she's getting you used to the camera and gathering reference material for her movies."

Come to think of it, Minami was always taking photos of her friends and the scenery last year. That might've been for her movies, too. As these thoughts crossed my mind, the door opened.

"Sorry we're late! Homeroom dragged on."

"Sorry 'bout that."

The same first-year girls I'd seen the other day came in. When they caught sight of me, their eyes widened a little, and they greeted me with a slight bow before they took their seats.

"This is Ichika," Minami explained to me, gesturing to the shorter girl. "She's a year below us, but like Aoi, we've been friends since preschool. She's an actress for our club. And the one with the long hair and laid-back attitude is Ena. We met in junior high. She's an actress, too."

"Uh, hi there," I said, turning to face the pair. "I'm Makoto Tsukishima. I was in the same class with Minami last year, so that's how I know her. I'll be joining the club starting today. Nice to meet you."

"N-nice to meet you, too!" Ichika answered for the both of them.

I guess they're going to be in the movie as well, I thought. *I wonder which one of them is playing the heroine.* I noticed that one of the girls—the one called Ena—was staring at me.

"Um, do I have something on my face?" I asked.

"I've been wondering, actually—do you have a crush on Tsubasa?" Ena asked nonchalantly.

The whole room froze in an instant.

I should've known better, but I glanced over at Minami. It was almost by reflex; it wasn't like I thought she'd told them. Startled, Minami seemed to sense something and shook her head. But it was too late: My reaction had given me away.

"Ah. Sorry… I didn't mean to put you on the spot…," Ena said apologetically.

"Tsukishima," Hayami snapped, staring daggers at me. "If that's what you're here for, then get out."

"What?"

"Get out. Now. Everyone, we'll start over from scratch. I'll rewrite the script, and—"

Thankfully, Minami cut in and calmed Hayami down. By then, the damage was already done, though. Everyone in the room had noticed my feelings for Minami.

"I won't hesitate to throw you out of our club if you so much as *try* to make a move on any of our members. And I don't just mean Tsubasa," Hayami warned me. "I'll even take it up with the school board or the police if I have to."

"Aoi, you're overreacting," Minami said. "Tsukishima isn't like that. We were in the same class last year, so he just sees me as a friend. That's all."

"Sorry for making things awkward, Aoi. I didn't mean to," Ena said in her easygoing drawl. "Hope you won't be mad at me."

They would've found out sooner or later, so I didn't blame Ena for asking. After that, we managed to pull ourselves together somehow and got down to business.

"All right, everyone," Minami said. "Since it's Tsukishima's first day, how about we start by reading through the script? We don't have to stick to the book that much on camera, but I want him to get a feel for the storyline."

"Oh, I actually read the whole thing yesterday," I said.

Minami's brows went up a little. "Really? Wow, way to go, Tsukishima. You're diving right in. I'm even more glad you're taking the role now."

I knew she was just saying that to be nice, but it still made me happy to get a compliment from Minami. It's possible that my reaction got on Hayami's nerves, because she decided to toss me in the deep end.

"Then let's start filming today."

"What? Already?" I looked at her in shock.

"You have the story in your head, right?" Hayami pressed, picking up the script. "I have permission from the school to film anywhere in the building, including the rooftop. And besides, it's your first time, Tsukishima; you have to get used to being in front of the camera and get a feel for the process. What—you got a problem with that?"

She pinned me with a glare. I didn't know what to say. The other three behind me were already prepping their equipment.

Somehow, I had a sneaking suspicion that Hayami was one person I should never cross.

Under Minami's leadership, the club swung into action for the day. They carried out their filming equipment—which they'd bought with their own money, saved up from part-time jobs—and got ready to start filming for *The Girl Who Dies from a Rare Disease* on the school rooftop.

Minami told me offhandedly that she would have preferred a

more evocative, artistic title for the movie. However, since their main aim for this project was to appeal to the masses, they settled on a title that would grab people's attention.

Everyone obviously knew what they were doing as they went about setting up the equipment.

"Well, then," Minami said casually, "like Aoi said, it'll be good to let you get used to the whole process, Tsukishima, so we'll focus on filming you today."

"Okay. I'm not sure I'm up to it, though."

"Don't worry. We'll do a scene where you won't really have to act. In the script, it's on page..."

I checked the page she pointed to. It turned out that Ena would be playing the role of the heroine. In the scene, the protagonist had just learned about the heroine's terminal illness, and he was supposed to gaze up at the sky all alone. Then his friend—played by Ichika—would come and cheer him up. Apparently, Minami had picked a scene where I wouldn't have to deliver any lines so I could get used to being in front of the camera first.

The filming was more professional than I'd expected, with a setup featuring several cameras in different positions. But they weren't those bulky cameras that I'd imagined—they were all using their smartphones.

"You can get interesting new angles and shots with phones, since they're small, and you can put them practically anywhere," Hayami explained calmly, noticing my surprise. "Plus, the apps are useful, they're more affordable than big cameras, and the quality's not bad, either. Commercial film crews use them, too."

I got the impression that Hayami and Minami were pretty

particular when it came their art. Since I'd read up on the basics of filmmaking beforehand, I knew that people normally made what was called a storyboard: a blueprint for the scenes. Minami and Hayami didn't use storyboards, though. According to them, storyboarding could make them feel too bound by it and keep them from discovering anything in the process of filming.

Instead, the two of them moved between the phones, exploring different perspectives to shoot from. Each phone had an app on it that enabled screen sharing, so they could check all of the angles from a single laptop.

After a quick rehearsal to check everything was working, Minami called out to the crew, "All righty, then. Let's get started. Just relax. Roll camera. Roll sound… Action!"

Minami had told me not to worry about acting and to just think about something sad instead. So I stood there, gazing up at the sky, thinking sad thoughts. I was getting pretty seriously depressed by the time her voice rang out. "Cut! You're doing great, Tsukishima."

"Uh, I was just standing here looking at the sky," I replied sheepishly.

We filmed more scenes without dialogue. Since Minami wanted to try different shots, I struck different poses, like leaning back against the small shed and gripping the fence on the edge of the rooftop, but nothing more complicated than that.

In between takes, Hayami asked Minami, "What do you think about cutting all the protagonist's lines so he's silent throughout the whole movie?"

Ena was coming up with ideas, too, even though she wasn't in any of the scenes being filmed today. She showed the others a video she'd recorded. "I tried getting a bird's-eye view with a selfie stick. Do you think we could use the shot somewhere?"

It was invigorating to see how they put their heads together and created the movie on the spot from the ground up. The air was taut with tension, but I felt excited to step into a whole new world. There was just one problem, though…

"Next up, let's try the part where the friend cheers up the protagonist," Minami announced. "There's a couple of lines you have to say in this one, Tsukishima, so good luck. Just talk like you normally do—Aoi will pick up your voice, and we'll deal with the noise from the wind later, so you don't have to speak loudly."

First, they got the shot of Ichika as the friend coming out onto the rooftop. Then, in the next shot, she walked closer to the fence where I was, and asked if I was okay. I turned around and answered, "I-I'm, uh— I'm— Yeah."

I'd completely botched my line. I clearly had a whole lot of work to do before I could even think about acting.

That night, I sat in my room, watching a movie that Minami had lent me.

After I'd stumbled over my line, we tried a few retakes, but every time, I'd either mumbled or said it weirdly. In the end, they decided that I could do a voice-over. I would record the line separately, and they'd stitch it onto the scene in the editing stage.

Minami assured me that voice-overs were totally standard, so it wasn't a problem at all. But I felt so useless that I made up my mind to practice vocalization skills and learn more about acting. According to Minami, though, it was better for me not to study acting methods. She explained that their movie was on the quiet side, so they wanted to strip down any hint of acting to the bare minimum.

"See, you turn into the character," Ena said, giving me tips. "Think about how you'd react if you were that person and try to show it in a natural way—so it's like you try not to *act*, if you get what I mean."

I kind of understood what she meant, but not really, so Minami lent me a movie that could serve as an example. It was a bit of an unusual film. The storyline and the characters had been set, but all the dialogue was improvised by the actors, who went with the flow and said what felt right in the moment. Most of the main characters were played by amateur actors, but the movie had still won awards internationally.

In the movie, the actors coughed on-screen. Their voices were low. Sometimes they talked over each other. Still, the whole thing somehow felt very raw and real. I felt like I was right there with them, and the story had a strange power that pulled me in. The scenes were beautiful, too. Even though it was an hour-and-a-half-long movie, it felt like it passed by in a flash.

After that, I watched the film that Minami's group had made in junior high school—the one that had won an award at a competition. It was thirty minutes long, like the movie we were making now. I was blown away by Ena's performance and magnetic presence on-screen; she seemed like a totally different person from the girl I knew.

Ena was also going to play the heroine in *The Girl Who Dies from a Rare Disease*—and I was supposed to be the protagonist. I was worried that I had absolutely no business being in their crew. Not only did I know zilch about movies and acting, but

I couldn't even get through a single line without tripping over my tongue. Not to mention—

"She's cute."

"Whoa!" I'd had my earphones in and been too absorbed in the movie to notice Dad standing right behind me. I hadn't even heard him come into my room, and I hit pause in a knee-jerk reaction. Dad laughed, a knowing expression across his face; he was probably making some weird assumptions about my panic.

"Sorry. Didn't mean to scare you. I see your dirty video has some plot," he teased.

"No, it's nothing like that."

"Ah, so mostly plot with a few dirty scenes, then."

"Is that any better?"

"Details, details! Don't worry about it," he chortled. "But really, what movie are you watching?"

He must've known it's just a normal movie, I thought, slightly disgruntled. "Um, just something my friend made back in junior high."

"Your friend? Well, how about that..."

I hadn't told my family about joining the filmmaking club. I had a few reasons for keeping it a secret, but mainly I was too embarrassed to say that I was starring in a movie.

"Anyway, did you want to tell me something?" I asked.

"Oh, just came to let you know I've taken a bath already, so it's all yours."

"Okay. I'll go in in a minute. Is Mom home?"

"Not yet—looks like she'll be a bit late tonight."

Both my parents had jobs, but these days, Mom was working longer hours than Dad. Since Dad worked from home and had a flexible schedule, he took care of most of the household chores.

"Don't forget to soak up to your shoulders and count to a hundred, all right?" Dad added.

"I'm not a little kid, you know."

He laughed and left my room. I quietly watched his retreating figure.

Dad might not look like it now, but he used to be an investment-fund manager with a glowing track record. At least, that was what I'd heard—back then, I barely saw him around, so I didn't really know him all that well.

When I was little, my parents worked in the inner city; Dad was especially busy, constantly working day and night. However, when I was in elementary school, going in and out of hospital, he seemed to come to some sort of realization and quit his job. When my health stabilized, we moved away from the city to a town with cleaner air, and he chose a different line of work he could do from home.

At our new place, Dad was always home when I got back from school. He always took good care of me, protecting me from everything—almost too much. And he was always ready to laugh wholeheartedly, as if pain and sadness didn't exist in the world.

...How's Dad going to cope when I'm gone?

The question I'd been trying to suppress crossed my mind. I tried to shake off my anxiety, and at the same time, I strengthened my resolve to do my best acting in the film—not just for my sake, but for my parents', too.

The best thing I could do to repay my parents might just be to show them that even after I'd gotten this diagnosis, I still had my own world and hadn't given up on living. That became another reason why I wanted to leave the film behind. *One day, when I'm gone, I want Mom and Dad to watch it. And then, maybe...*

I clicked play on Minami's film.

I want to make a good movie, I thought. *I'll try not to get in the crew's way, at least.*

6

The next Thursday after school, we shot a scene with some dialogue. Aoi gave me a new script—apparently, she'd revised it so that I would have as little to say on-screen as possible. Thanks to the articulation exercises they'd taught me, I somehow got through filming with Ichika for the day, even with several retakes. It took a huge weight off my shoulders when we were done.

I managed to handle the filming on Friday, too, though I still made lots of mistakes.

The problem was the shooting on Saturday. It was going to be my first time acting with Ena. The scene was set in the nurse's office, and in it, the heroine would tell the protagonist about her terminal illness and how much time she had left.

The nurse gave us permission to use her office if we did it on a Saturday, so that morning, we met up at the clubroom. We carried our equipment to the nurse's office, said hello to the nurse, and started setting everything up.

The nurse looked surprised to see me there and flashed a grin in my direction. We promised her that if any students came to see her, we'd let her know, and she left for the faculty office.

"All righty, Tsukishima and Ena, could you come over here by the bed? I'll fill you in on the plan for today," Minami said, then walked us through what we'd be doing.

I had seen Ena's acting in their previous movie. It was definitely not just her looks that made her stand out; there was a depth to her performance that I would never have guessed from her usual self off-screen.

"So, Tsukishima," Minami said, "you don't have to pretend to be anyone else. Just imagine how you'd react if you found out that the girl you had a crush on didn't have long left to live. Don't exaggerate; try to make it look natural, if you can."

I nodded, feeling tense.

"Ena might go off script, depending on how the scene goes, so don't feel like you have to stick to what's written, either. If you memorize the lines too closely, you'll stumble when you forget them, and the dialogue ends up sounding stiff. Whatever you do, try to be authentic."

Minami had given me the same piece of advice every day we'd filmed: that I could go off script if I felt like it. For an amateur like me who barely even knew how to act, it was a big help. It still made me nervous that I never knew what was going to happen until we played out the scene, but I found myself having fun with it all the same.

Hayami double-checked that everyone was in place, and we were ready to roll.

"Let's have fun with it," Minami called out.

Ena sat down on the bed, and I stood in front of her.

"Right, here we go. Roll camera. Roll sound... Action!"

The moment Minami announced they were filming, the air around Ena seemed to shift. "You heard, right? I'm sick," she murmured softly.

I was startled by the change in her. Before me now sat a completely different person: someone who seemed to have given up all hope and couldn't care less what became of her.

"They said I have six months left. It doesn't even feel real... Do people's lives really end just like that? After fifteen years living a normal life like anyone else?"

Ena continued her monologue. For a moment, I was so absorbed in her performance that I forgot where I was. The person in front of me wasn't Ena anymore, but a classmate suffering from an incurable disease with only a short time left to live who'd given up on everything...

What could I say to a someone like that? Offer my sympathies? Try to console her?

I tried to say something back to her, but I felt the words stick in my throat. I couldn't figure out why. Was it because I wouldn't have wanted to hear any attempts at consolation, in her place?

"Cut!" Minami called, and I came to my senses.

Everyone was watching me with concern, and it finally hit me that I hadn't said my line. "Oh, sorry!" I blurted out.

"It's totally fine, Tsukishima. Don't worry," Minami assured me with a smile.

"I do that all the time, too. It's nothing to worry about," Ena chimed in.

I pulled myself together for the next take. Telling myself to focus on the filming, I timed my delivery to match up with

Ena's and said my line almost word for word from the script. But it fell flat—I could already tell before I'd finished speaking. Since I was trying too hard to follow the script, the words and my intonation came out stilted. That made me tense, and the more nervous I got, the more strained my acting became.

We went through take after take after take.

I was caught in a vicious cycle, my field of view narrowing around me, until Hayami suggested, "Maybe we should take a break, Tsubasa."

I'd lost count of how many times I'd done the scene. Poor Ena. I apologized to her, knowing I looked pathetic.

"Don't worry about it. It's okay," she said with a smile. A crooked grin was all I could muster in response. Ichika was filling in as an assistant today, and she handed me a drink. I thanked her and stepped out into the hallway to get some air.

This was all-new levels of pathetic, even for me. Yes, Minami had invited me to join the club, but it had been my decision to say yes, and they'd let me in. I was utterly ashamed.

We had ten minutes to rest, so I headed to the covered walkway that led to the gym. I took a deep breath to calm myself down.

I have to do better. Don't mess up next time. Stop getting in everyone's way.

I closed my eyes and took a few more deep breaths, and then I heard a calm voice.

"Hope you're not beating yourself up."

Startled, I turned around to find Hayami walking in my direction. She was looking straight at me.

"No one's expecting you to be a great actor or anything, so

you don't have to be good," she said. Her clear voice rang out over the sounds of the school: the baseball club shouting out in the distance, basketball shoes squeaking on the floor in the gym, the sound of balls bouncing.

Before I knew it, Hayami was right in front of me, and we were standing face-to-face. In her own razor-sharp way, she was trying to tell me something. I summoned my courage and met her gaze.

"What do you mean, I don't have to be good?" I asked.

"Exactly what it sounds like. When we got a prize for our film in junior high, a director who was on the judging panel told us that Ena's IQ as an actor is way above everyone else. There's only a handful of people like her out there, but you're not one of them."

"But...I still feel like I need to give it my best. I don't want to hold everyone back."

"Then here's my advice: *Don't.*"

I was speechless. Hayami definitely wasn't one to mince words, but I knew she was giving me advice.

"You don't have to try hard. In fact, you don't have to *try* to do anything. You might think I'm stepping over the line right now, seeing as I'm just the assistant director, but I can tell you're freaking out, Tsukishima. Your mind's going a hundred miles an hour thinking about what you have to say, what you shouldn't say, all that stuff. Just forget about all that and be yourself."

For some reason, my own acting started to play in my head, as if I were watching myself from the side. It wasn't real, just a construction of my imagination, but I thought *freaking out* summed it up pretty well. I'd been trying too hard the whole time. I stood in a daze as her words hit home.

"Aoi," Minami called from a little ways off. Apparently, she'd been watching us talk.

"What's up, boss?" Hayami asked.

"I came to make sure you weren't bullying our lead actor," Minami joked.

"Don't worry. You wouldn't tell him what he needed to hear, so I'm doing it now: Don't be artificial."

"You don't have to say it like *that*."

"All right, all right. My bad." The corner of Hayami's lips twitched up in a wry grin. With a brief wave of her hand, she walked off, leaving us behind.

"Are you okay, Tsukishima?" Minami asked with a caring smile. Her warmth was almost overwhelming, like a droplet of pure sunlight. She'd probably come to check on me. It could've been her role as the director that made her so attentive, but I also felt her kindness.

"Yeah. I'm okay."

"Just don't put too much pressure on yourself—we can do it over however many times we need."

"You're right. Still…I feel like I'm starting to get it."

We chatted as we walked back to the nurse's office. I felt refreshed, as though I'd pressed a reset button for my headspace. My body even seemed to feel more relaxed. Maybe Hayami's advice had helped me loosen up.

I apologized to Ena again for all the retakes and told her that this time, I'd try being myself. Minami gave me a smile and told me to have fun with it.

"Okay, here we go," she called out. "Roll camera. Roll sound... Action!"

The next moment, Ena had already transformed into her character and was saying her lines. I knew I was standing face-to-face with a talented actress acclaimed by pros, but I just tried to be my ordinary self. *What would someone who's just been told she doesn't have long left to live need to hear? What would be the natural thing to say in a situation like this?* As these questions circled in my head, I tried to come up with something that I would say in real life.

Except...there was something off about the scene unfolding in front of me. I'd been through this myself.

"Uh, I..." My voice came out hoarse. That was okay; that could happen in real life. I just had to be myself, to say what I would say in this situation. "I think you should probably get mad."

Ena's eyes widened a little in surprise.

When you have to accept that you only have a short time left to live, you don't give in to despair that easily. You can't just let go. I knew that for a fact.

"It's easy to lose hope. Giving up won't change anything, though. You only make the people around you and yourself miserable. So...you should get angry."

I was ignoring the flow of the script, but I kept going anyway.

"You had your own dreams, your own hopes... You had things you wanted to do. You sit here and say, 'Why me? This is messed up,' but that doesn't mean you should give up. You should be mad."

Ena's face changed as I went on. It didn't feel like an act; she was responding as her character would've done, with anger and fear welling up inside of her. "What do *you* know?" she demanded.

"I can tell it's all just an act," I said.

"What? How?"

"You're going to *die*. You've got six months left to live? How can you act so *normal*? Why are you pretending to give up on life? It's not that easy to let go. You should want to take it all out on people. You should hate everyone going on with their ordinary lives. And that's going to make you hate yourself... But even with all that..."

The words I had scribbled in my dark notebook crossed my mind: *I want to live longer.*

"You should want to live longer and keep fighting right up until the end."

The next moment, Ena got up from the bed and whacked me with the pillow in her hand. As I stared at her, startled by her sudden reaction, she threw the pillow at me.

"You have no idea what you're talking about. How dare you act like *you* know how I feel." Her eyes filled with tears. "Don't you get it? It's easier just to give up."

"Easier? How is that easier?"

"Because...then I don't have to get my hopes up. I can't let myself feel anything. I don't want to hate anyone or get jealous. If I just keep my heart locked up, I... I—" A single teardrop drew a line down her cheek. "I don't have to hope that maybe one day I'll get better, and I might live longer... If I start to hope, it'll just end up hurting."

I forgot to breathe. In front of me right now wasn't Ena, but a girl who'd just found out she was going to die. I was face to face with my own past self.

"Cut!"

Minami's voice pulled me back to reality. For a few seconds, I'd completely forgotten that we were filming a scene.

"Sorry, Tsubasa. I didn't follow the story in the script," Ena said with a smile. She was already back to her usual self, wiping away her tears as though nothing had happened. "Sorry about the pillow, Tsukishima. I guess I hit you pretty hard."

"No, I should be the one apologizing. I went totally off script. Sorry." I'd tried to be my usual self, but the take we did just now would have to be scrapped. It had somehow slipped my mind that my usual self was more like the dying heroine than the protagonist. Thinking I should remember that next time, I turned to the others to apologize again and found that Hayami and Ichika were staring at me in surprise.

"Um, sorry. I know we don't have all day…and it's not like we can use any of that. Acting normally is actually pretty hard."

"Uh, that's not it…" Hayami seemed at a loss for words for a change, so Minami took over.

"I think this is good in a different way. *Really* good," Minami said. Her usual smile had been replaced by something more serious. I wasn't sure whether she was just saying that to cheer me up.

"Oh, really? You really think we can use that?" I asked hopefully.

"Yup. But wow, I never expected a performance like that out of you, Tsukishima. I want to go with that take, so we can tweak the scenes that come after this one." Minami gave me a smile in spite of the slightly awkward atmosphere in the room.

"Yeah, you really caught me off guard, too," Ena chimed in with a grin. Ichika smiled along with them.

The four of them put their heads together and decided to use the footage we'd just recorded. They came up with a new storyline for the next few scenes on the spot so that it would connect to the heroine's outburst, and then we shot some more scenes according to the new plan.

With lunch and breaks in between, we finished filming in the nurse's office before sunset. We thanked the nurse and went back to our clubroom. While the rest of us were charging and putting away the equipment, Minami checked the footage we'd taken that day on the laptop and made some edits. It was only meant to be a quick round of editing, so she was done in less than half an hour. She played the footage for us so we could all see how well it flowed together.

"I think you should probably get mad."

I watched myself speak. It felt weird seeing myself like this. I looked so serious, and my voice sounded higher than I thought, so I felt a bit embarrassed. I fully expected Minami to tease me and that Hayami would have something scathing to say about my improv.

But instead, Minami said earnestly, "It's…a really good scene."

The screen switched to a shot from a different angle, capturing the moment Ena hit me with the pillow.

"My dialogue and acting might feel a bit clichéd," Ena commented. If you asked me, I would've said her performance was gripping, but she critiqued herself with an unforgiving eye.

"I think you acted like how your character really would," Minami said calmly. "It's definitely not too over-the-top."

"You think?"

"How did you come up with those lines?" Minami asked.

"I think Tsukishima pulled them out of me."

Ena and Minami were breaking down the performance, reflecting on it like true professionals. Meanwhile, Hayami was staring at the screen without saying anything.

"Don't you think we got a great scene, Aoi?" Minami asked.

Hayami didn't answer at first; her gaze remained fixed on the screen. Eventually, she said, "Well...I guess it's pretty good."

It was hard to tell if she really meant it.

7

After that day filming in the nurse's office, the way I looked at acting changed a little.

No matter what I did or how hard I tried, I was an amateur—nothing more, nothing less. With that firmly fixed in my mind, I stopped bending over backward to try to give a "good" performance; instead, I focused on responding to what was happening in the scene in an honest, sincere way.

When I started doing that, I felt like I kind of got the hang of it, if only a little. But that was because the performance they wanted from me was something very ordinary that anyone could've done.

Still, I always looked forward to our filming sessions after school. And I felt like everyone in the club was gradually starting to accept me as one of their own.

One week after we began filming, I was walking alone to my next class when Ichika called out to me.

"Oh! Makoto."

Ena was with her, being her usual chill self. Apparently, they were in the same class.

"Hi there," I said.

"Are you heading to your next class?"

"Yeah. I've got one of my electives. What about you two?"

"We're on our way to the science lab."

"Hey, buddy," Ena said with a grin. She'd started calling me *buddy* at some point, maybe because she'd warmed up to me. At first, Ichika told her not to be rude to a second year like me, but I'd told her I didn't mind. "Looking forward to filming after school."

A little surprised, I replied, "Yeah. Me too."

Before I joined the filmmaking club, I'd avoided talking to other people as much as possible because I didn't want to make anybody else sad when I died in the not-too-distant future. But here I was, building new relationships and getting to know people.

Now, I actually wanted to be closer to them and know more about them. I felt as though a shaft of light had pierced through the melancholy darkness I'd locked myself away in, and suddenly everything was brighter.

I went to see the nurse to let her know how I'd joined the filmmaking club. It wouldn't have even crossed my mind if not for her push that day. Honestly, I felt nothing but gratitude for her.

The late-afternoon light filled the nurse's office, and emotion filled her voice.

"So, Tsukishima, you've found a place where you belong here at school—other than the rooftop, that is."

"It wasn't just the rooftop," I replied with a sheepish smile. "I felt at home in your office, too."

"This isn't where you *belong*, though. It's just a refuge. The only thing you'd find here is a cup of coffee and a nagging auntie."

"It still made me feel better—actually, I wouldn't have felt so comfortable here if this wasn't a place like that." I really meant what I said. The nurse chuckled, and I laughed, too.

Later in our conversation, she told me that I didn't have to come to her office anymore—that I should nurture the space I wanted to be in. I would miss her and this place, but her advice wasn't exactly a surprise. I nodded, gave the nurse a bow, and walked out. Eager to join in the filming, I made my way to the clubroom—the place where I wanted to be.

My life started changing little by little. I was actually excited to wake up each morning.

I submitted my application for the filmmaking club after my homeroom teacher said it was a requirement to join. It was official now.

Club wasn't all fun and games. Sometimes I got a scolding from Hayami: "Hey, Tsukishima, how many times do I have to tell you? This is the *third* time now."

Regardless, I was glad I had the chance to do something with everyone. This kind of thing would've been unthinkable for me back in the days when I used to tick off the items on my bucket list one by one, all by myself. And on top of everything else, I got to talk to Minami almost every day.

"You look like you've been enjoying yourself more lately, Tsukishima," Minami told me one day when we were in the clubroom after a filming session. I'd stayed behind to help pack up, and Minami was editing the footage by herself.

"Oh. You think so?" I said.

"Yeah. You used to be more...I don't know. You were a bit aloof back in first year, like you'd taken a step back from everything."

I stopped what I was doing. When I looked up, our eyes met.

Back then, I'd been dragged down by my past, worried that I'd turn back into the sickly person I used to be. Perhaps because of that, I'd distanced myself from everything going on around me—just like Minami said.

But when I looked back now, I didn't really get what I'd been so afraid of. There'd been nothing wrong with my body. I wished I'd had the courage to join in with everyone else, to dive right in without being scared. Back then, before I'd had this shadow of fear looming over me, I could've gotten to know people without worrying about the consequences...

"I just didn't know how to talk to people, that's all," I said with a self-deprecating laugh, looking away. Minami seemed surprised by my reaction.

My feelings for her hadn't changed, but I was also perfectly happy with our friendship now. You could even say it was too good to be true. I had an excuse to be close to my crush on a daily basis.

Every single day, I felt alive. I was living life to the fullest, always conscious of my illness, Minami's presence, and my newfound love of filmmaking.

Time flies when you're having fun. Three weeks had passed since we'd started filming, and that Friday was the last day of filming on the school grounds—though I wished it would never end. We were planning to film outside the following week. Our monthlong shoot was almost drawing to a close.

Since our schedule was tight, we had been shooting scenes every day except Sunday. However, for our third week, Hayami announced that we'd be taking a break the following day, on Saturday. The news came after we'd finished putting things away in the clubroom, and Ena and Ichika got excited and immediately started planning an outing for the weekend.

Eventually, Ena, Ichika, and Hayami went home, leaving me and Minami alone together. She was doing more editing work, and I was double-checking to make sure all the equipment was charging. I wondered what I'd do on Saturday. I had an appointment at the hospital in the morning, but nothing in the afternoon. Just as I was thinking about this, Minami spoke up as though she'd just remembered something.

"Hey, Tsukishima."

"Yeah?"

"Are you free tomorrow?"

"Um, I'll be free in the afternoon—from around eleven, actually." I tensed up a little bit; Minami was in the middle of editing, so I was worried that she'd found some sort of problem with my acting and was going to have to reshoot a scene. But what she said next came totally out of left field.

"Good. Wanna go on a date?"

"Uh, sure. I can do th— Wait...*what*?"

8

On Saturday morning, I went to the hospital with my parents for a checkup. Dad suggested rounding off the outing with a nice lunch somewhere, but I had to tell them I had other plans.

I'd promised Minami that I would meet her at noon at a park near a busy shopping arcade. Not wanting to be late, I hurried to our meeting place and ended up arriving ten minutes early. It was my first time meeting up with a girl outside school, so I'd wanted to get there before her, but Minami was already there, sitting on a bench.

I'd been floored when Minami had invited me out the day before. But as it turned out, it wasn't a *real* date she had in mind; she had her own plans.

"*You must be tired from filming every day. Plus, I want to do some research,*" she'd said.

"*Research...?*"

"*Yep. We're gonna shoot a date scene in the park next week. I want to learn about dating and romance both for the film and for myself, so how about we go on a practice run before your big scene with the heroine?*"

In other words, this "pretend-date" was study material for the film we were making, as well as for Minami herself, who was worried that she didn't understand anything about romance. I was still happy to hang out with her, though, no matter what the reason was.

"Oh, you're filming, Minami?" I asked, smiling.

She'd had her phone camera pointed at me as I walked into

the park. Minami had told me beforehand that she wanted to capture some scenes on our date, and she smiled as she stood up.

"Hey, Tsukishima. Can you ask me, 'Were you waiting long?'"

"Huh? Oh, sure. Um… Were you waiting long?"

"Don't worry. I just got here."

"I saw you waiting, though. You were sitting here already when I came."

"But it's like the typical thing to say, isn't it? On a date."

She was wearing a casual, sporty outfit that really suited her. I realized it was the first time I'd seen her in her own clothes instead of a school uniform. She could have been a model in a magazine, or one of those people who post their glamorous lifestyles on social media. I would've taken her for an actress, not a director.

Minami put down her camera and filled me in on her plan. "So, I was thinking we'd start with lunch at this place I've been meaning to check out, then walk around the city for a bit, and end up back here at the park. Could we have a quick meeting about next week's shoot after that?"

"Sure. Sounds good to me."

"Great, let's get going, then." She casually slipped her hand into mine.

"M-Minami, what're you—?"

"Huh? Don't couples hold hands on a date?"

"Uh, isn't that normally later on, when they're actually going out?"

"I did some research, just in case, and apparently it's not unusual to hold hands on a first date."

I was the only one getting flustered; Minami didn't seem

to feel anything in particular. That was proof enough that she didn't have any romantic feelings toward me, but I was nervous anyway.

"I'm guessing this is a first for you, Tsukishima."

"Well, yeah... Not for you?"

"I must've held hands with someone in preschool."

"I don't think that counts, usually." We were still holding hands as we chatted. I felt hot with nerves and hoped my hand wasn't sweating too much. "Um, Minami, I'm not sure if we should—" I tried to come up with some sort of excuse, but she just smiled at me.

"C'mon. Let's go, Tsukishima."

"Uh, hang on—"

And so, Minami pulled me along by the hand, and we melted into the bustle of the city streets. Our first stop was a trendy burger joint that Minami had had her eyes on for some time. We got in before the place got crowded and each ordered their specialty burger.

At some point, I forgot about being nervous and started looking forward to the meal, since I didn't know what to expect. When the burgers came out, they were humongous—the buns, patties, and veggies were all stacked up like a tower.

Minami wanted to see me bite into it, so I rose to the challenge. But as soon as I sank my teeth into the bun, I couldn't move; the filling would've all come tumbling out if I did. Minami was surprised by my struggle but laughing gleefully all the same.

After lunch, we wandered around town. A refreshing breeze swept through the streets, putting a spring in everyone's step. Minami suggested we check out some shops selling stationery and whatnot, so I let her guide me by the hand.

At one place, I found a flashy pair of sunglasses for a dress-up party. I couldn't help myself and put them on. Minami put on a weirder pair with a nose and bushy mustache hanging from them, which made me burst out laughing.

Minami was full of surprises, and I was never bored with her around. Brimming with curiosity and life, she enjoyed herself without worrying about what anyone else thought of her, as though she was always conscious of the fact that she only got one shot at life.

She filmed parts of our date—being mindful not to disturb the people around us or the shops—and I did the same, filming her with my phone.

Minami simply opened her arms to life. Maybe that kind of open-minded innocence was the most important quality you could have in life: to take things as they come and still find pleasure in the world around you.

Once we'd explored enough of the streets, we bought something to drink and came back to the same park we'd met up in to take a break. We sat on a bench side by side.

"You know, I think you're kinda like my dad," I said. The words seemed to come out of me on their own.

"Oh, I am? How so?" she asked eagerly. For a moment, I thought it might not have been the most tactful thing to say to the girl I liked, but she didn't seem to mind at all.

"Um, well… You're always so innocent and full of life."

"That sounds more like a little kid."

"Oh, I meant it in a good way."

"I know. So your dad's like that, too, huh? Kinda makes me wanna meet him."

Sitting on the bench, we talked about our families. I found

out that Minami had a brother who was a lot older than her and had an office job.

"What about you, Tsukishima? Are you an only child?"

"Yeah."

"I had a feeling you might be. It kinda seems like your parents raised you with a lot of TLC."

"Yeah, I guess. When I was little, I got sick all the time, so I worried them a lot. And—" I stopped myself just before something I didn't mean to say slipped out. It wasn't just when I was little—I was still making my parents worry now. Though they never let it show in front of me, I knew they must be in pain, knowing their son would die from an illness before them… There was no way around their suffering.

As I was sinking deeper into my thoughts, I heard a familiar *blip* from Minami's phone. I looked around to find her taking a video of me. "What's up?" I asked.

"Oh, I just thought it was a good shot and started recording without really thinking about it."

"Really? Well, the park looks nice, at least."

"…Sometimes you go somewhere else, don't you, Tsukishima?"

"Huh?"

"One moment you're here; the next you're gone. It's like… when you disappear like that, it reminds me that people aren't so simple. We come in all kinds, and every one of us is carrying their own load, in their own way."

Maybe I disappeared from the face of the earth when I thought about death, leaving only my shadow behind—and Minami had been watching that shadow. I stayed quiet, wondering what to say in reply.

"By the way," she went on, "what you said in that scene in the nurse's office—it was really powerful. How'd you come up with that?"

It had been a while since we shot that scene, but I still felt a bit embarrassed when I remembered my improv lines. I thought about how to explain it to her without giving away too much. "I knew you and Hayami wanted the acting and dialogue to be really natural, so I tried to be myself, just as I am…and that's what came out."

"So, from your perspective, it didn't make sense for her to give up hope so soon after she found out she'd die?"

Even though I knew Minami was just asking me what I thought about the scenario, my heart skipped a beat.

"Not that it 'didn't make sense,' exactly… Though, I guess I felt there was something more to it—something more real than what was in the script. It's surprisingly easy to let go of hope, but then there's nowhere else to go," I said, thinking back to my past self.

Minami looked somewhat taken aback. "Have you ever felt *that* hopeless about something?" she asked.

I quickly looked at her. "You mean like my fashion sense?" I said with a wry grin, trying to lighten the mood. It wasn't a great joke, but Minami went along with it anyway and laughed with me.

After that, we had a quick meeting about next week's shoot. We already had permission to film in this park. The others had scouted out the location beforehand, but in order to make things run as smoothly as possible on the day, Minami asked me to stand in different spots, checking the angles of the shots and things like that.

Once we got through everything we needed to, we headed to a video game arcade nearby. This time, it had nothing to do with the movie; Minami was genuinely curious about going there together as part of her research into dating. We had fun playing a claw machine and two-player games and took videos of each other while we were at it.

We left the arcade at around sunset and walked to the train station, the deep red sky stretching over us. We could've said good-bye then, but Minami wanted to capture the scenery against the setting sun, so we kept walking to the next station over. When she'd gotten enough shots of the scenery, Minami turned her camera back onto me. I thought it would be a lot more worthwhile to film *her* instead, though—she looked like she'd stepped right out of a movie—so I took some video of her, promising to give her the data later.

We followed the railroad tracks, and before long, our conversation drifted back to the movie we were filming.

"You know, Tsukishima, your character was supposed to be a really ordinary guy—the sort of guy you'd find anywhere," said Minami, looking at me. "But after that scene in the nurse's office, he turned into someone who *looks* like any other ordinary guy, but who's hiding something deep inside of him."

That's probably because I am *like that*, I thought. I was a run-of-the-mill guy through and through—except for my terminal illness.

"We could keep going with the script as it is now, but personally, I want to take your performance from that scene and make it part of the story somehow. We can't really make any big changes, but I've been thinking about how we could do something like that… You have any ideas, Tsukishima?"

Since I'd never collaborated on a creative project before, I didn't have anything worth calling an idea. Still, I wanted to contribute, so I stopped filming and pondered her question. One idea hit me. I almost blurted it out but hesitated and closed my mouth again.

Minami had seen it, though. "What is it? Just tell me—it can be anything," she pressed.

I was still unsure whether I should say it, but eventually, I gave in. "Okay. How about this? The movie is about a heroine who dies from a rare disease, but what if the protagonist is sick, too? And...what if he's hiding it from everyone?"

Though it might've sounded far-fetched, it was my reality. I'd offered it up to Minami in the hopes that she might find it even a little bit useful. Minami stopped in her tracks. I stopped alongside her.

"Could you tell me more?" she asked.

"Oh, okay... Let's say the protagonist also doesn't have much longer to live, though he's keeping it a secret. And that's why he can understand the heroine's pain and what she's going through. So when she tells him about her illness in the nurse's office, he tells her exactly how he feels, which makes the heroine open up about her own feelings. Something like that."

I was scared that Minami might detect the truth behind my words—that I was in that exact same situation—but I figured she wouldn't connect the dots. Minami listened to what I had to say and stayed silent for a while, deep in thought.

Then she let out a soft laugh. "You might be onto something."

"Really?"

"Yeah. The title would make the audience think it's just the heroine who's dying, but the protagonist is actually sick, too.

And he keeps it a secret right up until the very end. Because... he doesn't want the people around him to be sad?"

"Maybe." I thought about it not as the protagonist, but as myself. "No, I'm sure that must be why."

Minami started mulling over what kind of scenes we could add to the movie if we made that change to the plot and how we could tug at the heartstrings of the audience. We had to keep any additional scenes to a minimum, and I became her sounding board while also making some suggestions of my own.

We walked to the next station, building up the script all the while. We still weren't ready when we got there, so we kept right on walking to yet another station. It was twilight by then, and stars were starting to glimmer in the sky.

Eventually, we managed to put all our thoughts into words. Since we lived in opposite directions, we parted at the station. I got on my train, sat down, and was gazing out the window when I got a text from Minami:

"Thanks for today. I'm going to do more thinking about the script and how to direct it for the movie."

Her sincere message made me smile. We texted back and forth, going over the ideas we'd shared with each other on our walk, and we came to the question of how to tell the other club members about this change in the story.

"What do you think about keeping this a secret from everyone?" Minami asked. *"Shooting and editing the extra scenes won't be too much work, so I'm thinking we could make two versions of the movie without anyone knowing. Then, when we're finished, we show both and ask which one they prefer."*

Apparently, Minami wanted to take everyone by surprise.

But that wasn't the only reason she had this idea; she figured that if the others could compare the two versions without any preconceptions, they could judge them based purely on their merits.

I told her I had no objections. Now I was even more excited than before to see the finished film.

9

The following week, we started filming after school again. It was my first time doing it outside the school premises. We had to do some reshoots because of my slipups, of course, but we still got the shots we needed on schedule.

I wished it could go on forever, but we were quickly approaching the end.

On Saturday, the last day of filming, we shot the climactic scene at a hospital. Hayami's mom was a nurse, so we got special permission from the hospital to use an empty room. The filming mostly revolved around the heroine. I was surprised that the hospital we used was the same one that I regularly went to, but I didn't have much time to dwell on the coincidence. Ena performed all her scenes without a single retake, and while Ichika and I had some nerves, we both also managed to get through all our scenes before the time was up.

For everyone else, it was a wrap; Minami and I still had work to do. While the others were off having lunch, we shot the extra scenes in secret. We'd rehearsed the scenes countless times beforehand, and I didn't have any lines, so one take was enough for each. Minami suggested we also get an establishing shot of the protagonist standing outside and looking up at the hospital, which was going to be necessary for the flow of the story. We captured all the additional footage without getting caught by the others, and we gave each other a high five.

Just as Minami had planned in the beginning, we wrapped up the filming just before July. By then, our end-of-term exams were coming up at school. Summer vacation would be just around the corner once they were over, but the filmmaking club was under more pressure than ever, with the deadline for the indie film competition drawing closer. Minami and Hayami were up to their necks in editing work, and the rest of us helped as much as we could.

I never saw either of them study for the end-of-term exams, but when the test results came out and I asked how they'd ranked, Hayami's scores were better than mine. Though Minami had told me she'd done badly in math, she still managed to steer clear of a failing grade.

As for me, my scores were pretty average. More importantly, my health was perfectly stable—so much so that I almost could've believed my terminal illness wasn't real.

It had been the beginning of March when the doctor had first told me that I had one year left; four months had passed since then. Luckily, I hadn't had any noticeable symptoms so far, but they would start to appear when the disease progressed to the intermediate stage. Sometimes I got scared thinking about that, but I went about my life as usual.

Each day glided by, quietly but unremittingly advancing toward summer.

Minami was working on the edits for the alternative version of the film at her house, and I took some of the audio equipment home to record voice-over that she needed for the extra scenes.

The two movies—the original version and the alternative version—were both steadily nearing completion just in time for the beginning of summer break. The team told me that they usually had a party and a preview screening whenever they finished a movie, so Ena checked with her parents and got permission for us to celebrate in her room.

On the day of the preview, I stood rooted to the spot in front of Ena's house. I was stunned—some might even say overwhelmed—by how modern and fancy it was. I'd never set foot in a house like that before. I managed to find the doorbell, and Ena let me in.

Ena told me that her family was out for the day and that the rest of the club members were already there, whipping up some food for the party in the kitchen. She led me through her expansive house to a room on the second floor—a luxurious suite that combined two rooms into one, which turned out to be Ena's.

Soon, the others finished cooking and came up to Ena's room. "Hey, Tsukishima, you made it," Minami said cheerfully.

"Feels weird to see you here," Hayami joked.

"Hi, Makoto," Ichika said.

It was time for the preview to begin. Apparently, it was customary to have a short speech from the director before the show, so everyone prompted Minami to stand up and say a few words.

"Well, this is the first film we've made with the five of us, so I hope you all enjoy it. Oh, just make sure you don't die of laughter... Get it, 'cause it's about death?"

"Come on, Tsubasa, let's watch it already," Hayami said.

Ena turned off the lights, and Minami sat back down on the sofa between me and Hayami. Minami clicked on the laptop, which was connected to the projector, and the movie started to play.

Our faces were all illuminated by the light from the projector. I could feel Minami looking at me, and she grinned when my eyes met hers; she was clearly getting a kick out of this. Meanwhile, I was a bundle of nerves. Not only was it my first time seeing the movie all the way through, but Minami was starting with the alternative version—the one she and I had made in secret.

The opening scene of the film was already different from the original script. It showed the protagonist coming out of the hospital and looking back at the building.

"Uh...Tsubasa, what's this?" Hayami asked with surprise.

"No talking during the movie," Minami playfully scolded, and Hayami watched silently after that. Conscious of my racing heart, I kept my eyes glued to the screen.

Despite its plain title, *The Girl Who Dies from a Rare Disease* was bursting with emotion. The high schooler protagonist goes about his ordinary life and meets the heroine, who's in a different class. She seems calm and mature but also sullen and has trouble getting on with those around her. The protagonist gets to know her through their mutual friend, Ichika's character, but the heroine keeps herself inside her shell and won't open up to anyone.

One day, the heroine collapses in front of the protagonist. He carries her to the nurse's office, where he hears about the heroine's incurable disease as she lies there unconscious. When she wakes up and realizes he knows the truth, she acts like it's no big deal, but the talk takes an unexpected turn. They end up in a heated argument, and for the first time, she lets out her true feelings.

After that, the heroine begins to change little by little. She starts opening up to the protagonist. They go out together, having dates around town and at the park; they stay behind chatting after school; they run across the sports field as fast as they can—things they can only do while she's still strong enough to do them.

The heroine, who used to run track, stands on the field, gasping for air. She loves the feeling of the wind whipping past her when she runs. It makes her happy to be covered in sweat. She feels lucky just to be alive. With tears in her eyes, she says, "I want to live more."

She ends up being hospitalized after her disease progresses. Her condition gets worse, but the heroine is satisfied, glad that she could live life to the fullest even at the end. The protagonist visits her in the hospital, but she asks him not to come anymore. The heroine knows she's approaching death, and she wants him to remember her as she was.

She forces herself to smile and bids farewell to the protagonist. "Thank you...for living with me. It's because of what you said that I could keep my hopes up till the end. Good-bye. I think I might have fallen in love with you."

A few months later, there's a funeral for the heroine. Her friend comes to talk to the protagonist, and she tells him that the heroine looked happy right up until her last breath. The friend hands him a photo that the heroine had loved enough to put up in her hospital room.

It's a photo she took of herself and the protagonist while they were joking around one day. In the picture, she's smiling brightly like any other teenage girl.

The story comes to a close, and the end credits start to roll. The movie was originally supposed to end there, but after the credits, the extra scenes we shot start to play.

In the same hospital room the heroine had been in, the protagonist gazes out the window, wearing a patient's gown.

"When I met her, I already knew I only had three more years to live."

He delivers a soliloquy in a voice-over, accompanied by subtitles.

"She was in the same situation as me, and I made up my mind to be there for her.

"But all the while, my own time was running out, too."

In the end, the protagonist gazes at the photo of the heroine and him together.

"Sunny days. Rainbows. Coffee." He silently thinks about all the things he loves. *"Dad's cooking. Mom's smile. And...you."*

The film comes to an end with one last spoken line by the protagonist:

"Thank you for living with me."

No one moved once the movie finished. After a while, Ena got up to turn the lights back on. A few more seconds of silence went by, and then Hayami finally exhaled deeply and looked at Minami.

"So, are you going to explain?" she asked quietly. She was calm; there was no anger in her voice.

"Did we surprise you? I wanted to do something with Tsukishima's performance in the nurse's office, and we came up with the idea of changing the protagonist's side of the story," Minami said.

"...I figured it was something like that," replied Hayami. "Well, I can see how the earlier scene makes more sense like this."

"So, what did you think, Aoi? Didn't it make the movie better?" Minami asked.

Hayami was silent for a while. I was starting to think she might actually be angry after all, but it turned out I was wrong. With another sigh, she said, "Ena, can you turn the lights off again? And, Tsubasa, let me borrow your laptop."

In the darkened room, Hayami started going over the movie from the very beginning, focusing on the extra scenes and what came before and after them. When she was done, Ena switched on the lights again.

"About the opening scene," Hayami began thoughtfully, "the transition is a bit slow at the end. And if we're going to do this, we should go all the way. I know it's not your style, Tsubasa, but I think we should add a shot showing how the protagonist regrets time slipping away. That'll make it easier to understand. I'm pretty sure we could use some of the spare footage we shot. Also—"

Hayami raised several more points that stood out to her, like how we should refine the audio track of my voice-over that I'd recorded at home. Every critique she gave us showed she had fully grasped and accepted what we were trying to do.

"If we make all those tweaks...I think it works, to be honest. It was pretty cool."

Minami and I looked at each other.

"Yeah, I thought it was great," Ena chimed in. "What a plot twist."

"I—I really liked it, too," Ichika added.

We decided to watch the original version to compare the two, but in the end, everyone agreed that the alternative version was better.

"Hey, Tsubasa." Hayami turned to Minami, her expression tense like she'd come to a decision. "The submission deadline is in three days, right?"

"Yup, that's right," Minami replied casually.

"Uh, how are you so chill? Anyway, I guess we gotta do what we gotta do. Let's dig up everything we have to fix. And I think we better change the synopsis for the movie, too. I'll take care of that, so—"

"Is it just me or do you look kind of excited, Aoi? What's up?" Minami cut in.

After a pause, Hayami said, "I'd been wondering about Tsukishima's performance, too—and you tied it in really well with those extra scenes. I want to use the changes you came up with, Tsubasa...and as long as we're submitting something, I want us to aim for the top prize."

"I like the way you think," Tsubasa said. "But I'm so hungry. Can't we put off the work till tomorrow and eat for now?"

"Huh? But, Tsubasa, it's your fault the film's not ready yet."

"C'mon, we're here for a party, aren't we? I mean, it's not like we can really celebrate the film being finished anymore—but let's let our hair down a bit!"

Hayami pulled a face that said, "What am I going to do with you?" but in the end, she caved in with a shrug, and the party commenced.

We went down to the kitchen and carried up all the food to Ena's room, and then we raised our glasses in a toast. With everyone in high spirits, I forgot about how nervous I had been earlier and thoroughly enjoyed myself. Ena and Ichika chatted with me, too, and I felt really at ease with everyone. The lively party got a bit weird when Ena brought out the *amazake*; apparently, it was something of a tradition for Ena to make Hayami drink some sweet sake at their premieres.

Hayami started slurring her words at me, and Ichika, who'd drunk some with her, was soon cracking up over nothing. Meanwhile, Minami and Ena sipped the *amazake* peacefully, watching the other two get tipsy. Eventually, the room grew quiet, and everyone except me and Minami nodded off to sleep.

"Ahh. This is how our parties always end up," Minami said with a warm smile, watching the trio of girls sleeping soundly.

"Really? They're like this every time?"

"Pretty much. We're only drinking *amazake* now, but I'm a bit worried about what's gonna happen when we grow up. How crazy would they get with *real* alcohol?"

Still, Minami's eyes were full of love as she gazed across at her friends.

I'm sure the four of them will stay friends, I thought. *Even when they move on from drinking* amazake *to real sake, nothing else will change. They'll always be close...*

I felt a pang of regret that I wouldn't be a part of that. The thought of my illness crossed my mind, and I fell silent, sinking into loneliness.

"Hey, wanna get some fresh air?" Minami asked. Ena's room had an impressive balcony. The two of us slipped out and stood side by side in the soft moonlight.

"I'm glad we convinced Aoi—it looks like everything will work out," Minami said. "I had so much fun putting the movie together, and I thought those extra scenes were the highlights. What about you, Tsukishima? How did you like your first attempt at filmmaking? Did you have fun?"

Seeing her easygoing smile from the corner of my eye, I reflected on my own experience. "Yeah... I had a lot of fun, too. I never even imagined I'd ever be in a movie. Honestly, I'm really grateful that you invited me to join in..." Those few words weren't enough to express everything, but it was still how I genuinely felt.

The filmmaking club had given me an achievement I never could have touched by checking off my solo bucket list. I had even come to hope that I'd be able to keep spending time with Minami and everyone else for as long as I could. Except...

The words I'd heard from my doctor the other day were hanging over me:

"You aren't at the critical stage yet, but there's still a chance that symptoms will start appearing during summer vacation. So you should prepare yourself for that possibility."

I'd joined the club in mid-May, and two months had whizzed by in the blink of an eye. My days with the girls had been packed with excitement, but the time limit had come quicker than I'd expected. There was nothing I could do about that, though.

It was probably best to start distancing myself from the club. I'd finished my role, too, so it made sense to break it off now. I just had to find the right timing.

"You're gone again," Minami said.

"What?" I noticed her looking closely at me.

"You disappeared somewhere else."

"No...I haven't disappeared. I'm right here." I smiled, trying to sound cheerful, but didn't know if I'd convinced her.

"You're something of an enigma, Tsukishima." Minami let out a quiet laugh. After a pause, she went on. "You're close with the nurse for some reason, but you don't get smug about it or anything, and you helped us out making the movie... You're really nice, but sometimes you disappear..."

The air around her shifted slightly. At some point, I'd turned to face her.

"And that's not all," she continued. "Back in first year, when the girl was getting bullied... I tried to be secretive about being friendly toward her—I didn't want to make her stand out even more. I was even careful just saying hi to her. But you noticed me, Tsukishima. How come?"

I hadn't expected Minami to think anything of that. "Yeah..." I hesitated. "I could see you were being subtle about it. Still, it was obvious to me," I said honestly.

"Why was that?"

"Because I was watching you all the time. I don't know when I started to, but I just couldn't look away."

It was a clear, starlit night; only the darkness, the moon, and the stars were watching us. As I stood there, aware of the beautiful sky above our heads, Minami smiled at me.

"I have a feeling that maybe your words would've bounced

off me if I'd heard you say that before—when I didn't get what romance is. For me, it was something that existed just in songs and movies." Then, suddenly, she asked, "Do you want to go out with me?"

My eyes flew to hers. Every sound in the world seemed to be drawn in by her gaze. I was too stunned to speak.

She smiled again. "What it means to fall in love with someone—I think I might know what that feels like now, just a little bit. Maybe it happened because you're similar to the type of guy I like. You're shouldering a kind of sadness, and you look like you're hiding something… We're not in a movie, though, so I know I must just be imagining it. But right now, you're all I can see, Tsukishima. And more than anything else…I have the most fun when I'm with you. If that's not love, then I don't know what is."

I couldn't believe this was actually happening—except my throbbing pulse and the breeze blowing against my skin was proof that I wasn't dreaming. I didn't know what to do. Not even in my wildest dreams had I ever dared to hope for *this*.

But I didn't even have a year left to live. If I said yes to Minami here, she would eventually have to grieve the death of her boyfriend. And if she found out about my illness…

"Maybe you've got things mixed up," I said, desperately trying to suppress my own feelings. "You might just like me as a friend or as a club member. Maybe that's why you have fun when I'm around…"

Minami fell silent. After a little while, her cheeks softened in a smile. "So, how about we test it?"

"Uh, test…what, exactly?"

"Let's try kissing. And if my heart beats faster, that means

I like you, Tsukishima—no... Makoto. And then we'll know nothing is mixed up."

Minami leaned over, closing the distance between us. Her idea should have made me feel shy and flustered, but somehow all I felt was fear. I had the feeling that if I let this happen, there would be no turning back.

This must be some sort of practical joke. A prank that only Minami was in on, where she'd pull out at the last minute. She'd see my wide-eyed face, burst out laughing, then tease me for it...

The next moment, a softness I'd never felt before touched my lips.

I felt as if I'd tasted the entirety of life in a single moment.

Minami drew back and opened her eyes, looking at me with a shy smile. "My heart was going crazy," she said. "I knew it. I really do like you a lot, Makoto."

Ah... Why now? I thought. After all this time having God ignore my wishes, one wish that shouldn't be granted was about to come true. I hadn't even dared to write it down in my notebook.

I knew deep down that I shouldn't continue on this path. But it was the first time in my life that a girl I liked had told me she liked me back.

Am I allowed to have this once-in-a-lifetime experience? I wondered.

I don't know yet how things are going to change for me. Still, when the time comes, I'll find a way. I'll choose to live my life in a way that won't make her sad. So...

"I like you, too, Minami. With all my heart."

My words fell quietly in the air like a lonely prayer. Like a teardrop.

Minami smiled at me, as if to scoop up that prayer. "So, you'll be my boyfriend?"

"Yes."

"That makes me really happy, Makoto."

The girl I'd fallen for was someone who made movies. She was a kind person with a beautiful soul, and right now she was looking at me as if nothing else in the world mattered.

I might not be able to see where our story would lead, but I couldn't stop it from moving forward.

Scene 2.

Aoi Hayami

1

At what point do you stop being a child and start being an adult?

The thought drifts across my mind sometimes.

When I was little, I thought grown-ups knew a lot of stuff. They taught me how to solve problems in my homework that I didn't get. They knew all kinds of games. I could rely on them, and I felt safe when I was with them.

I guess the answer to that question depends on who the child sees as a grown-up—for me, it was my father.

He was an aspiring film director, and as far as society was concerned, he was jobless. We were always together at home. He had a habit of saying, "Because I'm the grown-up," and whenever I didn't have school, the two of us would watch old movies all day long.

At one point, my "grown-up" father started lying to me. Maybe he'd already been lying a long time before that, and I'd just been too little to see through his lies.

If growing up meant being able to see through people's lies, I wanted to stay a kid forever.

But the grown-up in front of me kept right on lying.

I loved him a lot. He was always gentle. He was important in my life, and I wanted him to be by my side forever.

One day, he just disappeared. I was in elementary school. Before he left, he said, "I'm going out for a bit. I'll be back before you know it." He had that same pained look he always had on his face when he lied.

It was August already. Two weeks had gone by since school let out for the summer. So much had happened since then—actually, it had already been hectic before summer break started. We hurried to revise our movie according to Tsubasa and Tsukishima's new idea, and we somehow made it right in time for the submission deadline for the indie film competition.

It would've been ideal to make movies with more wiggle room in our schedule, but sometimes we'd end up like this—especially if Tsubasa came up with something new—and we'd keep revising the movie right up to the deadline. But I knew that those last-minute ideas always made the film better.

I'd never forget the time when the four of us made a movie in the summer of our third year of junior high, and we submitted it to a contest for junior high schoolers. That time, just like now, Tsubasa had proposed a change right before the deadline. We worked together to make it happen, and as a result, our movie won an award.

I hadn't thought I'd get emotional, but when we heard the news, I just couldn't help myself. I'd discovered how thrilling it could be to work together with a team you trust to achieve a single goal. I got hooked on the creative process.

Since then, we threw ourselves into filmmaking with even

more fervor than before. Once in a while, Tsubasa would come up with a new idea right before the deadline, but I'd come to accept it as a sort of superstition. Whenever that happened, it always led to something good.

So this time around, I had a hunch that the same thing might happen again. Maybe this movie would also turn out to be something special…

"Now then, let me just say one more time—hey, Aoi, are you listening?" Tsubasa called out to me.

I'd been lost in thought, sitting at the desk in our clubroom with my chin resting in my hand. I looked up at her. She was standing in front of the group, the commemorative plaque in her hands.

"Yeah, yeah. I'm listening," I told her.

"Okay then, once again… Congrats to us for snagging the special prize at the indie film festival! We did iiit!"

It was a pretty strange cheer, and Tsubasa thrust her fist into the air as she said it. Everyone except me followed her lead, raising their fists with a hesitant "W-we did it."

"Uh, you want us to all cheer 'We did it'?" I asked dubiously.

"Oh, would you prefer 'We won'?"

"That's not what I meant, but that *might* be a little better."

"All right, then, one more time—"

"Again?"

"Why not? We can do it a hundred times. It's something to celebrate!"

In the summer indie film festival, anyone of any age or any level of experience could submit a film to be part of the public competition as long as they passed the preliminary selection.

Almost fifty films were shown in a small theater over the space of a week or so. The audience cast their votes, and the top ten films were judged by a panel. Since there were so many films, even the most die-hard film lover would find it hard to watch every work in the running—which meant that the race had begun when the titles and blurbs were displayed on the festival website.

Our film, *The Girl Who Dies from a Rare Disease*, got a special prize at the festival. We'd also passed the preliminary selection last year, but our movie had failed to garner enough attention and hadn't got many votes. This year's outcome was a major achievement. I should've been overjoyed. And yet…

"All righty, then, let's do this one more time. Congrats to us for bringing home the special prize at the indie film festival! We wooon!"

We all chanted, "We won!" When I glanced at Tsukishima, he was grinning sheepishly with his fist in the air. Why was it that I couldn't fully bask in the glory of our win? Probably because of this guy: Makoto Tsukishima.

Just as I was shooting him a look, Tsubasa said, "We got the prize thanks to *your* idea, Makoto. Plus, you were the leading actor. You should be shouting the loudest!"

"What? No, it was all of you—you let me be a part of the project, and I was just tagging along."

At some point, Tsubasa had switched to calling Tsukishima by his first name. And that wasn't the only thing that had changed: As hard as it was hard to believe, they were actually going out now.

Tsubasa, the same person who used to say she didn't get what romance was all about, was officially going out with someone…

Tsubasa and I have been friends since preschool, and we've been making films together since our fifth grade of elementary school. Our tastes are similar. What we consider beautiful or ugly align pretty closely. That's why Tsubasa always counts on me to give her my opinion; whenever she comes up with an idea for revising a movie, I'm the first one she talks to. At least, that's how it had been up till now.

This time, I found out afterward that the new idea had come from Tsukishima. I'd assumed it was Tsubasa's, so I was shocked, and it also kind of got on my nerves.

"So, Director. About our next film," I said a bit awkwardly, seeing the two of them getting along.

"Oh, right, sorry. Our next movie. Let's see..."

Prompted by my remark, Tsubasa started describing her idea for our next movie. Ena was listening eagerly, all smiles, and Ichika was drinking in her words with the attentiveness of a diligent student.

Ena had been one of us since junior high school. When Tsubasa and I were in second year, we got wind of a rumor that an incredibly cute girl had transferred to our school, so we went to ask her to be in our movie.

"*Why are you making a movie? What's the point?*" Ena had said.

Back then, Ena never smiled; she was surly and ice-cold. The gossip around school was that her father was a VIP at some famous company and that he'd recently gotten remarried.

"*There's no* point. *The meaning is in the making,*" Tsubasa answered without batting an eye.

"*That still doesn't make any sense,*" Ena said frostily.

"*Of course it doesn't. You're not* trying *to get it,*" Tsubasa said.

Ena had turned us down at first, but Tsubasa didn't give up. It hadn't been easy, but with Tsubasa's persistence, Ena eventually gave in. Even so, I had the feeling that Ena had only pretended to begrudgingly give in; I think she secretly wanted to make something with Tsubasa. Back then, Tsubasa was the only person Ena would talk to. Ena had put up thick walls all around her, shutting everyone else out. Only Tsubasa, with her carefree attitude, could march right through those walls as if they weren't there.

Later on, I came to understand that Ena hadn't locked herself up in her shell because she'd wanted to. There was a reason why she had to be that way.

One time, she'd suddenly showed us her weak side. "*My father...wanted a son, not a daughter,*" she told us. For her, saying that out loud must have been like sending out an SOS. She must have wanted to call for help so badly. "*But Mom couldn't have any more children... He was fine with it until I got to junior high, but it turns out he just couldn't give up on the idea. He's a piece of garbage. He arranged the divorce and got himself a new wife before I even knew what was going on and told me I shouldn't see my mom again.*"

Losing someone you love, your parents getting divorced—things like that happened in movies. I already knew firsthand they were both part of real life, too, though. Like me, Ena couldn't live with both her biological parents. She seemed especially close to her mother, so it was hard for Ena to be separated from her.

We were just junior high kids. There was nothing we could do to help Ena—or so I'd thought.

One day, when we didn't have school, Tsubasa had called Ena

to come out for a film shoot. Ena didn't seem to know what to make of Tsubasa's sudden suggestion, but we made her get on the train with us, and we headed for the town where Ena used to live with her mother.

Happiness comes in all sorts of different forms; that's another thing I learned from movies. Both Ena's parents and mine must have parted ways because each person had different ideas about what happiness is.

"I don't know about all the complicated stuff...but it's obvious what makes Ena happy, don't you think?" Tsubasa mused as we waited for Ena in a café in the unfamiliar town.

When Ena had seen her mother again, she'd cried. The three of us had been walking toward Ena's old house. Tsubasa had been stopping Ena from turning back, and just at that moment, her mother had come outside. She noticed Ena and stopped in her tracks, shocked. Then she started running toward her daughter.

I'd watched scenes like that in movies before, and once again, I was struck by the fact that films really did reflect reality.

"Mom," Ena murmured in a daze. Her mother pulled her into a tight embrace, and Ena sobbed loudly.

"I'm glad you could see your mom again," Tsubasa told her. Then we had left Ena and her mother alone and gone into a café nearby to wait.

Tsubasa was sitting there with her big, carefree smile, so I told her what I thought: Happiness comes in different forms. And that had been Tsubasa's answer: It's obvious what makes Ena happy.

Ever since that meeting with her mother, Ena started to change. While Tsubasa and I were waiting at the café, Ena had talked with her mother for the first time since her parents' divorce and told her everything, including how much she still loved her.

We didn't hear the details, but it sounded like her mother had taken a step back after the divorce so that Ena could get used to her new stepmother sooner. It was clear that Ena's mom still loved her daughter from the bottom of her heart—we'd seen it in the way she ran over and hugged her tight.

Ena's mother had given her the name, written with the kanji for *smile* to express her hopes for her daughter. Ena said she wanted to be true to her name and never forget to smile, no matter what happened in life. That way, she could remember what her mother wanted for her, even when they were far apart. And that's how she became the Ena she is now, always holding on to that positivity.

"*Ena looks more comfortable in her own skin than she used to,*" Ichika had once said.

Ena stood out at school, while Ichika, on the other hand, was fairly nondescript. Tsubasa and I had been friends with Ichika since we were little. She tagged along with us everywhere, so when we started making movies in fifth grade, she helped us out as an actor. We knew that Ichika had a pure soul and that she was more earnest and hardworking than anyone else.

So that was how we became a team: Tsubasa, the genius type, bold and impulsive, who knew how to get things done; the beautiful Ena, who was actually the wisest of all of us; Ichika, who never skimped on her efforts and gave her all to everything she did; and me, who had no special talent to speak of but at least knew a lot about movies.

The filmmaking club was just for the four of us. As soon as

Ena and Ichika entered the same senior high school as Tsubasa and me, we registered as an official club, and luckily the school approved our application without a hitch. They even gave us a clubroom and a small amount of funds for our activities. This room was a castle for just the four of us. At least, it had been for me. But now…

"Aoi? Are you listening?" Tsubasa called out.

I snapped out of my reverie and replied calmly, "Sure. We're submitting to the Eiga Koushien Competition again this winter, right? It's going to be a medium-length film, so it'll take time to shoot it. Ideally, we should settle on the concept during the summer break and start filming once school starts to stay ahead of schedule. So, if we have ideas about the story or anything else, we should speak up anytime. Does that about sum it up?"

Tsubasa nodded, looking pleased. "Oh good, you *did* hear everything I said."

"I'd never miss a single word you say, Tsubasa."

"Can you say that again? I wanna film you. It was a nice line for a 'trusted partner' kinda role."

"Sorry, what? I didn't quite catch that."

"What happened to you hearing everything I say?"

We had a brainstorming session about our next film after that. We were lucky enough to have an AC in the room, but it was an old one, so it didn't work so well. We were practically sweating as we sat around the laptop.

The sky we could see from inside the room was a deep, bottomless blue. Cicadas chirped furiously outside, as if they knew how short their lives were.

During the meeting, Tsubasa spoke freely, and Ichika diligently offered her own opinions. Sometimes Ena joined in with a sharp observation. When Tsubasa asked him for his thoughts, Tsukishima responded thoughtfully. As for me, I organized everyone's suggestions and got them back on track when the discussion seemed to veer off course. The whiteboard was filling up with all kinds of ideas.

But at some point, the ideas dried up and we started talking in circles.

"Hey, Tsubasa, how about we take a break?" I said. Since we'd run out of drinks, someone had to go get more. We played rock-paper-scissors to decide who should go. Tsubasa and I lost, so it was on us to go to the vending machine.

As soon as we stepped out of our clubroom, we were swallowed up by the heat. It felt like a sauna.

"Whoa, it's so hot. Sure feels like summer!" Tsubasa exclaimed happily. She wasn't faking it; she really did seem to find the fun in any situation.

We walked side by side, just as we'd always done. Tsubasa had her phone out to take footage of the summer scenery, but this was just business as usual, so I didn't mind. I'd gotten used to it by now.

Do people just get used to everything, given time? Would I get used to having five people in the filmmaking club?

The vending machine was right by the gym. We stepped into the shade where it stood. Tsubasa put a few coins in and pressed the buttons for the drinks that everyone had requested.

It was then that I finally realized we were by ourselves. This was my chance to say something.

"Hey," I blurted out.

"Hmm?"

"Why are you going out with Tsukishima?" I wondered how

my quiet voice could echo so loudly with the shrill chirping of the cicadas all around us.

Tsubasa looked back at me. "Huh? 'Cause I like him," she said casually.

"Do you...mean that?"

"Yup. We went on a date to the zoo last week, and I was like, 'Ah, I really do like him.'"

"Oh yeah? What stole your heart, then?"

"I feel like there's darkness hiding inside him."

"What? He's not a movie character, you know."

"I'm kidding. I mean, that's how it started...but now I feel really peaceful when I'm with Makoto, and my heart starts racing—you know. There are all these little moments when I can tell he really cares about me. I guess he made me realize I'm in love."

"Whoa. Seriously?"

"What else? He's super kind. He has this air about him that's actually a bit like your dad—" Noticing my grimace, Tsubasa stopped herself.

"Like *who*?" I said.

"Uhh, sorry. Never mind."

"You're paying for my drink, Tsubasa."

"Aww. Oh well, guess I gotta suck it up. What do you want? Black coffee?"

We got a can for everyone; Tsubasa carried three, cradling them in her arms, and I carried one in each hand.

"Brr, they're cold. Let's hurry back," she said. When we turned around, we found Tsukishima coming toward us. "What's up, Makoto?"

"Oh, nothing. Just thought maybe you'd like a hand with the drinks." He took two cans from Tsubasa's arms.

"Ooh, thanks. Makoto to the rescue."

"Well, they'd be easier to carry if I hadn't joined the club, so I can go get the drinks from now on."

"I wonder how many you can hold."

"I don't know, I guess I could handle five at least, if I tried."

"Hey, Tsukishima," I cut in. When he turned around, I shoved two more cans in his hands. "Then you take these, too. You better not drop any."

He looked taken aback, but then a wry smile crossed his face. "Oh, okay. Sure thing." Tsubasa giggled at how obedient he was and took one of the cans for him.

2

In the end, we didn't make any big decisions about our next film that day. But we kept discussing the direction we wanted to take, and eventually it started taking shape. We thought of having Ichika play the lead role this time.

Having Ichika as the protagonist sparked our discussion: What kind of film would work well with Ichika as the main character? What kind of story would draw out compelling dialogue from her? Little by little, we built up our vision for the film.

Apparently, Tsubasa and Tsukishima were going on dates after every club meeting. I happened to hear about it because Ichika was eager to ask them how things were going.

Tsukishima couldn't come to the clubroom sometimes

because he had errands to take care of at home, but otherwise, he was a steady presence at our meetings.

One weekday in August, I stumbled across Tsukishima at the hospital.

Both my mother and stepfather have regular jobs—my mother, who remarried when I was in sixth grade, works as a nurse.

The day I saw Tsukishima, I'd gone to Mom's workplace to bring her something she'd forgotten at home. Back before my parents divorced, my jobless father and I used to go to the hospital together to bring her things.

My father had dreamed of becoming a film director. He was a kind man, but he had trouble making a living. In the end, he never managed to become a professional director, and when I was in fourth grade, he wandered off somewhere and never came back.

He left quite a few things behind for me: a whole lot of DVDs and books about movies, some filming equipment like his old camera, and a sort of sixth sense for detecting lies.

My father had lied to me a lot. He told me that he was so close to becoming a professional director and that things were going well between him and my mother. From little white lies to blatant falsehoods, he told them all. Before I knew it, I'd picked up this weird knack for seeing through people's lies. I learned how their tone or attitude changes, how their eyes look when they're not telling the truth.

On the day he disappeared, my father had said, "*I'm going out for a bit. I'll be back before you know it.*" As soon as he said it, I knew he was lying. And I was right. He never came back.

This skill of mine comes in handy, though. When a group

of girls are making movies, people try to cozy up to you when you'd rather be left alone.

One guy had told us, "*I genuinely like the movies you make, Tsubasa. It'd be great if we could make something together.*" That was a lie. He'd only been interested in getting close to Tsubasa.

Another guy said, "*You really do make interesting movies. Can I have your numbers? I'll introduce you to a producer I know.*" That was a lie, too. He wasn't talking to us because he appreciated our filmmaking skills, but because he liked how we looked.

Thanks to my father's example, I could pick out lies from truths. I'd been doing my best to protect everyone in the club because the three of them were really important to me.

Now, back to the day I saw Tsukishima at the hospital. I was sitting in the café in the building, watching people pass by while having a cup of coffee. There was a branch of a popular coffee shop just inside the front entrance of the hospital.

So many people came and went at a hospital. Countless lives intersected in a place like this, and so much was happening underneath the surface, invisible to strangers. I was gazing at the flow of people absentmindedly when I spotted a familiar face.

That was a surprise—it was Tsukishima.

He was walking toward the exit with a woman, probably his mother. She looked somewhat downcast, and he seemed to be trying to cheer her up.

I worried if something had happened to them. I almost kicked myself for worrying about Tsukishima.

He glanced at the café. I thought it'd be awkward if we saw each other, so I looked away. Apparently oblivious to my presence, he led his mother into the café.

"So, what are you having, Mom? How about something sweet?"

"Hmm, maybe I'll have a donut. Would you halve it with me, Makoto?"

"Sure. Um...cheer up, Mom. If you're worried about the sickness, I'm sure it'll be okay."

"...Honestly, I should really pull myself together or your father's going to tease me for making *you* cheer *me* up."

"Dad always jokes around, though."

"That's true. He really does."

The two of them got in the line leading to the counter. It wasn't my style to eavesdrop, so I got up quietly, put away my tray, and left without Tsukishima noticing me.

Though I'd tried not to listen, I couldn't help guessing that Tsukishima's mother might be concerned about her health. And her son was being attentive to her, trying to take care of his family as though it was the most natural thing in the world. Just as Tsubasa had said, Tsukishima was probably a nice guy—though I didn't particularly want to know anything like that about him.

I didn't tell anyone that Tsukishima's mother might be ill. It looked like Tsukishima hadn't told anyone either. Tsubasa seemed unaware of anything troubling him as she happily taught him about filming techniques and how to edit footage.

Since Tsubasa asked me to, I taught Tsukishima the basics of scriptwriting and the filming process. Ichika was interested in writing screenplays, too, so I taught them both the methodology behind it.

One day, before the Obon festival in mid-August, Ichika, Tsukishima, and I were in the clubroom by ourselves. Tsubasa and Ena, full of energy even in the scorching heat, were out location-scouting and getting some fresh air. Ichika seemed to have just as much energy as well.

"Ooh, I have an idea! How about we put a plot twist using a smartphone into the script? The dates you see on a messaging app are actually linked to the device itself, so—"

"That's the trick you were telling Tsubasa about before, right? Movie scripts are different than novels; it's best to keep them as simple as possible. The key is not to try to cram too much in," I explained, borrowing the words of a director I'd read about somewhere. Tsukishima and Ichika were listening closely.

Ichika had always had a preference for literature; she was a big fan of romance and mystery novels. It turned out that Tsukishima had also used to read a lot when he was in junior high, so the two of them got along well. They were quickly becoming fast friends.

I finished my lecture on writing scripts, and we decided to take a break. Ichika went to the restroom, leaving Tsukishima and I alone in the clubroom. He was staring at the tabletop calendar in his hand, lost in thought.

"Hey," I said. It wasn't that I couldn't stand the silence. Nor did I have any intention of saying anything like "Take good care of your family" or "Count yourself lucky that you've still got both of your parents with you." But somehow, I found myself overstepping a boundary, and I asked him something that was no business of mine: "Did you have any troubles over summer break?"

"Oh..." Tsukishima's eyes widened a little. He put the calendar back on the table. "Why do you ask?"

"Sorry. I just can't keep quiet when something's bothering

me, so I thought I'd ask. You know my mother's a nurse, right?" When I mentioned her workplace—the same hospital we filmed at last term—Tsukishima's expression grew solemn. "I took her something she'd forgotten at home the other day, and I saw you with someone. I'm guessing she's your mom. She looked like she was feeling down…so I wondered if something bad had happened to her."

I could tell Tsukishima was tense, but as I explained, he suddenly looked relieved.

"Ah…right. I see. Sorry for making you worry," he said.

"No, I'm the one who was apologizing. I know I'm digging into your private life."

"Still, I feel kinda bad. Um…my mom's fine. She's perfectly healthy."

For a moment, I suspected that Tsukishima had lied to reassure me—that his mother actually did have some sort of serious illness and that he was covering it up to avoid making us worry. Except I couldn't detect any trace of a lie in Tsukishima's words.

When people tell lies, they try to make it believable to convince other people that it's true. To do so, they tend to talk a lot, or make gestures they don't usually make, but Tsukishima showed none of those signs.

"Okay. That's good to hear," I replied.

"Yeah."

If nothing was wrong with his mother, why had she looked so down? Had they been visiting someone? Maybe an acquaintance of theirs had a deadly illness…

"By the way, how long are you planning on being with Tsubasa?" I'd been on the fence about asking this question, but

I knew I'd gone too far. It wasn't my place to ask something like that. "I mean, you didn't even think you had a chance with Tsubasa in the beginning, did you?" It might've been because I was trying to make it less awkward, but my tone took on a sarcastic sting. *Ugh, I'm so awful. How do I become a better person?* I thought, but I couldn't stop myself. "You said you didn't come here to get closer to her, but look at you now."

I noticed that Tsukishima had gone quiet.

"Yeah, I know... You're right," he said hesitantly. "I'm surprised, too. I didn't want to go out with her, and I didn't think I could, either."

He smiled weakly, as if he didn't know what to do about it. At the same time, he also looked kind of lonely, and as I wondered why, he went on.

"But it's all right. When the time comes, I'll break up with her. So don't worry."

"Huh? Wait, what do you—"

"Oh, but that doesn't mean I'm not completely serious about going out with her now. I want to make her happy and protect her in my own way, so..."

"That's not what I was asking about," I said, but before I could press him on what he really meant, Ichika opened the door. Tsukishima and I both looked up at her.

"I'm back," she said. "Um, is everything okay? What's up, Aoi?" She seemed puzzled by the sudden intense attention.

I was still frozen in place when Tsubasa and Ena came back from scouting, saying stuff like "It's sooo hot out there. The AC feels like heaven" and "I feel like my makeup's melting off my face."

In the end, I didn't get to ask Tsukishima what he had really meant. Judging from my interactions with him so far, I knew he wasn't the kind of guy who said whatever popped into his head just to placate whoever he was talking to. Besides, I didn't sense any lies in anything he'd said. That meant that what he'd said about Tsubasa must've been the truth: *"When the time comes, I'll break up with her. So don't worry."*

Just what had he meant by that?

3

Three days later, I texted Tsukishima: *"Can we meet up? I want to ask you about the other day."*

I'd been thinking about our conversation, but I still couldn't make heads or tails of it, so I'd come to the conclusion that I should just ask Tsukishima head-on. If I could get him to talk to me face-to-face, I could tell when he was dodging my questions or lying.

It was the middle of August. Since it was the Obon season, our club was on holiday, too.

"Would it be okay to talk over the phone? Or text?" he wrote back.

"I want to talk to you in person."

"Okay. When's good for you? How about today?"

"Can't today. Are you free tomorrow?"

"Tomorrow? Hmm..."

"You've got plans? The day after tomorrow works for me too."

"No, nothing in particular."

"Then let's do tomorrow." I wrote the time and place before

he could get out of it. *"Don't be late, okay? And don't even think about canceling on me."*

Maybe I'd been too forceful. His reply didn't come immediately. There was a pause, as though he was unsure about something, and then he wrote, *"Got it. See you then."*

The next day, I waited for Tsukishima at the meetup spot—my favorite café. Though the place was usually crowded, it was quieter today; people were probably traveling to see their families for the Obon holiday.

Tsukishima showed up five minutes before our meeting time. He looked slightly nervous, probably because he thought he was in trouble. We ordered drinks and chatted a bit, then sometime after our order came, I brought up the question I'd been waiting to ask.

"So, about what you said the other day. What did you really mean?"

"What did I say…?"

"That you'd break up with Tsubasa when the time came."

Tsukishima fell silent. He seemed to be struggling to find the words. Eventually, he braced himself and looked me straight in the eye. "I meant exactly what I said," he answered. "To tell you the truth, I have to transfer to another school in the winter because my family's moving. It's really far away."

"What?" I murmured. Sometimes the most important life changes struck you from out of the blue. He took me by surprise, and I couldn't help showing it in my reaction. But it wasn't just what he *said* that startled me; it was that this was unprecedented. Tsukishima had never once lied to me in the time I'd known him. But for the very first time, he'd just lied straight to my face. At least, that was what I'd sensed.

"When did you find out?" I asked.

"Over summer break. I didn't expect it, either. I was shocked." He laughed with a helpless shrug, trying to lighten the mood.

I didn't know how to respond to his behavior, but I moved the conversation forward anyway. "So does that mean you're breaking up with Tsubasa because you have to move far away with your family?"

"Yeah. I guess that's about the long and the short of it."

"And…Tsubasa doesn't know about it, does she?"

"Sorry. I know I have to tell her sooner rather than later, but I haven't found the right time yet."

"Why? What are you waiting for? You should tell her as soon as possible," I pressed, swallowing back the rest of the sentence that crossed my mind—*if what you say is really true.*

Tsukishima clammed up again. Eventually, he replied, "Because this, right now, might be the happiest time of my life… Maybe you'll laugh at me if I say something like that." His face twisted into a pained grin, as though he was trying but failing to laugh his sadness away.

This time, I was the one to go quiet. I couldn't get a read on him; I was even more confused now. Why did he laugh like he was about to cry? If he was so happy, he should look for a way to stay here at the same school. It might be difficult, but there had to be a way. And even if that failed, it wasn't like he *had* to break up with Tsubasa. Lots of couples kept going long distance. So why did he make a face like that? Why did he give up so easily on his own happiness?

I didn't get it at all. I had so many questions whirling around my head.

"Tsukishima…can I ask you something? That story about moving, is that really—"

Just as I was about to confirm whether my intuition was right—and if so, why he decided to lie—something even more bewildering happened.

Tsukishima turned pale, the blood suddenly draining from his face. He seemed to notice the change, too, and there was fear in his eyes. It hit me that he'd been acting a bit odd since he'd arrived at the café.

"Sorry. I-I'm not feeling so good today," he blurted out.

"What? Wait, you okay, Tsukishima?"

What happened next looked like an act. Tsukishima thumped both arms down on the table and slumped over face down. "I'm really sor—," he murmured.

The next moment, his whole body went limp and he stopped moving completely.

I called his name, but he didn't react. I reached out to touch his arm. It was cold, but he was sweating at the nape of his neck. Something was really wrong.

I asked a waiter to call the ambulance right away, while Tsukishima was slumped in his chair, unconscious.

4

The ambulance came within ten minutes, and the paramedics urged me to ride with him. I wondered whether I should let Tsubasa know, but I called the school first on the way to the hospital. I talked to a teacher on duty, who told me he would alert Tsukishima's parents and that I should wait for them at the hospital. The nurse assured me that Tsukishima was safe, but he didn't wake up.

Tsukishima's parents came in no time: his kindly mother, who I'd seen before at the hospital, and his father, who looked like a generous, good-natured man. They looked frantic as they rushed to his bedside.

Since it was the first time I'd met them, I briefly introduced myself as the vice president of the filmmaking club that Tsukishima was a member of, and I apologized to them for making Tsukishima meet up with me at the café.

His parents seemed surprised to hear that Tsukishima was involved with the filmmaking club at all. Apparently, he hadn't told them much about it. When I answered their questions—that Tsukishima had just joined last term and that he'd been acting in our movie for us—they seemed even more taken aback.

"So that's what he's been up to," his mother said. "He did tell us he joined a club, but making a movie…? He must be new to everything—I hope he hasn't been making things difficult for you."

"Not at all. In fact, it was our president who dragged him into it in the first place… And I'm not sure if you've heard, but thanks to his hard work, we even won a prize in a summer film festival."

I was surprised at my own words recognizing Tsukishima's contributions to the club. I wasn't just saying it because I was talking to his parents, and it wasn't out of guilt for pushing him too hard, either. I was simply telling the truth, explaining

Tsukishima's presence objectively to a third party. Whether I liked it or not, that prize wouldn't have been ours if not for him.

"A prize? He didn't tell us anything about that...," his mother replied with a wry smile while I was still reeling from my own admission. At first, I hadn't really thought Tsukishima resembled his parents much, but looking closer, his mother's facial expressions were just like his. I could see traces of him in his father, too. All three of them had a gentle, kindhearted air about them.

They asked me not to tell Tsukishima that we'd had this conversation about his club activities, since they didn't know why he'd been keeping them a secret. Tsukishima was still lying in bed, unconscious.

"Um, by the way—does he have some kind of chronic illness?" I asked. "He said he wasn't feeling well today just before he blacked out."

His parents looked at each other. After a slight pause, his mother turned back to me and told me gently that he used to get sick often when he was little, but it wasn't something you'd call a chronic illness.

"Don't worry, he'll wake up in a jiffy," his father added with a smile. "He's...perfectly healthy. There's nothing to worry about."

My thoughts went still hearing his father's words and seeing his reaction. I wondered why. There shouldn't have been anything to suspect in what he said. But even as I told myself that he must be telling the truth, all the lies I'd heard and my finely honed sixth sense were sending me signals.

I can't stop myself from sensing what's left unsaid. I can feel it in my gut. That's why it hurts sometimes—it's always been that way.

"I see. I understand. I'm sorry for asking about something so private," I said. After chatting with his parents a little while longer, I went back home.

I couldn't bring myself to ask them about Tsukishima's story about transferring schools.

5

Tsukishima didn't wake up while I was at the hospital, but he sent me a text that night, apologizing for putting me through all the trouble. He explained that he'd fainted because he was anemic. He also asked me not to tell Tsubasa anything about his collapse or his move in the winter.

I agreed, but after that incident, I found myself observing him through a different lens. I had a feeling that he was hiding something. Tsubasa had joked that one of the reasons she'd fallen for Tsukishima was because there was a darkness inside him. I could sense that shadow, too—hidden behind his faint smile or in his eyes as he gazed silently off into the distance. I felt it even when he sometimes told us casually that he couldn't come to club that day because he had to run some errands at home.

I mulled over what he'd said before he passed out:

"Because this, right now, might be the happiest time of my life... Maybe you'll laugh at me if I say something like that."

What was Tsukishima hiding?

I stumbled across the answer to that question when I least expected it.

It was ten days before the end of summer vacation. The organizers of the indie film festival had turned the prize-winning films into commemorative DVDs, and Tsubasa had received our set in the mail. We decided to watch them all the way through to reflect on each film's strengths and weaknesses, so we gathered in the clubroom. Of course, our own work—*The Girl Who Dies from a Rare Disease*—was among them.

We went through the films one by one, and eventually it was time to watch ours. Everyone was in high spirits; Tsubasa was teasing Tsukishima, and Ena and Ichika were grinning together.

The scene in the nurse's office appeared on the computer screen, with Tsukishima's lines: *"It's easy to lose hope. Giving up won't change anything, though. You'd only make the people around you and yourself miserable. So...you should get angry."*

I was stunned. For the others, it was just another scene in a movie. But for me, it was completely different. Everything made sense now.

What was Tsukishima hiding? I couldn't believe the answer had been staring me right in the face.

"*You're going to* die," Tsukishima said to the heroine on-screen. "*You've got six months left to live? How can you act so* normal? *Why are you pretending to give up on life? It's not that easy to let go. You should want to take it all out on people. You should hate everyone going on with their ordinary lives. And that's going to make you hate yourself... But even with all that... You should want to live longer and keep fighting right up until the end.*"

At the time, I'd wondered why Tsukishima had gone in that direction. Some actors can turn into a character as if they were possessed, but those kinds of actors are rare. Before shooting that take, I had told him to be himself instead of trying to act, but I figured he'd thought more deeply about who the protagonist was, and that was what he'd come up with.

But maybe I'd had it all wrong. Maybe Tsukishima really was just being himself. Those words might have been based on his *own* experience, which meant he was going to…

When we finished watching all the prize-winning films, Tsubasa and Ichika were excited, ready to dissect each work from every angle. Since we had coupons for a family restaurant in front of the train station, we decided to discuss it over lunch.

Everyone was chatty as we ate, Tsubasa most of all. I was the only one who was quiet.

We stayed there till sunset, then headed home before it got dark. I parted with the others, telling them I wanted to stop by a bookshop. But instead, I went to a park nearby and sat down on a bench.

After a little while, a text message pinged on my phone.

"I'm alone now. Where should I meet you?"

It was from Tsukishima. While we were still at the diner, I'd secretly texted him that there was something important I wanted to talk to him about, and I'd asked him if we could meet one on one later.

I messaged him where I was and waited. Soon Tsukishima came by himself. He had a serious look on his face. He noticed me on the bench and walked over to me. I got up, and we stood face-to-face in the empty park.

"So," I said.

"What's up?" he replied. The sun was dipping below the trees.

"Tell me...are you going to die?"

Tsukishima froze. His face turned to stone; he didn't betray any emotion.

I'd wavered about whether to pry into his personal affairs, right up until the words actually left my mouth, but I just had to ask. It was important to know for the future of our club, too. He was silent for a while, taken aback by my sudden question.

"Where did you get *that* idea? Are you still worried about what happened the other day? I just passed out that time—no big deal." He laughed, apparently trying to turn my question into a joke.

I didn't say anything. I knew what silence could do in situations like these.

"Besides...everyone dies," he said.

"True."

"Seriously, what's gotten into you?"

"How much longer do you have to live?"

Tsukishima's face stiffened again.

"The protagonist in our movie—that was about you, wasn't it?"

A breeze drifted through the park. The sky was a violent red, as if the whole world was on fire.

After a long pause, he said, "I... I don't know what you're talking about."

His acting was terrible, and I think he knew it, too.

I gave him a brief version of how I'd come to my conclusion, leaving out the conversation I had with his parents. I told him about my hunch that he was lying about moving, my assumptions about his collapse, and how the movie we'd rewatched had clinched it.

Tsukishima listened without saying a word. He neither

interrupted nor refuted me, nor did he try to laugh it off. He seemed to accept reality, and when I finished my account, he had an awkward smile on his face.

"I thought lying would be so simple…but it's harder than I imagined," he said, turning his gaze to the sunset. I stared at his profile as he narrowed his eyes a little, as if the light was too bright. Or maybe he was in pain. "But I'm a bit relieved, too, somehow. I guess it's because I don't have to keep lying to you, at least… It's a funny feeling."

Tsukishima did look somewhat relieved; the shadow hanging over his face had cleared. I didn't sense he was hiding anything, in his expression or his words.

"If Tsubasa were here, she'd wish she'd filmed you saying that," I joked to relieve the tension.

He smiled back. "She'd probably pull out her camera and ask me to say it again. And I'm an idiot, so I'd say the same thing all over, even if I felt embarrassed."

"Yeah, probably."

"…Hm? Which bit were you agreeing to?"

"What Tsubasa would say, and that you're an idiot."

We burst out laughing. I realized it was the first time we'd laughed together like this. I felt so open and unreserved in that moment. One thing we had in common was that Tsubasa Minami was precious to us. That was the pure and simple truth, and that was enough to help us understand each other.

Tsukishima's smile faded, and he looked straight at me. After a moment's hesitation, he told me the name of the illness he had: a long, difficult name that I'd never heard of. "I found out back in March this year. They told me I have one year left."

He spoke as quietly as falling snow, and I could feel a chill on my skin even in the summer heat. That snow swallowed up all the sounds of the world. All of a sudden, I didn't know what to say or think. Even in my confusion, even in that strange silence, everything he'd said was coming together in my head.

"I want to ask you something...," I said. "Why did you make up that excuse about moving?"

"I was going to break the news to everyone eventually," Tsukishima replied, his gaze still fixed on me in the gathering twilight. "I'm sure it's sad when someone close to you passes away—it must come as a shock. I don't want you guys to experience that. So I've talked to my homeroom teacher and the nurse at school, and when I get too sick to go to school, the official story will be that I had to transfer to a different school on short notice...and I'll just disappear."

"And Tsubasa doesn't know?"

"Like I said, I haven't told her anything about that yet."

"What about your illness and how much time you have left?"

Tsukishima averted his eyes. "She doesn't know that, either," he said, his voice heavy with regret and grief.

Before I knew it, I'd stepped forward and grabbed him by the collar. It was a cliché straight out of a manga or TV show, but here I was, playing it out.

"Why did you start going out with Tsubasa, then?" I snapped before I could stop myself. "It's obvious she's going to be miserable when that happens. She really likes you now. She's always said she doesn't get a thing about romance, but she genuinely likes you. So if you just go off and disappear—if you die—she'll be a wreck. Can't you see that?"

As soon as the words tumbled out of my mouth, I regretted it. I knew it was just about the worst thing I could've said to him. I let go of Tsukishima's shirt and apologized, lowering my eyes to the ground. "Sorry," I mumbled. "I know you're the one who's hurting the most… That was awful, what I just said."

"It's okay. It's normal to care about your friend."

I raised my head. Even at a time like this, he still wore a smile on his face. But a moment later, his expression became more complicated.

"Don't worry, I'll keep my disease a secret from Minami. I promise I'll make sure she never finds out. And once we break up because of me 'moving,' I'll just become a blip in her past as time goes by. If we end it like that, she won't be hurt too badly…I hope."

Even though he was talking about something so serious and sad, Tsukishima still forced himself to sound positive.

"Really, don't worry about it," he went on. "I'll keep everything hidden till the end—both my illness and my death. According to my doctor, I'll pass out more and more often and for longer stretches of time as my illness progresses. And eventually, I'll pass out one last time, and I won't wake up anymore. But I can usually tell when I'm going to black out. If I don't miss the signs, I can keep it a secret. The fainting started only recently, during summer break. I hadn't gotten the hang of it yet when we met up the other day—I'd told myself I was going to be okay, and I ended up passing out in front of you…but from now on, I'll make sure that won't happen. So…"

Tsukishima trailed off. He'd been keeping the cheer in his voice as best he could, but the smile he was trying to give me now was a failure.

"Or do you think I should just disappear from Minami's life

right now?" he asked. "I could pretend I have to move before school starts up again. And I could go without saying good-bye to her..."

It hurt to see Tsukishima like this. I knew that face well; Tsukishima reminded me of my father whenever he thought his dream of becoming a film director would always be beyond his reach.

Memory pulled me back, and the image of myself as a small child flashed through my head. The one who's left behind waits for the one who went away, hoping against hope that he might return someday. It didn't matter to me that my parents had divorced; I still thought that my father might come home. That we could all live together again. But as time went by, and I began to understand, I realized that would never happen.

And what about Tsubasa? If Tsukishima disappeared, would she wait for him? Would she chase after him? In time, would he become a part of her past, as my father had for me?

At what point do you stop being a child and start being an adult?

"Don't you dare," I said.

Even if they can see through the lies of a grown-up, it makes no difference: A child is still just a child. They should only fix their eyes on their own happiness. They shouldn't have to sacrifice themself or give up on what's important to them.

I realized I was angry. I'd probably wanted to rage at something for a long time. I'd wanted to fight back against the injustice I perceived—what had made a child become an adult at such a young age, that had left her with no other choice but to grow up.

"I'm sorry...for what I said back there," I told him. "I know why you're going out with Tsubasa—it's obvious. It's because that's what makes you happy. So you just reached out and seized your chance at happiness. That's what people are supposed to do."

Right now, Tsukishima was living as normally as possible and spending time with the girl he liked every day—something he wouldn't trade for the world. He was keeping his illness a secret because he truly cared about Tsubasa. Even though he was just a teenager, he was acting like a grown-up because he didn't want to make her grieve.

"I want you to hold on to that happiness for as long as you can," I said. "You're going to die, Tsukishima. You know that? You really might not have much longer to live."

I couldn't stand it that he was prepared to throw away his chance at happiness. Tsukishima should be more selfish in the way he lived his life. He should be happy by Tsubasa's side before he lost that chance forever. I was sure that was the right thing for Tsukishima to do.

Besides, it wasn't just Tsukishima who cared about Tsubasa—she was also my best friend. *I* could help take care of Tsukishima. *I* could help him keep his secret.

"People who don't have much longer to be happy shouldn't be so quick to give up on that happiness. I'll help—not for your sake, but because it's the right thing to do for a fellow person. And for Tsubasa so she won't have to grieve."

Tears were streaming down my face. I didn't understand why—it wasn't just because I'd seen my past myself in Tsukishima. I didn't even really care about him. Or so I'd thought. Until now.

Maybe somewhere deep down, there was a part of me that did care about him. I knew by then that this boy standing in front of me was kindhearted. He spared no effort in doing the things he set out to do. He was honest and loyal. And that was why I'd come to accept him as the fifth member of our crew.

"You're one of us, Tsukishima. Promise me you won't let go of your own happiness. Okay?"

Tsukishima was speechless, probably surprised to see my tears. The silence stretched on.

He seemed to hesitate but finally responded, "Okay. I never knew how kind you were, Hayami."

I slapped him lightly on the arm and promised that from now on, he could always rely on me.

6

When people open their eyes, they can take in so many things around them: light, the scenery, a town, the people. The macro and micro goings-on of everyday life. But there are some things you can never see, no matter how hard you look, like the inner lives of the people around you, their anxieties, and their illnesses.

At the park that day, I asked Tsukishima to tell me all about his disease. I needed to know to be able to support him, so I wiped away my tears and got ahold of my emotions.

In his current condition, he would lose consciousness about

once every few days. The onset would be sudden, but it would usually happen on a day when his body temperature was low in the morning. I told him that he shouldn't push himself too hard on those days and that he should stay home and not come to the club. I assured him that I'd cover for him as naturally as possible.

There was one problem, though. It was easy to come up with all kinds of excuses during the summer holidays, but once school started, that would get a lot more difficult. We needed to come up with a strategy while we still had time. Tsukishima had an idea, so we talked it over in depth.

Four days later, Tsukishima was absent from the club, saying that he'd caught a summer cold. Everyone was worried about him, but since it was just a cold, they weren't too anxious. I was the only one who knew that Tsukishima had actually blacked out.

The next day, in the evening, Tsukishima sent me a text. He said he'd been out cold for about thirty hours—from the previous morning until just then—but he said he would come to our club meeting after school the following day. So far, his bouts of unconsciousness had happened at irregular intervals and never on consecutive days.

Just as he'd said, he showed up at the clubroom that afternoon.

"Oh, you're here, Makoto. How's your cold?" Tsubasa asked. She didn't seem to suspect anything.

"Sorry for making you worry. I'm all right now."

"Want me to come over next time you're sick? I'll take real good care of you."

"Uh, that's okay. Don't wanna spread it around." Tsukishima

was his usual self, too; he didn't betray any signs that he'd just had a blackout.

When I saw my chance, I delivered the line that Tsukishima and I had agreed upon beforehand. I was secretly nervous, but it was important to say it so we could handle things better in the future.

"Come to think of it, you're pretty pale, Tsukishima—is your health okay? I don't think you've mentioned anything...but you strike me as one of those guys who used to get sick a lot when you were little," I said, trying to make it sound casual.

"Oh, um, well... I've mentioned this to Minami before, but I used to have a bit of a weak constitution back in elementary school."

Tsukishima's mother had also told me about this, but it seemed to catch Ena and Ichika off guard.

"Really? Are you all better now, Makoto?" Ena asked.

"Uh, yeah, I'm fine. That's all in the past. But it's been extra hot this summer, so my parents are getting a bit overprotective of me... I might have to miss school or the club sometimes to go to the hospital—just to make sure I'm not getting sick like back then. That's why I was away a few times during the break, too," Tsukishima explained apologetically. His response was natural; I would've been surprised if anyone could see through the lie. Besides, it was a private matter, so the others didn't want to be too inquisitive.

"Make sure you get plenty of rest, and don't push yourself too hard, Makoto. And let us know whenever you need to take time off," Tsubasa reassured him, having already known about his condition.

That gave Tsukishima and me the cover he needed to keep up his normal life.

When summer vacation came to an end, the club held a discussion about the filming schedule for our next movie. I was ready to present my idea.

"So, about our next film—I want Tsukishima to assist me instead of being an actor."

We'd included him as an actor during the planning stage, along with Ena and Ichika. However, as the screenwriter, I could suddenly decide to cut him from the script. This way, if something happened to him, he could miss club without feeling any pressure. It felt a bit forced to suggest such an idea, but we'd thought about that as well.

"About that, Aoi—I'm all for doing the shooting without pushing Makoto too hard, but I still want all three of them in the movie, now that he's part of the crew."

Tsubasa was reluctant to leave Tsukishima out; if we shot the film just with Ena and Ichika, there was a good chance that we'd end up making movies just like the ones we made before.

"Let's do that next time. We have to brush up on our skills first. You know it's gonna be hard to win a prize at the Eiga Koushien this winter. Besides, you always go for the more artsy ideas, Tsubasa—the same thing happened when we were brainstorming for this movie. That's not gonna improve our chances."

"Well...I guess you've got a point...," Tsubasa mumbled, not totally convinced.

"That's not all," I added after a pause. "We're a crew of five now. Isn't it better for Tsukishima to get a feel for different roles in filming, not just as an actor? It'll be worth it in the long run, when we make more movies together."

A momentary hush fell over the room. Tsubasa, Ichika, and even Ena were all staring at me, wide-eyed—I'd practically given Tsukishima my seal of approval as a member of the club.

"What happened to you, Aoi? Did you eat something weird?" Ichika blurted out. But when I shot her a look, she got flustered and didn't say another word. I let out a sigh.

"Anyway, that's my thinking. Let's have three actors for our next movie after this one, and in the meantime, we'll improve our skills as a crew." I could sense Tsukishima's eyes on me.

"Hmm..." Tsubasa gave the idea some thought, but after a little while, she seemed satisfied. "Yeah, I guess you're right," she said with a laugh. "That makes sense. I'm sure we'll have a lot more chances to make movies together next year—and even when we're in college. From now on, we're a crew of five."

Tsubasa beamed at Tsukishima, never doubting for a second that the five of us would keep making films together in the future.

Tsukishima smiled back. "Yeah, I'm sure we will," he said.

I must have been the only one who could sense he was hurting inside.

At some point, the cicadas' intense chirping had quieted, and a cool breeze occasionally blew in through the open window.

Summer was quietly fading away for each of us.

Scene 3.

Tsubasa Minami

1

Life is too short to achieve something but too long to do nothing.

That's a famous quote I heard once.

This is just my theory, but I believe that for every person, there are words that effortlessly transform their life. Everyone encounters them at some point, even if those words have taken root so deep that they can't be recalled without conscious effort.

For me, that line was the one that stuck. I don't remember when I read it or heard it the first time, but I came across it somewhere, and by the time I was in fourth or fifth grade of elementary school, it had become a part of me, a shadowy idea in the back of my mind.

Life is too long to do nothing.

Yet each day passes by, one after the next, unceasing.

What really planted that seed inside me was when I went on a field trip in fifth grade. We went on a tour of a factory and watched products getting assembled on moving conveyer belts. The other kids in my class didn't seem particularly impressed, but for some reason, I was mesmerized by the process. Even though I was just a little kid, I wondered vaguely whether my own life was going to follow a track just like one of those conveyer belts.

Life is too long to do nothing, yet each day passes by, one after the next...

You drift through life, following a predetermined course, and your life ends up just like anyone else's.

I felt like I was riding on a conveyer belt. Not just in the grand scheme of things, but also in my day-to-day life. I woke up, went to school, chatted with my friends, sat in class, and then it was time to go home. Most of the day just slipped away on autopilot. The days passed by as if I were simply sitting on a conveyer belt.

One day, I wondered where this conveyer belt was taking me. Who was I going to become?

I suddenly became afraid of those uneventful days that kept streaming by. I didn't know how, but I wanted to gather up my courage and jump off the conveyer belt.

It was my childhood friend Aoi who gave me a way out—movies. We'd been friends since preschool, and we'd always been together. I tended to have my head in the clouds, so Aoi, the down-to-earth, reliable one, would help me out. My parents were relieved that Aoi was around to look after me.

Sometime after the factory trip, I confided in Aoi about my abstract anxieties. The very next day, she came over to my house with a DVD and said, "I'm not sure what to do about your worries, but do you wanna watch this with me?"

The DVD had once belonged to her dad. I'd often seen Aoi watching some sort of hard-to-follow movie with him when I'd gone over to her house. Her dad was kind, and he used to buy me sweets, but he disappeared without warning when Aoi and I were in fourth grade.

We watched the movie Aoi had brought over together. Up until then, I'd only ever watched anime or comedy flicks, so this was my first time watching a serious foreign film. I suddenly felt like a real grown-up; my heart pounded, and my eyes were glued to the screen.

The protagonist was an earnest, mundane man who worked at a run-of-the-mill company. A few minutes into the movie, he said, "Every day goes by as if I'm riding on a conveyer belt."

I was riveted, stunned into silence by the realization that there was someone else in the world who had the exact same thought that I'd had.

The protagonist has a girlfriend who's beautiful but tough on him. One day, she tells him, "Imagine we stay together—you and I are going to get married, make a home for ourselves, have children, and carry on like that until we're buried in our graves. It's like we're riding on a conveyer belt. I couldn't stand a life like that." And she dumps him.

The protagonist looks down at his feet in a daze.

I'd done the same gesture before—staring at the conveyer belt running beneath the soles of my feet, but unlike me, the protagonist makes an effort to change. He used to make movies when he was a student; he'd set his heart on becoming a film director, but he'd long since given up on that dream. Now, trying to turn his life around, the protagonist starts making films again. At first, he struggles by himself, but he gradually finds friends who help him with his movie.

I was blown away by the film. For the first time in my life, I felt like strangers weren't complete strangers to me. This movie was proof that there were people out there who had the same thoughts that I did. Cinema opened my eyes.

Before I knew it, I found myself captivated by film. From that day on, I started watching all kinds of movies with Aoi. There were so many DVDs in her house that we couldn't even get through all of them, as well as lots of books about old cameras, filming equipment, and film production.

It was a natural progression for me to feel the itch to make movies myself. Since then, my life has suddenly spun into a dizzying flurry of activity.

I roped in Ichika, who lived nearby, and I asked my parents to buy me a filmmaking kit that was designed for elementary school kids. Following the kit's instructions, the three of us made a movie titled *Ichika's Adventure*.

This movie—the first movie I'd ever made in my life—was a clumsy attempt at filmmaking, but it still filled me with excitement. Aoi, Ichika, and I would get together almost every day to watch movies or record videos on our phones. The filmmaking kit also included software for editing videos on a computer, so I practiced using that, too.

At our junior high school, there hadn't been any clubs related to movies, so Aoi and I joined the literature club instead. Claiming that it was one aspect of creative writing, the two of us studied how to make movies and taught ourselves to use professional editing software. We shot a lot of different movies, starting with homages to our favorite works.

Ichika came to our junior high when we were both second-years there. Two became three. Ena transferred in from a different school, and I managed to coax her into joining us. Three became four.

Then, in the summer of my third year in junior high, we won an award in a film competition for junior high kids. We were overjoyed. Aoi, who was always as cool as a cucumber, cried at the news and said, "Let's keep making movies with the four of us."

In high school, too, Aoi and I kept making movies. For me, cinema was life. I don't know when it disappeared, but I'd stopped seeing the conveyer belt under my feet.

One day, a classmate told me, "You're a bit odd, Tsubasa. Don't you have any interest in romance?"

There was something I'd been neglecting because my head was too full of movies. When I looked around, my classmates were falling in love, dating, and getting a taste of that fresh school-life drama that made people's hearts go wild.

I knew a little about romance, at least. I'd seen love stories in movies and heard about it in songs all the time. A boy even asked me out. But I still didn't know how it felt; I'd never fallen in love with anyone.

Somewhere deep down, I felt a pang of desire to fall in love like I'd seen in all those movies or heard about in songs. I thought it might be enriching to love someone. I wanted to experience it both to keep making movies and to live my life to the fullest. But it wasn't so simple to *like* someone like that…

"Okay, cut!" I yelled out.

The heat of the summer was nearly gone, and fall was almost here. As soon as summer vacation was over, we'd gotten started on our new film, *The Withered Sunflower*, to submit to the Eiga Koushien Competition in the winter.

We had asked Ichika to play the leading role—an ordinary high schooler—and as soon as I called "cut," Ichika let out a huge sigh. "Phew, that was nerve-racking." She smiled at Ena, who was also acting in the same scene.

As I checked the footage we'd just shot, Aoi and Makoto

made sure the filming ran smoothly. Aoi asked him about the next scene, and Makoto replied, "Scene twenty-two, right? Once the footage check is done—," and on they went like that, checking that everything was done right.

We were filming in one corner of the grounds at the back of the school. I turned around to look at Makoto.

I'd never known how happy you could feel just by looking at someone.

I had confessed my feelings to Makoto, and we'd started going out before summer break. I hadn't asked him out because I was trying to learn more about romance; we were together because we liked each other—a real, genuine couple.

Makoto must've sensed my eyes on him, and he looked up at me. He gave me a bashful grin. I felt warm affection overflowing inside me.

"Hey, Makoto," I called out before I could stop myself.

"Yes? What is it?" he asked, acting in his role as assistant to the director.

"Nothing much."

"Oh, okay?"

"I just felt like saying...I really like you."

I had something I wanted to do, friends to do it with, and someone who was special to me. I felt happier than ever. I had everything I could ever want right here and now.

Makoto's face turned bright red, and Aoi marched over to me with a sigh.

"Hey, Boss. Could you stop flirting with your assistant and move on to the next scene?"

"Sorry, Aoi. I like you a lot too, you know."

"Huh?"

"Oh, aren't you telling me off 'cause you're jealous?"

"Sometimes I can't help but think...you're crazy, Tsubasa."

"Crazy about movies, you mean? Yeah, I can own that."

"Uh, there are limits, you know. You're with me on this, right, Tsukishima?"

"What? Oh, but I... I really like how Minami gets excited about movies."

"Ugh."

Ichika came over, asking "Ooh, were you just talking about love?"

Ena followed close behind, also chiming in: "So, who's crazy about who? Who's jealous? Tell me, tell me."

The more things I found to like, the happier I felt. These sort of everyday moments, when the five of us spent time together, made me happier than I'd ever been before.

We continued with the filming, and thanks to Aoi's organizational skills, we managed to tick off everything on our schedule for the day. In the glow of the sunset, we cleared away our equipment and went back to the clubroom. As we were putting our gear back, it struck me that we'd never taken a photo together.

"Hey, wanna take a pic with all five of us?" I asked.

Everyone seemed to wonder why I suddenly wanted to take a photo, but I ushered them into their seats, then fixed my phone on a stand in front of them. I set the camera to timer mode.

"All righty, everyone get ready. Smile!"

Ten seconds later, the shutter sound rang out, and this moment in time was saved as a collection of data. In the photo, Aoi was smiling like she had no choice but to listen to my whims, and Ena and Ichika were huddled together with big smiles. Makoto looked happy, too. I was beaming next to him, practically bursting with joy.

When I got home, I shared the photo in our group chat. Everyone reacted in their own way. Reading their replies and gazing at the picture, I wished that we would always stay as happy as this. And I believed with all my heart that we would.

But I should have been more attentive. There had been so many hints already, but I was careless, hopelessly blind to what was going on around me.

Back then, I'd had no idea that Makoto was pushing himself just to keep up with our daily filming.

2

It was October, when the cool autumn air had settled in, that I noticed something was wrong with Makoto.

The filming for our new movie was all going according to schedule. In fact, we were ahead for once. But that day, we noticed a mistake in the script during a shoot—just a small problem we needed to revise. Since it would be simple to fix if they looked at the reference material, the screenwriter, Aoi, and her assistant, Makoto, went back to our clubroom, and the rest of us decided to go ahead with filming the other scenes.

Much to our surprise, we finished shooting earlier than expected. Aoi was usually the one who made sure the filming ran smoothly, so sometimes our shoots would drag on if she wasn't there. The three of us headed back up to the clubroom, hoping to surprise Aoi and Makoto, but we found Makoto alone in the room. Unusually for him, he was slumped face down over the desk. Aoi was nowhere to be seen.

"Oh, where's Aoi?" Ichika asked.

"Looks like she's gone off somewhere," Ena replied. "Is Makoto asleep? I guess he must be really tired."

"Maybe 'cause Aoi's working him so hard," I joked. The three of us pictured Aoi bossing Makoto around and giggled.

Careful not to wake Makoto up, we put away our equipment. Since we couldn't do any more filming without fixing the script first, I told Ichika and Ena they could go home.

"Awesome," Ena said happily. "Wanna stop by a café, Ichika?"

"Good idea. It's past time we had some girl talk!"

I waved good-bye to them, and I was left alone with Makoto. I wondered where Aoi had gone, but she hadn't called me, so I assumed there was nothing to worry about. I sat down in the seat across from Makoto and watched him sleep.

My eyes turned to his hand resting on the desk.

Something had changed in me ever since we'd started going out. I hadn't had a problem holding hands with him before, but now I felt too shy to do it.

On the other hand, Makoto was asleep. I hesitated a little, then reached out a hand toward his. It was just a small, simple gesture, but I could feel my heart racing. The tips of my fingers hovered over his. Holding my breath, I took his hand in mine.

"Huh…?" I'd expected to feel excited and embarrassed, but surprise pushed everything else aside. Makoto's hand was as cold as ice—so cold that I thought I must be imagining it. I drew back in shock, then took his hand again. It was cold. My senses hadn't been playing tricks on me.

I jumped up and put my hand close to his mouth. He was breathing, of course, but something was wrong. It seemed shallow.

"Um, Makoto?" I shook his shoulder, trying to wake him up.

Just then, I heard footsteps and urgent voices coming from the hallway. The door opened and Aoi came in, followed, to my surprise, by the school nurse.

"Oh, Tsubasa? You're done already?" Aoi was startled to find me in the room.

"Yeah, we finished earlier than we thought—but Makoto, he's really cold."

"Calm down, Tsubasa. It's okay," Aoi said reassuringly. "He's…just asleep."

"He's sleeping?" Bewildered, I looked at Makoto again. Aoi was silent for a few moments, as though she was making up her mind about what to say. When I turned my eyes back to her, she reluctantly opened her mouth to explain.

"Uh, to tell you the truth…Tsukishima said he's got insomnia."

Insomnia…? I was confused, and I struggled to understand the situation at first. Aoi seemed hesitant to disclose Makoto's condition, but she told me haltingly that Makoto was taking prescription medicine for it, and that he had asked her to keep it a secret from me so I wouldn't worry. Apparently the medicine had significant side effects, so sometimes he would fall asleep for long stretches of time even during the day, and his body would go cold.

Apparently, Makoto had told Aoi about his insomnia when she'd appointed him as her assistant. But it was the first time Aoi had seen the side effects of his medicine for herself, so she'd called the nurse just to be safe.

The nurse gave me a small smile. "People might think that all there is to insomnia is a lack of sleep...but it's much more serious for the person suffering from it. And sometimes the medicine that's prescribed is very strong."

"So that's what it was...," I murmured.

"It'd be a pity to wake him up when he's finally gone to sleep... I'll take him to my office so he can rest there. Don't worry, if he stays asleep much longer, I'll call his parents."

The nurse quickly checked over Makoto, then carried him out of the clubroom on her back.

I got a text from Makoto the next morning: *"Sorry about yesterday. I heard you found me sleeping like a rock."*

Since Makoto's insomnia might get worse if he worried about it too much, I pretended not to know about his condition, just as the nurse had suggested, and went along with his story that he had simply dozed off.

But ever since I found out, I often found myself worrying about Makoto. Was he pushing himself too hard? Was he trying to be brave for our sake?

I did a bit of research into insomnia, too. It wasn't a rare condition, and it could happen to high schoolers. Stress was the worst enemy for insomniacs, so I talked with Aoi to cut back his workload for the club.

Makoto didn't bring up his insomnia, but he missed school and the club on some days, most likely to go to the hospital. I'd noticed he'd been going to the hospital for a while now, but since I knew he'd been prone to sickness in the past, and he'd told me himself that he was fine, I'd never bothered asking him about it. I wondered whether those visits had been because he was having trouble sleeping. Even though I was his girlfriend, I'd had no idea he was suffering so badly.

Though I was concerned about Makoto, our filming was going well. We all worked in close accord to keep things moving. Ena's acting was great, and it drew out natural responses from Ichika.

"Cut!" I called out. "Good job, everyone. I'll check the footage."

Two weeks had gone by since I found Makoto asleep in the clubroom. We were filming in the park near the school, and once I confirmed that everything was okay with the footage, we started clearing away our equipment.

Hoisting everything onto our shoulders, we walked back to the school. Makoto was with us, bringing up the rear as he discussed the filming schedule with Aoi.

"Filming's going so smoothly so far," Ena commented.

"Yeah, we're doing great," I said. "Thanks to you and Ichika."

"Oh, it's all thanks to Ena," Ichika said. "I'm the one making you do retakes."

I thought Makoto wouldn't want too much attention on his condition, so I hadn't said anything about it to Ena or Ichika. Even as I was chatting with them, I was anxious about whether he was doing okay and kept glancing back at him.

Ichika noticed my glances and sidled up to me. "By the way, Tsubasa, how's it going with Makoto?"

"Huh? What do you mean?"

"You know, you two are together, so…"

"Ooh, Ichika wants to know all about the sexy stuff," Ena teased.

"N-no, that's not what I meant!"

Ichika had enjoyed talking about romance and people's crushes ever since she was little, and even though she was in high school now, nothing had changed. I thought it was cute, but I wasn't sure what to say about my relationship with Makoto—I couldn't give away anything about his insomnia.

"I think things are going well," I said. After a pause, I decided to share my honest feelings. "But I guess sometimes I get a bit worried that I'm a burden on him and I don't realize it. Like, what if it's one-sided, and I like him much more than he likes me…?"

Ena and Ichika stared at me, wide-eyed.

"You are the classic teen girl in love, Tsubasa…," Ichika said.

"You really are head over heels for him," Ena added.

"Oh, was my reaction *that* good? Maybe I should've filmed myself. It could've been good reference material for a love story."

"Phew, now that's the Tsubasa we know and love," Ena said, and we all laughed. They started asking me about where Makoto and I had gone for dates lately, but we hadn't done anything special since the fall term started, what with the filming and Makoto's errands at home. Sometimes we went to a café or a video game arcade after school, but we hadn't gone out on the weekend in a long time.

When I told them that, Ena suggested in her usual laid-back tone, "Well, we're on top of the filming schedule, so how about you guys go on a date this weekend?"

"But we still have a lot more to film…"

"The director needs a breather sometimes, too," pressed Ena.

"A breather, huh…?" A break might be good for me, and especially for Makoto. Though I didn't know what was causing his insomnia, we needed to let our hair down, forget about everything else, and just hang out once in a while.

Encouraged by Ena and Ichika, I tried asking Makoto out on

a date when we were back in the clubroom. I was nervous, but I wanted to invite him before I got cold feet.

"Um...Makoto, do you want to go out with me on Sunday? We've both been busy lately, so we haven't gone anywhere. I...I'd like to go to the amusement park with you."

It was a bit out of the blue, but Makoto said yes. He wavered a little at first, so maybe he had something he had to do. But Ena and Ichika backed me up, and in the end, we decided to take a break from filming on Sunday so that Makoto and I could go on a date. I was worried I'd pressured him into it, but he said that wasn't the case

"Are you sure you don't mind, Makoto?" I asked.

"I've got no other plans if we're not filming...so of course I don't mind. Let's go out."

"I don't want you to push yourself. You're feeling well enough?"

"Yeah, totally. I'm glad you invited me."

We promised to meet in the square in front of the train station downtown at nine in the morning on Sunday.

Ena and Ichika watched us with satisfied grins. I thought Aoi would poke fun at me and Makoto, but she just looked at us without saying a word.

When I got home, I started picking out my outfit for the date, even though it was still three days away. I looked up the amusement park online, searching for things I thought Makoto might like. I just wanted Makoto to have so much fun that he forgot about his insomnia for one day, at least.

Then, on the day of our date, I heard that Makoto had gotten into an accident.

3

As soon as I woke up on the morning of our date, I felt restless and was tingling with excitement. I usually don't pay much attention to my makeup, but I took my time with it to calm my nerves. The cosmetics that Ena had recommended to me went well with my skin, and I felt like it was going to be a good day.

I put on the outfit I'd picked out. I wanted to try wearing something a bit more feminine for a change, so I'd settled on a skirt and matching top instead of my usual pants. Once I was dressed, I examined myself in the mirror and couldn't suppress a smile. *Good thing I bought this skirt the other day*, I thought. *I wonder if Makoto will tell me I look cute.*

I couldn't sit still, so I left the house before I needed to and got to our meeting place ten minutes early. The square in front of the station was bustling with people, all waiting there to meet someone. I sat down on a bench, joining the crowd.

I couldn't wait to see Makoto, but even just sitting there waiting for him didn't bother me. After all, I knew that eventually, I'd get to see him. My head was full of ideas for the day as I sat there, bright-eyed and bushy-tailed.

"Sorry to keep you waiting."

I heard a voice nearby and glanced up, my face already breaking into a smile—but it wasn't Makoto. A man who looked like he was in college was talking to one of the women sitting next to me. I checked my watch; it was five minutes until our meeting time.

Knowing how conscientious Makoto was, I thought he was bound to come soon. I took out my phone so I could pretend to be surprised when he arrived.

I waited for the sound of his voice. *Has he seen me already? Did he notice that my outfit's different today? Maybe he's walking over right now...*

"Sorry I'm late!"

I reflexively looked up, but it wasn't Makoto this time, either. It was another man smiling at the woman on my left. They held hands and cheerfully strolled away.

Feeling restless, I waited for Makoto to appear. He could show up any minute now.

But he didn't come. When I checked the time, it was already nine. I looked all around me. I thought for a second that he might be hiding somewhere, but there was no way Makoto would play a trick on someone that would make them worry.

I hadn't received a text from him yet, either; maybe he was running late. I wrote to him so that he wouldn't have to come in a hurry: *"I just got to the square. No rush!"*

After that, I kept looking around the square then back at my phone, but Makoto didn't come, and my message stayed unread.

Five minutes passed. Then ten minutes. I started to feel slightly anxious: This kind of thing had never happened before. *Where could he be?* I wondered. I tried calling him, but he didn't pick up. Just as I was starting to worry that something had happened to him because of his insomnia, I heard an ambulance siren blaring in the distance. I looked up and in the direction of the sound. Normally I wouldn't have given it a second thought, but for some reason, the sound seemed to ring in my ears.

I looked down at my phone again. He still hadn't seen my text.

I felt strangely on edge. My throat had gone dry. Ten more minutes went by; still no word from him.

What could this mean? He's just running late, right? Yeah, that must be it. I told myself that he'd see my text and call any minute now. But no matter how long I waited, nothing changed.

I felt a chill. The worst-case scenario crossed my mind, but I desperately tried to convince myself that I was just overreacting. *I'm reading too much into this. It's just my imagination running wild.*

But would Makoto ever break a promise for no reason?

My body was rigid with nerves, and suddenly I heard someone running toward the square. I glanced up and locked eyes with the person who was frantically searching for me.

"Tsubasa!"

It was Aoi. She rushed toward me, panting heavily.

"Aoi… What are you doing here?"

"I overheard you guys talking about where you'd meet in the clubroom. Anyway, that's not important right now. I have something to tell you, but I want you to stay calm." She inhaled deeply, trying to steady her breathing. "Tsukishima got in an accident. My mom called me—she said he's in her hospital."

My mind went blank. *Makoto, in an accident…?* I wished my concerns had all been for nothing, but there was one piece of good news.

"Don't worry, it was just a scrape," Aoi said. "A motorbike blindsided him. His phone broke, but he's all right."

"What? A bike? He's not hurt or anything?"

"That's what I heard. So there's nothing to worry about."

A sigh of relief escaped me. My mind was still blank, and I didn't know whether I was happy or scared, but I gradually got myself together as Aoi talked me through the situation again. Makoto had gotten in an accident, but he hadn't been hurt badly. I hadn't been able to reach him because his phone was smashed.

"I'm glad he's okay... I was worried sick that something bad might've happened to him. Wait, do you think he hit his head? I've heard that you might seem okay at first, but it can get worse afterward."

I couldn't shake off my anxiety. I told myself not to panic, but no matter how hard I tried, I couldn't quell my worries and doubts. Maybe my sense of urgency showed on my face, because Aoi was watching me with concern.

"You could talk to my mom if you want," she said with a reassuring smile.

"Oh. Can I?"

"Sure. That should put your mind at ease—I've already told her we might call."

I hesitated, but I was close with Aoi's mom. I would just worry until I heard the whole story, so I nodded, taking up their kind offer. Aoi rang her mom and handed me her phone.

"Oh, Tsubasa? Are you all right? You must've been shocked to hear the news," said Aoi's mom. Just hearing her relaxed voice comforted me, and I realized how tense my shoulders had been.

"I'm okay. Sorry for calling you when you're busy at work."

"Oh, don't worry, dear. It's only natural that you're scared for him. So, about the accident—"

Aoi's mom was probably used to describing all sorts of injuries; she gave me a short, clear explanation of Makoto's situation. Just like Aoi had said, he only had a minor injury, and there were no signs of impact to his head. I wanted to rush over to the hospital to be by his side, but Aoi's mom told me that, just to be safe, Makoto was getting a thorough checkup over the course of the entire day, so he couldn't see any visitors. She offered to pass on a message from me instead, so I asked her to tell Makoto not to worry at all about our date.

"You know, Tsubasa, when I heard you got a boyfriend, I have to say I was surprised," Aoi's mom said, a hint of emotion creeping into her voice. She knew me well, having watched me grow up since I was little. "He seems like a kind boy."

"You talked to Makoto?"

"No, I just saw his face... I don't think he knows I'm here."

We talked a bit more, and I was relieved to hear her reassure me that Makoto was fine. Since I didn't want to get in the way of her work too much, I thanked Aoi's mom and hung up. When I handed the phone back to Aoi, she was staring at me in surprise.

"Are you crying, Tsubasa?" she asked. I noticed for the first time that my eyes were damp.

"Oh, I guess so. Wonder why. I must just feel...relieved. Like, now I can let my guard down."

"Tsubasa..."

"You might laugh at me, but he's just not the kind of guy who'd break a promise, so I was really worried... And there's that insomnia thing, too. I was wondering whether I'd asked too much of him and that's why this happened… I don't know, my head's a mess." I wiped my tears away before adding, "Sorry, forget I said that."

Aoi was quiet, but not long after, she let out a soft laugh. "You're turning into a Makoto fanatic."

"Oh, I get a second title on top of 'film fanatic.'"

"More like getting *branded* than getting a title."

"Well, you know what? If you fall in love, too, you'll get it soon enough."

"Whoa, life is freaky. Never thought I'd hear *you* say something like that, of all people."

"Me either." We laughed as we always did, chasing away the somber mood.

"Hey, wanna go to a café or something?" asked Aoi. "I ran all the way over here—I could use a drink."

We decided to stop in at a nearby café. As we sat and chatted, Aoi teased me about my date outfit, and I started to calm down. Since I had the whole day free now, we went shopping.

Aoi got a message from her mom later in the morning and shared the news with me. "They got the results from the tests they did this morning. There's nothing wrong with Tsukishima, as expected. And Mom also said she passed on your message."

The two of us spent the rest of the day together. Now that we were out, we figured we might as well go watch a movie that was creating a lot of buzz. Afterward, we went to a café to discuss our thoughts on the film.

Aoi seemed to be waiting for more news from her mom, as she kept checking her phone the whole time.

That evening, I got a call from a public pay phone. I was suspicious for a second, but realized it must be Makoto, who'd broken his phone in the accident. Aoi had asked her mom to give him my number.

"Hello?"

"Oh, hi. Um, sorry for calling you on a public phone. It's Makoto."

As soon as I heard that familiar voice, a wave of relief washed all the way through me. I'd never thought of myself as quick to cry, but I felt tears pricking my eyes again.

"I just got my test results from this afternoon, and everything looks good. Hayami's mom told me what happened, so I wanted to call you," he explained. "I'm sorry we couldn't have our date."

"It's not your fault, Makoto. I'm sorry if I put too much strain on you."

"No, I should've been more careful. If I'd been paying attention, this wouldn't have happened."

We kept going in circles apologizing to one another, so we both laughed it off and agreed to let it go.

"Anyway, are you really feeling okay, Makoto? You're not hurt?"

"Oh, no, I'm completely fine. It was just a small scooter."

"Really? I thought you got hit by a motorbike."

"Uh, right… No, it was a scooter. Did you hear otherwise?"

"Sorry. Aoi said it was a motorbike, so I pictured something bigger." I asked about his phone, too, but he said that luckily, he just had to get the cracked screen fixed, so it should be ready to use again by tomorrow. He said he'd stay home tomorrow, but that he should be back at school the day after that.

We didn't talk about going on another date. I didn't want to put too much pressure on Makoto.

4

Two days later, on Tuesday, I peeked into Makoto's classroom first thing in the morning before homeroom started. He was back. We'd texted each other before leaving for school, but I was relieved just to see that he was really there.

Makoto caught sight of me and came out into the hallway. He seemed unhurt, as far as I could tell.

"I'm so glad you're back, Makoto. You look great—it's like nothing happened to you."

"Oh, yeah. I told you, I'm fine."

"So, how was it, then? Wrestling with a scooter."

"Um...I think it won."

We weren't really talking about anything at all, but we still couldn't help but grin at each other. It was these little moments that really felt precious to me.

"Um, I...I wanted to say I'm really sorry I missed our date on Sunday," he said sincerely.

"Don't worry about that—it's all good," I reassured him with a smile.

I'd invited Makoto out in the hopes that it'd be a nice change of pace for him, but to be honest, I'd also been really looking forward to it for myself. I was sure we'd have another chance to go again sooner or later. That was what I was thinking, at least—until he said something I didn't expect.

"So, I was wondering..." Makoto glanced around, as though to make sure no one was close enough to overhear. "By way of apology, if you're up for it...how about today?"

"Huh? What do you mean, today?"

"Do you feel like going to the amusement park with me? It might be less crowded on a weekday, too."

His suggestion came as such a shock that I didn't catch on at first. "You mean... What, are you saying we should skip school to go hang out?"

"Um, I guess it's a crazy idea, right? Sorry, I don't know what I was—"

"I'd love to!" I said, leaning forward. I wouldn't have imagined Makoto would be the type to suggest cutting classes to go on a date, but I was all for it. Even though he'd been the one to bring it up, I felt like I was way more excited than him. "That's a great idea, Makoto. Let's go! If we set off now, we should get there before noon."

"So...you wanna go?"

"Yesss, we're going!"

We came up with a plan on the spot. Since we might attract attention if we went in our school uniforms on a weekday, we decided to go home and get changed first, then take the train to the amusement park together. We decided to meet up at the school entrance and went back to our classrooms to get our bags. I saw Aoi when I got back to my desk, so I told her straight out, "Sorry, I'm gonna miss school today."

"Huh? But you're already here."

"I'm skipping school with Makoto—we're going to the amusement park."

"Uh, seriously? You're leaving now?"

"Yup, completely serious."

Aoi looked perplexed. I thought she might try to stop me, but she started packing up her things as well. "I'll come too," she said.

"You will?"

"Yeah, I'm gonna tag along. It's been a while since I went to an amusement park. Or did you two want to go just by yourselves?"

"Hmmm. Nah, you're more than welcome. Actually, it might be even *more* fun with the three of us."

"That's settled, then. No time to lose. I'll talk to the teacher about why we're absent."

I told Aoi to meet us at the school entrance, and she headed for the faculty office.

After a while, the bell for the start of homeroom rang. As everyone rushed to their classrooms, I made my way to the entrance hall with my bag. It was exciting being in the quiet hallway when I was supposed to be in class like everyone else, so I pulled out my phone and started filming.

"You were quick, Minami. Oh, you're recording?" Makoto showed up with his bag slung over one shoulder.

"Yup. It's not every day you get to see the place like this. By the way, is it okay if Aoi comes with us? Sorry, but I told her she could before checking with you."

"Hayami's coming?"

We heard someone running down the hallway toward us, and the next second, Aoi appeared.

"I sorted things out so me and Tsubasa can take the day off," she said nonchalantly. "We're all set now."

"Wow, Aoi. I knew you were good...but how'd you manage that?"

"I have my ways." Aoi turned to Makoto. "I guess you heard from Tsubasa—I'm coming with you."

"Oh, sure. I don't mind, but are you sure you're okay with this?"

"It'll also be useful to collect some reference material for our future movies," Aoi said. "So I'll be your personal videographer today. You can pay for my entrance ticket and lunch, Tsukishima."

"Uh, why me?"

"I went through a lot of trouble for you on Sunday, you know. I think that's fair compensation. What, you don't think so?"

"No, you're completely right."

Seeing Makoto surrender so easily made me giggle. "You're such a pushover," I teased, and he smiled sheepishly.

"He really is," Aoi agreed with a shrug.

After that, we went back home, got changed, and met up at the same square in front of the train station where I'd waited for Makoto on Sunday. On the train, we chatted energetically all the way to the park.

The amusement park was even less crowded than we'd hoped for. There was hardly anyone in the plaza beyond the entrance gate, and the whole place was quiet.

As we were looking around in surprise, Aoi made a cutting remark. "Well, it's almost November, it's pretty chilly, *and* it's a weekday, so I guess it's mostly just people who skip school on a whim who're here today—right, Tsukishima?"

"...Sorry you had to go along with my whims," he said apologetically.

"On the flip side, we basically have the whole place to ourselves," I chimed in.

We didn't have to wait in line for the rides, and we could film as much as we wanted. We had the run of the empty amusement park, and we could enjoy it to our hearts' content.

"All righty, we're gonna go on every single ride in the park," I announced. "C'mon, Makoto!"

"Uh, *all* of them? I'm not so sure about that—"

"President's orders, Tsukishima," Aoi said, shutting him down.

I grabbed Makoto's arm and pulled him through the park, while Aoi filmed us with a grin on her face. I wanted to make him laugh so much that he'd forget about his insomnia.

Our first stop was the merry-go-round. We rode the horses and Aoi took a video of us.

"Mooom, look at meee!" I called out, waving to Aoi. She waved back with a chagrined smile on her face.

I asked Makoto to do the same, so on the next go-around, he timidly said, "M-Mom, look at me," and waved his hand.

"I'll get you for that later," Aoi said, flashing him a smirk. That freaked Makoto out, and I burst out laughing.

Aoi made him get on the spinning teacup ride next, claiming it was time for some payback. I stayed on the ground to film them. When the music began, the other empty teacups started spinning slowly. Meanwhile, Aoi and Makoto's teacup spun like crazy, and Makoto let out a scream.

Once they got off, we watched the video I'd taken; it was

completely absurd. Aoi couldn't stop herself from cracking up, and then Makoto and I doubled over laughing, too.

We kept going around the park after lunch. With almost fifty rides in total, it was almost impossible to fit all of them in. Still, we enjoyed the attractions and took a lot of videos of one another with our phones. The whole day was filled with pure joy, and I felt perfectly content.

Time passed by in a flash. Winter was on its way, so sunset came earlier now. As the sky became steeped in an orange glow, we got on the Ferris wheel to wrap up our day.

"I wonder what people think when they see one guy going around the park with two girls," I said once we were in the car of the Ferris wheel.

Aoi scowled. "We look like friends, right? They probably think the guy's going out with one of us, or that all three of us are just really close."

"Come on, Aoi, we *are* all close. Don't make a face like that," I teased her.

"Huh? You're including me and Tsukishima in that?"

I'd known Aoi long enough to know her little jabs at Makoto didn't mean she disliked him. The same went for Makoto. They actually got along well.

The car we were in arrived back down on the ground, and we walked into the plaza. I gave a big stretch. It had been such a perfect day. I'd managed to do almost everything I'd been hoping to do with Makoto on Sunday—except for one thing.

As I was thinking about that, Aoi said she wanted to go to the toilet, and she left me and Makoto by ourselves. We decided to sit on a bench near the Ferris wheel and wait for her.

I gazed at Makoto's hand resting on the bench. I gathered up my courage and gently took it in mine. He looked at me in surprise. Though it was such a small gesture, it made my heart thump loudly.

"Um, you know, we haven't had much of a chance to hold hands lately," I stammered.

"Oh…y-yeah, you're right." He looked down, blushing a little. I could feel the warmth of his hand—completely unlike that time I found him asleep in the clubroom.

I thought my nerves would kill me if I didn't say something, so I tried to make conversation. "Um…I had a lot of fun today."

"Oh, yeah. Me too."

"Thanks for asking me out. You really surprised me. I never would've guessed you'd want to skip school like this—but I'm really happy you did."

"I'm glad."

We were still holding hands.

Though I was worried about his insomnia in the back of my mind, Makoto seemed to have enjoyed today as much as I had. I hoped we might have more dates like this in the future, assuming it hadn't been too hard on him; I wanted to share experiences, see the same sights, and laugh together with Makoto.

Just half a year ago, I had never even touched romance in my own life, and love had been a cryptic concept to me. It used to be something I craved, something I was impatient to explore. But now…

"I want to go everywhere with you, Makoto. I want to keep making movies together."

Before I realized it, I'd given voice to my wishes, squeezing his hand a little all the while. A part of me was still anxious not to be a burden on Makoto, but I told myself that it was okay, that Makoto would nod and say yes. I thought he might be shy about it, but I hoped he would say he felt the same way.

Except, for some reason, Makoto's shoulders grew tense; I could only sense it because I was holding his hand. I waited for his answer, but he was silent for a while before answering.

"I'm sorry. I… I have to move overseas this winter."

I'd been caught completely off guard, and at first, the sentence made no sense to me. "What? You're moving?" I murmured once my brain had finally grasped the meaning.

A pained expression crossed Makoto's face. "Yeah. For my parents' work. So once I go…" He hesitated, then seemed to make up his mind and said firmly, "I can't make movies with you anymore."

5

Makoto is moving to another country. We won't be able to make movies together anymore.

I was shocked, but I think I managed to stay calm. "Oh… okay. You're moving away…"

"I'm sorry. I should've told you sooner. It was decided during summer break, but it's been so great making movies with you all that I just couldn't find the right time to tell you."

I must've looked like a lost child: anxious, unsure. I opened my mouth to try to say something in response, but nothing came out, and I shut it again. I wanted to tell him, "No, don't go anywhere. I want to be with you," but it wasn't easy to just come out and say that to his face. Maybe this was partly where his insomnia had come from…

"Makoto. I…I…" I didn't know what to do, but I wanted him to know how I felt. But before I could say anything more, someone else spoke.

"Even if we can't make movies together, that's only going to be for a year or so, right?"

Startled, I looked around to find Aoi walking across the plaza toward us. Apparently, she'd heard our conversation.

"I guess you can't stay in Japan by yourself now 'cause you're still a high schooler, but what about when you're in college? Or are you gonna go to college abroad, too?"

Makoto looked somewhat unsettled by Aoi's words. "Um…I haven't thought about that yet."

"So you can persuade your parents to let you go to the same college as us, or at least somewhere in the same prefecture, right? That way, we can still make movies together."

Aoi was looking not just at Makoto, but also at me.

Though I was still a bit stunned by the news, I thought about what Aoi had just said. *If Makoto goes to college overseas, then there's nothing we can do…but if he's in Japan, somewhere close enough, she's right—it wouldn't be too hard to keep making movies together. Still…*

"Right. Case closed," Aoi declared. "So don't look so sad, Tsubasa. It's not like you have to break up with him just because he's going away. Though you'd have to do long distance."

I finally figured out that Aoi had been concerned about me and trying to cheer me up. "Did I really look *that* sad?"

"Uh-huh. Just like that time you got so excited about the dessert in our school lunch that you knocked it off your tray and accidentally stepped on it."

That had *actually happened*, I remembered. It had been like a scene right out of a manga.

"Uh, are you saying I'm on the same level as a dessert?" Makoto asked hesitantly.

"Are you kidding? You're lower than dessert. *Way* lower," Aoi said.

"Ouch."

"You kept your mouth shut about something this important, so don't complain. Sheesh, you could've told us a lot earlier. I've already taught you so much about movies. Were you seriously just gonna let that go to waste?"

"Sorry…"

"I don't want your apologies; I want reparations. You better pick a college in Japan, all right? In the same prefecture as us. Got that?"

Cowed by Aoi's fierce attack, all Makoto could do was agree. "S-sure. You got it."

Aoi must've been startled by the news, too, but I guessed she'd said all that to lighten the mood around all of us. My eyes met Makoto's. He hadn't completely brightened up, but he did laugh.

I still hadn't processed everything, but maybe Aoi was right; maybe we'd only have to be apart until we started college. If that was true, I'd still be lonely, but at least I'd only have to wait a little over a year.

"Anyway, let's get going, Tsubasa," Aoi prompted, snapping me out of my thoughts. "We should look for souvenirs for Ena and Ichika." We had told them we'd had to cancel filming for the day and promised we'd get them something to make up for it.

"You're footing the bill for this, too, Tsukishima," Aoi said as we walked toward the souvenir shops.

"Huh?" Makoto said, taken aback.

"You haven't told Ena and Ichika about your move, have you? Who do you think has to clean up after your mess? Hmm?"

"...I'd love to buy something for them," he said, defeated.

They were both trying to be jokey. I remembered back to this morning, when Makoto had surrendered to Aoi just like that, so I chimed in, "You really are such a pushover, Makoto." They both grinned.

After that, I tried to act like I always did. Aoi and I teased Makoto as we picked out souvenirs, and we headed back to the train station. Luckily, we found empty seats on the train, so we sat down side by side.

Aoi fell asleep. Maybe she was tired—or maybe she was just pretending to be.

Makoto and I were awake. I slipped my hand into his, and he turned to look at me.

"Makoto...come back for college. I'll be waiting."

He stared at me, then softly said, "I will."

The next day, after school, Makoto gave Ena and Ichika their souvenirs and shared the news that he would be moving in the winter. The pair were both surprised.

"Really?! What country are you moving to?" Ichika asked.

"Singapore, apparently."

"Aww, that's too bad. I thought we made a good team," Ena said.

"Yeah…but I'm planning to come back to Japan for college, so I hope you'll let me help you make movies again when I do."

Though they looked disappointed, the girls agreed that there was nothing he could do but go with his parents. Makoto, meanwhile, seemed to have made up his mind about coming back to Japan for college; he'd assured them that he would only been gone for a little more than a year.

Makoto told us that he would have to miss school fairly often from now on to get ready for the move. True to his word, he went home early the next day, and he didn't show up at the clubroom. I heard that his homeroom teacher had officially announced the news that he was moving to his classmates as well.

It still didn't feel real to me, but I had to face the facts: Makoto was going to go away this winter, and it was going to be hard to see each other until he came back to Japan for college.

The day Makoto left school early, I went up to the rooftop during the short break after fifth period. I used the key that Makoto had given me before; he'd told me that he didn't need it anymore.

A brisk wind blew across the deserted rooftop. I gazed up at the sky, standing near the fence.

"What are you doing all the way up here?"

I turned around at the sound of the voice and was a little surprised to find Aoi walking toward me.

"Oh, nothing much," I replied. "I guess I felt like gazing up at the sky."

Aoi came to stand next to me. After a beat, she asked, "Is this about Tsukishima?"

"...Was it that obvious?"

"Duh." She cracked a wry grin. "How many years have I known you?"

"Six years in elementary school, three years in junior high, and a year and a half in senior high. So, like ten and a half years?"

"You're forgetting preschool. Add another three years to that at least."

"That's a *long* time."

She smiled. "And how long has it been since you met Tsukishima? A year and a half?"

"Yup. If we just count the time he's been in the club, about half a year."

"So, what's on your mind?"

"Well..." I looked back up at the sky again and tried to describe how I was feeling. "I'm gonna miss him." It was as simple as that.

Aoi let out a deep sigh. "It's not like you'll never see him again... That's a bit much."

"You think?"

"I mean, I get why you'd feel lonely, since you'll be long-distance for a year at least. But it's not like you to be so down, Tsubasa."

"What *am* I like, then?"

"A film fanatic."

It never bothered me when Aoi called me that—in fact, I was grateful that she put up with my craziness and came along with me. I knew she looked out for me in ways I didn't even notice.

"But you know, maybe it's a good thing you got to experience all sorts of new feelings with Tsukishima," Aoi went on. "I bet it'll come out in the movies you make, too."

"Yeah...you're right."

"And like I said, it's not like you're saying good-bye forever. It's just a little over a year. Between making movies and taking entrance exams for college, that's gonna go by in a flash."

Aoi could be brusque, but she's always been kind at heart. I could tell she was saying all this just to cheer me up, and when I realized that, I loved her even more than I usually did.

"Thanks, Aoi, for always sticking with me."

She looked a bit taken aback. "What's gotten into you, Tsubasa? Did you eat something weird?"

"Sure did. I'm full of love and friendship."

"Oof, that's gonna give you heartburn."

I burst out laughing, and Aoi's lips curled up into a grin. She seemed relieved to see me smile.

"I'm gonna head back to class. Don't be late," she said, walking away.

I quietly watched her go, thankful to have her by my side.

6

The week after, Makoto was absent from school even more often than usual—which meant he couldn't come to the club, either. It was already October, and apparently, he'd already started preparing for the move. Since we couldn't be together as much as before, we texted each other instead. I was starting to get a feel for what being in a long-distance relationship would be like.

If my past self could've peered into the future, she would've been shocked to see me looking things up online and reading articles about long-distance relationships and prepping myself mentally for what was to come.

Long-distance relationships were more common than I'd expected, with a fair number of couples in relationships like that for more than three years. Compared to them, our case seemed trivial: just a year and a few months. Just as Aoi had said, that time would go by in the blink of an eye, since I'd be up to my neck with filmmaking and exams.

Even on the days Makoto couldn't come to school, he dutifully replied to all my messages.

I was texting him during a break one day when Aoi asked, "Who're you messaging? Tsukishima?"

"Yup. We're getting ready to go long-distance. Makoto is so sweet, he always replies every time I text him."

"Sounds like him. We've got end-of-term exams coming up next month though, so make sure you don't spend *all* your time messaging him."

"Yeah, I know."

The morning break was soon over, and it was time for third period. Though Aoi had just told me not to get too distracted, I couldn't help texting Makoto during class, too.

While I was staring at the blackboard as I waited for him to reply, I noticed something from my seat in the back of the classroom. Aoi, who sat toward the front, was going against her own advice and secretly using her phone. It wasn't just once, either; I caught her typing something several times during class. It was unusual for her to be texting someone so eagerly.

At lunch break, Aoi and I took our bento boxes to the club-room. Ena and Ichika came, too, just like normal. Aoi had wanted to keep these lunchtime meetups just between us girls, so Makoto had never joined us for lunch.

"Guess what happened today," Ichika said excitedly. "A boy from another class came to ask Ena for her number."

"Again? You sure attract a lot of guys," Aoi said casually.

"I don't know about that," Ena countered. "I can't hold a candle to Tsubasa."

"Who, me? Uh, I'm in the weirdo department, so I'm not really that popular."

"Wish I could say I was," Ichika said, making us laugh.

"Speaking of," I said, remembering Aoi's texting during class. "You get a lot more attention from boys than I do, Aoi."

"Huh? *I* do?"

"Yeah," Ena chimed in. "I wouldn't be surprised if you have a bunch of guys crushing on you. Especially the younger ones."

"No way. If Tsubasa's in the weirdo department, then I'm in the scary girls' group."

"Wish I could keep up with your girls' talk."

"You already are, Ichika," Ena said.

We chatted all through lunch break. Eventually, Aoi finished her lunch and got up to leave. "I'm gonna go back early to get ready for class. Don't go playing hooky, Tsubasa."

Once it was just the three of us, I asked Ena and Ichika, "By the way, were either of you texting Aoi during class today?"

"Hm? Not me," replied Ena.

"I wasn't either," said Ichika. "Did something happen?"

"I don't know for sure, but it looked like she was texting someone a lot. I've never seen her do that before." She could have been talking to someone in her family, but I had a feeling it wasn't. Ichika and Ena leaned forward eagerly.

"Ooh, really? Do you think it's a boy?" Ichika asked.

"Come to think of it, she's been checking her phone pretty often during filming these days, too," Ena said.

"Right? It's not like her, so I've been wondering..." Since I'd been messaging Makoto in between takes, I couldn't point fingers at anyone, but texting during filming was normally something Aoi herself didn't approve of.

We swapped ideas about who Aoi's mysterious correspondent could be. We were in the same class, but I still couldn't come up with a likely candidate. Ichika and Ena had no idea, either. We were still tossing up ideas when Ena let out a little sound as if she'd thought of something.

"What is it?" I asked.

"Oh, well—I know it's not good to snoop, but I just realized we might've caught her phone screen on one of the outtakes from the other day. When Makoto was away, and we were filming on the sports ground."

"You think we caught her phone on an outtake?" I asked in surprise.

"Yeah. I was filming the landscape while you were checking some footage, and I got a shot of Aoi while she was using her phone. I think the screen was visible. The footage didn't turn out great, but I've got it saved it on the laptop just in case."

I didn't want to spy on Aoi, but Ichika was already opening up the laptop. "Let's see."

"I know we've known her since we were kids, but isn't this stepping over the line?" I cut in.

"You really can't pass up a good love story, can you, Ichika?" Ena said.

"Aoi's not the type to put herself out there, so we have to help her out," Ichika said.

"Careful, Ichika. She's gonna make you cry like when we were in elementary school," I teased.

"Let's just look at the name! I have to know who she was texting." Ichika was peering intently at the screen. I got up to pull her away, but before I could step in, she let out a "Huh?"

"What is it? Did you find the name already?" Ena asked.

"Well, I did, but…she's just texting Tsubasa. See?"

"Really?" I looked at the screen, apologizing to Aoi in my head all the while. Ichika had zoomed in on the phone in Aoi's hand, and you could see a name at the top of the screen: *Tsubasa Minami*. So she had been talking to me. "You're right. It says Tsubasa."

"Aha, I knew you two were like that," Ena commented as Ichika sat back in disappointment.

But I was perplexed by the texts I saw on Aoi's phone—I recognized those messages.

I was lost in confusion for a moment. I thought of asking Ichika to check, but it would've been hard for anyone who wasn't part of that conversation to confirm anything. Ichika regretfully went away from the laptop while my eyes stayed fixed to the screen.

Breathing deep, I took another look at the messages. Aoi's phone showed a message thread with me. There was no mistaking that; my name was right there at the top. But one thing still puzzled me: The conversation on the screen wasn't one I'd had with Aoi, but with *Makoto.*

7

Lunch break was over. I didn't tell Ena and Ichika that anything was amiss. Instead, I mulled over my discovery by myself: Aoi's phone had messages sent between me and Makoto. Judging from the screen, it was the conversation as Makoto would have seen it from his end.

There were a few possible explanations for this: One was that Makoto could've sent Aoi a screenshot of our chat, and Aoi had been looking at the image on her phone. But that only made me wonder why he would do something like that.

There was one other possibility. The messaging app allowed a person to log into someone else's account as long as they knew their ID and password, meaning that people could hack into another person's account and take it over. Though I hadn't heard of that actually happening before, in theory, you could even keep an eye on other people's chats and pretend to be them. Either way, Makoto should have gotten a notification of the new sign-in. There was no way Aoi could've done something like that without his permission.

The next day, Makoto came to the clubroom. I thought of

asking him about it, but I was too scared to bring it up. It wasn't like I didn't trust him, nor was I suspicious of Aoi. But when I thought back, I remembered that they'd often been talking to each other in secret. I caught them making eye contact a few times, as though they were sharing some secret only they knew about.

Could Makoto and Aoi...be seeing each other behind my back? I wondered, but I immediately dismissed the idea. *No, they'd never hide something like that from me. I'm absolutely sure about that. So then, why are they being so secretive...?*

The following Monday, Makoto missed school again because he had to take care of some errands for the move. As an experiment, I tried texting Makoto during class while keeping an eye on Aoi in front of me. A few seconds after I'd sent my message, Aoi started tapping on her phone. She looked back up at the blackboard, and a reply came from Makoto at the almost exact same time. I sent a few more messages just to make sure.

There was no doubt about it now. I could hardly believe it, but Aoi was replying to me, pretending to be Makoto. She'd perfected his writing style; the messages she wrote sounded exactly like him. But why was she doing all this?

It had been raining since the morning. The four of us gathered in the clubroom after school, but I announced that we'd be taking the day off. I waited for Ena and Ichika to leave, planning to wait until then to ask Aoi about why she was using Makoto's account—though there was no guarantee she'd give me a straight answer. As I was mulling over how to get to the bottom of this, Ena and Ichika asked us if we wanted to go to a café. Apparently, they'd heard about a popular spot by the train station in the neighboring town.

Before I could answer, Aoi said, "Sorry, but if we're not filming today, I want to go to the library."

I decided to go with Ena and Ichika. We all walked to the nearest station underneath our umbrellas, then parted with Aoi at the station, since she was taking the bus to the library. I stopped short before we reached the ticket gate to the train. "Sorry, I just remembered I have to go to the faculty office." I told Ena and Ichika to go on without me, then hurried back to the bus stop.

Aoi was still waiting for her bus. I couldn't help but wonder—was Aoi really going to the library? Could it be that, for some reason, she was actually going to see Makoto? I hesitated, but in the end, I went to stand at the back of the line.

The bus came, and Aoi got on. I followed her, tense with nerves. Aoi had taken a seat toward the front, but she was looking out the window and didn't notice me as I made my way to the back. Even when the bus started moving, she showed no signs of having seen me.

We passed the first stop, then the second, then the third. The bus pulled in at the fourth stop near the library: Aoi stayed in her seat. Then, at the sixth stop, she stood up and got off the bus with a few other passengers. I shadowed her.

She'd gotten off at the stop in front of the hospital—the same hospital where her mom worked. I had a lot of questions spinning around my head, but now that I'd come this far, I couldn't turn back. Making sure to keep enough distance between us, I tailed her. Maybe the rain covered any sound I made, but she didn't notice me at all.

Aoi went into the hospital and kept going as though she'd followed the same path many times before.

I remembered one summer holiday in elementary school when I'd come to this hospital with Aoi. There was a room where the nurses could take breaks, and we went there to deliver something her mom had forgotten at home.

But now, it wasn't the break room where Aoi was headed. After a brief stop at the reception, she continued down the hallway. I thought someone might stop me, but I kept pace behind her. Luckily, no one called me out, but I lost sight of Aoi when she got on the elevator.

I almost gave up, but then I saw the elevator stop on the third floor, so I hurried up the stairs nearby. When I popped my head out of the landing on the third floor, I caught a glimpse of Aoi going into a room at the end of the hallway. Checking the signage, I confirmed that I was in the patients' ward; apparently, Aoi was here to visit someone.

Who could it be, though? She never mentioned anything like this.

I calmed myself down and walked toward the room that Aoi had just entered. When I reached it, I saw a nameplate hanging on the door inscribed with the patient's surname. It was a private room, and there was only one name written on it:

Tsukishima.

I didn't understand. It was the name of someone very close to me, but it didn't make any sense.

That's Makoto's last name...but it can't be him, I thought. He'd been missing school because he had to get ready to move. He hadn't been absent because he was sick—or at least, that's what I'd thought.

All of a sudden, I had a flashback to the afternoon when Makoto had fallen asleep in the clubroom and how Aoi had told me that it was a side effect of the insomnia medicine he was taking. I remembered how cold his hand had been…

Feeling anxious, I pulled out my phone and wrote him a text: "*Where are you now, Makoto?*" Almost immediately, it was marked as read.

"*I'm at home. Why?*" A reply came from Makoto's account, as if everything was normal.

Who was replying to me? Was it Makoto or Aoi? If I forced myself to believe what was written on the screen, then Makoto had to be home. There was no way he could be behind this door.

That means…whoever's in here must just happen to have the same name, I told myself. *That must be it. What am I thinking—why would Aoi text me back, pretending to be Makoto? I'm just making it all up in my head. It must be some kind of mistake…*

Making up my mind, I pushed open the door.

Aoi was inside, and she turned around in surprise. She had her phone in her hand, and I caught a glimpse of the text I'd just received from Makoto on the screen.

And in the bed lay Makoto—with his eyes closed, asleep in a patient's gown…

Makoto—who was supposed to be at home, getting ready for his big move—was, for some reason, in a hospital room.

Scene 4.

You Don't Know How Much Time I Have Left to Live

1

It was during summer vacation, at the end of July, when the symptoms of my illness started appearing and I lost consciousness for the first time. It was a few days after I'd gone on a date with Minami to the zoo. Until then, there hadn't been any serious abnormalities, and I'd been able to go about my life as usual. I didn't have to be scared of making promises. I was free to go wherever I wanted. Nothing held me back from doing what I normally did.

But a lot changed when the symptoms began. That day, when I passed out for the first time, I could sense it was going to happen, just as the doctor had told me. My body temperature had been low when I'd woken up in the morning. I'd been measuring my temperature every day, but that was the first time there had been a clear dip.

Feeling uneasy, I sat down at the breakfast table and told my parents about my temperature. The room went quiet for a moment.

"Okay. By the way, Makoto, what do you want for lunch today, somen or soba noodles?" Dad asked casually, making breakfast in the kitchen.

Mom didn't sound shaken, either. "Maybe I'll get noodles for lunch, too," she said, not taking her eyes off the newspaper. Both of them kept composed and talked to me without making a fuss. Honestly, I was grateful for that—thanks to them, I could take things at my own pace.

There's a condition called narcolepsy that makes you fall asleep without warning.

Like narcolepsy, my disease made me suddenly lose consciousness. The further the illness progressed, the more frequently I would black out and the longer I would stay unconscious. From the middle to terminal stages of my disease, I would be unconscious for several weeks at a time, and once I passed a certain point, I would spend more time unconscious than awake. However, I wouldn't notice symptoms daily until I got to the terminal stage. It wasn't an exact science, but there were different signs that I could watch out for on the morning it would happen and immediately before passing out.

After letting my parents know about my low temperature, I went to the bathroom and brushed my teeth, feeling jumpy the whole time. I was nervous as I went to the toilet, too, thinking how pathetic it would be if I blacked out there.

I managed to make it to the breakfast table, but when I thought about the doctor's instructions to spit out whatever I was eating so I wouldn't choke if I fainted during a meal, I completely lost my appetite. Even though the food Dad cooked was always healthy and delicious, I just couldn't bring myself to eat.

In the end, all I could stomach was some miso soup. When it was time for Mom to leave for work, Dad and I saw her off at the door. She looked back at me one last time before leaving, but she just smiled and said, "See you later," without mentioning anything more serious. I knew it was only because she thought I'd rather not talk about it; inside, she must have really been hurting.

We had an agreement with the doctor that whenever there was a warning sign of an impending blackout, I would go to the hospital so they could examine me for their research, so I got ready to leave. Dad called the hospital, and I texted Minami to let her know that I wouldn't be able to make it to the club meeting after school.

When we were both ready, we got in the car. I leaned the passenger seat all the way back so if I passed out on our way to the hospital, I wouldn't hit my head. The car quietly rolled out into the road. We'd already decided beforehand that we would avoid calling an ambulance unless it was necessary; we didn't want to take it away from people who were in life-threatening situations. I already had an action plan of what to do and where to go on the days with warning signs. Still, my heart was pounding with anxiety.

We reached the hospital, and while Dad was signing in at the reception desk, the nurse brought out a wheelchair for me to preempt any falls. With the nurse pushing me, Dad and I headed to the room I'd been assigned. Getting wheeled around was a pretty heavy blow to me psychologically; it made me feel completely helpless.

The private room was equipped with a bedside medical monitor, and as soon as I saw it, my body tensed up. The nurse told me that they had to gather data immediately before and after I lost consciousness, so I got changed into a patient's gown and let them attach the sensors to my body.

Somehow, I felt a sudden urge to see Minami. I wanted to go back to our clubroom.

I was sitting on the bed when my doctor came in. She had a quick chat with me and Dad, then took a sample of my blood. After that, she let us be by ourselves.

I knew Dad had brought his work laptop with him, so I told him not to worry about me and that he should feel free to do some work.

"All right," he said with a nod. He opened up his laptop on the desk, but just when I thought he'd started working, he turned around and said, "Hey, how about a game? I brought cards."

He had a deck of cards in his hand. I couldn't believe he'd actually brought it from home, and I let out a laugh but then shook my head no.

"All right, then," he said, smiling sheepishly as he turned back to his laptop.

I lay down on the bed and stared at the ceiling. I could hardly do anything but endure the passage of time, wondering when my consciousness would be snatched away from me.

One hour went by. Then two. Time felt heavy and slow.

But nothing happened.

Eventually, it was time for lunch. Even though I could feel my stomach rumbling, I was too scared to eat anything. I noticed Dad opening the backpack he'd brought with him, and I raised myself from the bed, wondering what was in there. He handed me a cooler bag. I opened it to find a round bento box with an ice pack and a small thermos bottle.

The bento was packed with my favorite *kinshi tamago*—shredded egg strips—as well as julienned ham and cucumber on top of a neat ball of somen noodles. I was stunned.

"There's homemade broth for the noodles in the thermos," Dad said with a smile. "I figured noodles might be easier for you to eat."

Tears pricked the corners of my eyes. When Dad had asked me what I wanted for lunch that morning, I couldn't even answer him. I hadn't realized what he'd wanted to do. Even so, he'd thought about what would be best for me and made me something that would be easy to swallow.

I poured some broth over the somen, picked up the chopsticks, and put a few of the thin noodles in my mouth. I only had to chew a couple of times for the noodles to slip down my throat. I wasn't scared to eat anymore.

"It's delicious, Dad," I said.

He grinned. "Glad to hear it." He'd made himself the same lunch, and we finished our meals without incident.

I didn't feel anything yet. And just like that, another hour passed.

I started thinking that it all might've just been in my head. Had I just imagined the warning signs? Had I fabricated the whole disease?

If that was true, I'd have nothing to fear. I could keep seeing Minami. I could keep making movies with the club. I could talk about the future with Minami, try to figure out which college to go to or what to major in, and we could study hard for our exams together...

If only I could do things like that. It would fill me with hope. I was shaken by my own thoughts. I dreamed of spending days living an ordinary, run-of-the-mill life.

But I had to face it: I was sick, and there was nothing I could do about it. It wasn't just a figment of my imagination.

Suddenly, the faintness arrived. My vision wavered. Everything blurred over. I tried to trick myself into thinking it was just some dust in my eyes, but a biting chill ran through my body. I felt cold, yet I could feel myself sweating. It was ruthless. I recognized the signs I'd heard about.

"Dad…I'm sorry." I squeezed out the words, desperately trying to let him know what was happening. Sweat beaded on all my pores, even though I was shivering with cold. I heard Dad's voice echoing somewhere far away.

"Makoto! Makoto!"

When I woke up, I was completely disoriented. The ceiling light was bright above me. I saw that I was in the hospital, and noticed it was dark outside. Time had skipped ahead, and I had trouble getting my thoughts in order.

"Makoto! You're awake!"

I looked around to find Dad nearby and realized that I was lying in bed. "Dad…"

He wasn't alone; Mom was standing next to him, watching me with concern.

I almost apologized, but I knew that would only make them sad. I might be unable to stop making them both feel miserable, but I hadn't been born to bring sorrow to the people around me. I wanted to laugh—I wanted to make everyone laugh.

So instead, I said, "Good morning—er, night." It was the best joke I could muster. The mood relaxed a little, and my parents' expressions softened.

"Morning, Makoto. Or good night," Dad replied.

"What a sleepyhead you are," Mom said.

Apparently, I'd been out for about six hours. My parents had talked to the doctor while I was unconscious; unfortunately, my illness was clearly progressing. Since the doctor had already collected the data they needed for their research, I was free to go, so the three of us headed home.

That was how the symptoms I'd been dreading began to appear. I had to find a way to live with my condition—and this became my mission in what was left of my life.

But I had a feeling that once I got the hang of it, it might not be so hard to make things work. The blackouts came suddenly, but there would always be warning signs in the morning. As long as I stayed away from school or the club on those days, it would inconvenience the people around me as little as possible. I could still keep my illness a secret.

Though it still made me anxious, I managed to deal with the second blackout better than the first. The third time as well. I checked into the hospital for my examinations, and Mom came to pick me up the day after. I tried to cheer her up.

People can get used to anything, given time. That was what I learned.

I also learned the hard way that if you get too used to something, it can trip you up when you least expect it.

2

It happened right around Obon, when we were more than halfway through summer vacation. Hayami had told me to come meet her at a café. A lot had happened between us in the lead-up to that, and I'd even said to her, "When the time comes, I'll break up with Minami. So don't worry."

I'd already been resolved to end things with Minami around the time my symptoms started appearing. There was no doubt that the sickness was eating away at my body, and I knew there would come a day when I wouldn't be able to go to school at all. I was going to tell everyone that I was moving somewhere far away and disappear from school when things got to that point. I'd break up with Minami, using the move as an excuse. It might make her sad at first, but it had to be better than finding out that I was dying.

But I'd been careless to say what I'd said to Hayami. It made her suspicious, so I had to meet up with her to talk about it. I preferred not to make plans with anyone if I could help it, but this time, I had no choice.

I was scared to measure my temperature that morning. I told myself that as long as the results were normal, everything would be fine—but life is cruel sometimes. My temperature was low: a clear warning sign.

I should've canceled my meeting with Hayami right then and there. But up until that point, my blackouts had always happened in the afternoon, and we'd agreed to meet in the morning.

Though my disease was progressing, I still felt healthy; it wasn't as if I was physically weak. I could go to talk with Hayami in the morning, come back home before noon, and then go to the hospital. I thought I could handle that much.

Without telling my parents about my low temperature, I went to the café. Hope and fear churned inside my gut in equal measure: hope that everything would be okay and fear of what would happen if I collapsed in front of her.

I felt relieved when I got to the café. All I had to do now was chat with Hayami, then go home. I could tell my parents I'd forgotten to measure my temperature that morning, then take it at noon instead and tell them it was low.

After a bit of small talk, Hayami asked me what I'd meant about breaking up with Minami. So I'd lied to her about transferring to another school in the winter. Right after that, it struck. I felt faint, and everything went blurry. As I felt a chill grip my body, I instantly regretted my decision to come. I should've known better.

Still, it was just that one time; I thought I'd be able to explain it away, tell her I used to get sick a lot when I was little, and that it was the heat that had made me pass out…

Ten days before the end of summer break, when Hayami asked me at the park whether I was actually going to die, it caught me off guard. I tried to sweep it under the rug, but in the end, even that failed. And then, for the first time since we met, we talked openly and laughed together without holding anything back.

That was also the first time I'd told a friend about my diagnosis. Hayami was stunned. I felt so helpless, knowing that all I could do was shock and upset the people around me, but letting her in on my secret led to something I'd never expected.

"*People who don't have much longer to be happy shouldn't be so quick to give up on that happiness,*" she'd told me. "*I'll help—not for your sake, but because it's the right thing to do for a fellow person. And for Tsubasa, so she won't have to grieve.*"

Hayami became my co-conspirator, helping me keep my secret. Having her on my side made a big difference, since I wanted to keep going to school like a normal kid for as long as possible. After that day, Hayami always stayed by my side whenever we were at the club.

But my disease was progressing faster than I'd expected. It was October, and the cool autumn weather had arrived when I realized just how bad my condition had become. I passed out in the clubroom after school.

I'd measured my temperature that morning, and it had been normal, so I felt confident going to school and staying for club activities. We'd discovered an issue with the script during filming, so Hayami and I were revising it in the clubroom by ourselves. All of a sudden, I felt the strength leave my body, and I got strangely dizzy. The whole room blurred. A familiar chill came over me, and I broke out in a sweat. I panicked and felt like crying.

Why now? I should've been okay today.

Hayami had noticed immediately and shouted my name.

When I came to, I was lying in a bed in the hospital. The sky was starting to lighten, and Dad was asleep on the sofa in my room, sitting up with his arms crossed. I didn't want to wake him, but I did anyway, and we alerted the nurse that I'd regained consciousness. Soon the doctor came to give me a thorough examination. Though the details were unclear, the disease was advancing more rapidly than they'd predicted. She told me that from now on, I should check my temperature not just in the morning, but during the day as well.

Before the examination, I'd read through the messages I'd got while I was unconscious. I was worried about what might have happened in the clubroom after I passed out, but apparently, the school nurse and Hayami had covered for me. I couldn't thank them enough. Hayami's message included some crucial information, and I read and reread it so I didn't miss anything:

"I had to come up with something to cover for you with Tsubasa, so I said you've been trying to hide the fact that you've got insomnia."

"I told her that your insomnia medicine has severe side effects, so once you fall asleep, it's hard for you to wake up again. And when that happens, your whole body goes cold."

"That's the story Tsubasa believes now."

The way Minami looked at me changed a little after that, most likely because she was worried. She seemed careful not to tire me out as well. I felt bad putting her through all that, but at least I'd avoided the worst-case scenario of her finding out about my illness. I had to keep it a secret at all costs; the last thing I wanted to do was to upset her.

Even so, I ended up making her sad because of something else...

"Um...Makoto, do you want to go out with me on Sunday? We've both been busy lately, so we haven't gone anywhere. I...I'd like to go to the amusement park with you."

At the end of October, Minami asked me out on a date to the amusement park.

We'd gone out a few times since we first started dating, including during summer break, but ever since my blackouts started, I hadn't been able to do much more than hang out with her after club meetings.

When Minami invited me out that day, she looked uncharacteristically nervous. She was usually carefree, the kind of person who said whatever popped into her head—but in that moment, she seemed anxious as she waited for my response. I didn't know what to do.

I knew that the most sensible answer was to say no. But when I saw how shy she looked, expectantly waiting for my answer, I just couldn't bring myself to turn her down.

I thought Hayami might get mad at me for agreeing to go on a date, but she was supportive when I talked to her about it later. "If that's what you want to do, Tsukishima, then don't feel like you have to restrict yourself. Just...don't give up on your own happiness, okay? I get that it was hard to say no, and that's partly on me for not shutting it down straightaway."

She encouraged me to be optimistic and see what happened on the day. If all went well, I might be able to go on the date without any trouble—it wouldn't hurt to hope for that small happiness, at least. She said she'd back me up if anything went wrong.

Her words gave me courage. On the day of the outing, I checked my temperature, praying for a good number. It turned out to be low. Disappointment and sadness washed over me, and I didn't want to believe it—but I had to face up to the facts and act fast.

I picked up my phone to let Hayami know and come up with plan B. I felt drained as I called her number, probably due to the emotional shock of it all. Hayami was as crestfallen as if I was canceling on her, but she immediately came up with a plan. "Could you tell Tsubasa that something urgent came up?" she asked. "I'll take care of the rest."

But just then, I started feeling lightheaded and realized I was about to black out. I cursed the bad timing—I hadn't even gotten around to contacting Minami yet. My eyes went out of focus, sweat covered my body, and I lost all sense of what I had to do.

"Hey, are you okay? Don't tell me—Tsukishima? Tsukishima!"

I woke up in the hospital, back again in my usual room. A bitter, frustrated laugh escaped me. The clock showed it was around four o'clock in the afternoon, and my parents were close by my bedside. They pressed the call button, and while waiting for the doctor and nurses to come, Mom handed me my phone. I had a lot of notifications: a handful from Minami, and the rest from Hayami.

I learned that Hayami had raced to my house to check on me right after our call. She told my parents that she knew about my condition, and the three of them found me unconscious in my room.

And that wasn't all. Hayami had then rushed to the square in front of the train station where Minami was waiting for me and told her that I'd gotten into a traffic accident with a motorbike. To make it sound even more convincing, she explained the situation to her mother, a nurse, who also talked to Minami about it.

Now wasn't the time to wallow in my own grief—Hayami had done so much for me, and even her mother had gone out of her way to help. First, I texted her to let her know I'd woken up. Then I called Minami from a public phone inside the hospital, since my phone was supposed to have been broken in the accident.

Minami sounded relieved to hear my voice. I slipped up a little when I said a scooter had hit me instead of a motorbike, but we chatted and joked about for a little while and promised we'd see each other soon at school.

Later that day, when everything had settled down, Hayami messaged me: "*Tsubasa was really worried when you didn't show up. She said she thought something must've happened to you because you're not the type to break a promise. I should've been more careful. Sorry I didn't stop you.*"

Hayami had nothing to apologize for—I was the one who'd made the wrong call. I knew that I would soon have to decide how and when to withdraw from my life at school.

3

The examinations took longer than expected, so I also ended up spending the day afterward in the hospital, but by Tuesday, I was well enough to go back to school. I went to see Minami, apologized about Sunday, then asked her if she wanted to go to the amusement park that very same day. I knew there was only a small chance I'd pass out that day, and more than anything else, I had something important to tell her.

Minami was taken aback, but she was excited to come with me. Hayami ended up tagging along, too, and we all skipped school together. The three of us had so much fun. I checked my temperature in the afternoon, but there was nothing abnormal about it, so I stayed until the evening. We finished the day with a ride on the Ferris wheel, and once we were back on the ground, Minami and I had a moment to talk by ourselves.

I finally told her what I'd been meaning to: that I was going to be moving overseas that winter with my family. I'd be lying if I said it hadn't hurt me to tell her that, but it was just something I'd had to do.

Since the news came without any warning, it hit her hard. I might've just imagined it, but I got the feeling she wanted to try to convince me to stay. Then Hayami came to the rescue once again: "Even if we can't make movies together, that's only going to be for a year or so, right?"

I was a little confused at first. Hayami knew the truth, so I didn't understand why she would make plans for the future, but I went along with it and said that I'd come back to Japan for college. Luckily, Minami believed me.

That night, after I got home, I called Hayami to ask what why she'd said that.

"It was for Tsubasa… She really likes you more than you think, Tsukishima," Hayami said, her voice heavy with worry and sadness. "If you end the relationship because you're moving, you'll break her heart. It's all happening so quickly, so there's a good chance she won't be able to give up on you. I'm guessing she was about to say she wants you to stay. So I tried to convince her that it was only until we get to college that you'll have to be apart."

I listened to Hayami without saying a word.

"People forget about things. With enough time, they move on," she went on unflinchingly. "That's just the way it is… So if you and Tsubasa are in a long-distance relationship, eventually you'll talk less and less, until you gradually fade out of each other's lives. That way, Tsubasa can let you go little by little. I'll help out, and I'll be there for her. Maybe it's harsh, but I'll tell her that you've found your own little world somewhere else."

Hayami laid out a well-considered plan to pull it off, asking me to give her my password for the messaging app. She offered to reply to Tsubasa for me so we wouldn't have a repeat of what happened before—even after I died.

When I thought about how much of a burden Hayami would have to carry, I couldn't answer her at first, but she ended up talking me around. I gave her the passcode for my phone, too, in case there was some sort of emergency.

I was running out of time; I had to prepare myself for what was to come. Considering the possibility that my illness might keep advancing faster than expected, I told the school and my parents that I would stop coming within the year, and the school agreed to announce that I was moving away with my family. I told Ena and Ichika about leaving, too.

A little of the weight lifted from my shoulders once I'd told everyone. Whenever my body temperature got low in the afternoon and I had to go home early, I could use it as an excuse: that I had to get ready for the move.

My disease continued to progress, and by November, there were times when I would stay unconscious for days at a time. The doctor told me that there was a chance the illness could enter the terminal stage before the year was out.

I felt content, though. I could still make movies with everyone and be with Minami. There was nothing more I wanted.

One day, I woke up in the hospital at night. I heard the gentle sound of rain outside. When I checked my phone, I noticed a strange message Minami had sent to me.

"Where are you right now, Makoto?"

"I'm at home. Why?"

Hayami had been replying for me. Like a true screenwriter, she could write in my voice seamlessly. Her texts sounded exactly like me. I was a bit puzzled to see that Minami had waited a while before replying.

"This is Tsubasa. I'm standing outside your house."

"What?"

"Just kidding. Did I spook you? It's raining today, so I thought it might sound like something out of a horror movie."

"You made me look out the window. I thought I'd see you getting drenched."

"If this was an old-timey movie, we'd be holding on to each other in the rain. Wanna give it a go?"

"Nah. We'd both catch a cold."

I read all the way through the messages and was relieved to see that nothing had happened. There didn't seem to be anything suspicious going on; the pause between Minami's replies must've been unrelated. When I texted Hayami that I was awake now, she told me that things had gone as usual.

The way she described that—"as usual"—made me think of day after day going by without change. I was gradually getting farther away from that reality. But that was exactly why I was so glad when I could go to school and show up at the clubroom like I used to.

I lived every day like there would be no tomorrow. I got by somehow, surrounded by people who cared about me and supported me. I managed to keep going like that until the end of November.

Yet I was hitting my limit. It was getting hard to go to school, both physically and emotionally, so I decided I'd done enough. Not only was my time in school over—so was the time I got to spend with Minami…

A few days before the start of December, I was well enough to go to the club after school. I helped out with their filming, and we carried the equipment back to the clubroom. After we finished putting everything away, I told them what I'd gone there to say.

"Sorry, I know this is really out of the blue, but my parents had to reschedule our move, so we'll be leaving Japan before the end of the year. And…I'll have a lot of stuff to do starting tomorrow, and things are going to get really hectic, so…"

Thank you, and good-bye. I got to live a happy life right up until the very end, and it's all thanks to you. You've all been so kind, warm, and all-around amazing. I can't thank you enough. I might not have said that out loud, but I let my voice carry how I really felt.

"So I can't come to school anymore," I said. I felt at ease, free of regrets. "This will be my last day in the filmmaking club."

A hush fell over the room. The only sounds I could hear were the hum of the heater and the laptop.

The first one to break the silence was Ichika. "Really? You have to leave so soon?"

I didn't want to be too dramatic, so I just looked at her, hoping the extent of my gratitude showed across my face. *Thank you for everything, Ichika. I was worried about a lot of things when I first joined the club, but you made sure I felt comfortable here—that made such a big difference. I'll never forget your kindness.*

"Aw, that's a shame. I can't believe today's your last day," Ena said.

I turned to face Ena. *It was truly an honor to act alongside you as your co-star. I wonder what the future holds for you. That's not for me to find out, but I'm keeping my fingers crossed that you have a brilliant career.*

"Geez, Tsukishima, what is it with you and last-minute news?" Hayami let out an exasperated sigh—but it was all an act: I'd already confided in her about this in private. I exchanged a look with her. *No words can convey how grateful I am to you, Hayami. If not for you, I wouldn't be standing here right now. Sorry for giving you so much trouble. But thank you for everything.*

Finally, I turned to look at Minami, wondering whether I'd find shock or sadness on her face.

"You've done so much for us, Makoto. Thank you."

It wasn't what I'd expected at all—she was smiling. I was taken aback, but then I noticed Minami was trying hard to put up a brave front. I hated seeing her like that. My words got stuck in my throat, but I forced myself to speak. "Sorry it's so sudden."

"Don't worry, it's not your fault. If your parents have to leave earlier, there's nothing you can do." She flashed me another smile. There was a soft glow to it that reminded me of another smile she'd given me long ago.

"Whoa, for once you sound like a grown-up, Tsubasa," Hayami quipped.

"Now, that's our leader," Ena chimed in. Thanks to the two of them, the mood in the clubroom was already brightening up.

Minami turned toward them, grinning. "Someone once said that at a time like this, a real lady puts on a smile and sees a man off without complaint."

"Huh? Who said that?" Hayami asked.

"An actress from an old movie."

"That explains why it sounds so dated."

"Wait, what? You think it sounds dated?"

"N-no, it didn't, Tsubasa!" Ichika cut in. "It just didn't make any sense!"

"You're not really helping, Ichika," Ena teased.

We all laughed, and I could feel my relief spreading through my body. Minami seemed to relax and revert to her usual self. She talked about what it was like when I'd first joined the club, cheerfully recounting some stories from our time together. I reminisced as well, enjoying my final day here with everyone.

They started talking about seeing me off before I left Japan. Ena and Ichika said they wanted to come to the airport to see me, but luckily, Minami talked them out of it, saying that they'd probably just end up getting in my parents' way.

"Besides," she added, "we'll see him again in just a little over a year. Right, Makoto?"

Hayami and I had already come up with a plan for what to do if the others started talking about seeing me off, but I was surprised that Minami jumped in to put a stop to it. I nodded back in reply.

We spent the rest of the time chatting about the past six months, swapping stories excitedly. Whenever our eyes met, Minami gave me a gentle smile.

It made me sad to think I'd never see them again. I wanted to spend more time together and keep walking the same path, even if we clashed every now and then.

But my time for looking ahead at the future was at an end. From now on, I would be looking back at the past, recollecting fond memories. We were headed in different directions; their lives were ahead of them, while my death was ahead of me.

"I'm really glad I met you all," I said one last time. I tried to make it sound casual, not like a final good-bye. They all looked at me, and Minami answered for everyone.

"We feel the same way—especially me. I'm so happy I met you, Makoto."

And so, I did what I had to do to leave school for good. I was ready to spend the rest of my days quietly without seeing any of them again—but something happened that neither I nor Hayami had foreseen.

"Oh, by the way," Ena said, "you said you're flying out before the end of the year, but are you still going to be here for Christmas Eve? We have a party at mine every year. Do you think we could see you one last time before you go?"

I wasn't sure what to say. I'd been pretending that Christmas didn't exist; I'd already given up any hope of doing anything special that day. It would've been great to have one last party with everyone, but in my current condition, I couldn't make any promises.

"That's asking a lot, Ena," Hayami interjected. "I'm sure Tsukishima has his own plans and stuff he's got to do."

"Aww, it doesn't hurt to ask," Ena replied with a pout.

I glanced over at Minami. She seemed to be taking a back seat, just watching the scene unfold. When she noticed me looking in her direction, she gave me a warm smile.

"I probably can't make it," I murmured, a little downcast. "But...if it looks like I can come on the day, would it be okay for me to just turn up? Oh, I'm sure you have to get things ready, though, so I understand if that won't work."

It might have been because there was something fragile, even melancholy, about Minami's smile, but I just couldn't help but cling to that one last scrap of hope. I lifted my gaze to look at the girls.

Once my illness reached the terminal stage, I wouldn't be able to cover it up. Regardless, even if my body betrayed me before Christmas, I still wanted to keep something to hope for. This was probably going to be my very last wish.

"Of course you can. Feel free to pop by anytime!" Ena said, beaming.

"Hope you can make it," Ichika added.

"Well," Hayami said, watching me with a caring look in her eyes. "Only if you don't push yourself too hard."

We took a group photo together, which Minami shared with me, and then it was time to go home. The five of us walked down the path to the school gate in the sunset. Everyone went their separate ways until eventually I was left alone with Minami.

"Wanna walk with me for a while, Makoto?" Minami asked. She'd been growing quieter the closer we got to saying good-bye.

I nodded, and we started walking in the opposite direction to the train station. We decided to go to a nearby park, and as we were walking side by side, Minami took my hand. Now that it was just the two of us, she didn't talk much. She even stayed quiet while we sat on the bench in the park. But we could feel each other through our linked hands.

Sometimes her hand squeezed more tightly around mine. Though she'd kept it hidden while the others were around, Minami seemed like she didn't want to say good-bye. I squeezed hers back, hoping that I'd always remember the feeling of her hand in mine and our time together right now.

Eventually, the sun dipped below the horizon, and dusk gathered around us. When I looked up, I saw stars starting to glimmer in the sky.

I once read that the light we see from stars was actually emitted many, many years ago. There's so much distance between the stars and the earth that it takes all that time for the light to reach us here, so what we're actually seeing in the sky is the light from the past.

Though I didn't mind the silence between us, I found myself telling Minami about the stars, because I was going to become part of her past, too—though, of course, I didn't say that last part out loud. I couldn't help wishing that once in a while, she might remember the winter of her second year in senior high, when someone held her hand in a park and talked to her about starlight.

"'The light from the past,' huh? That's an interesting way to put it. It could be good in a movie."

"Are you sure you didn't want to film that?" I asked playfully.

Minami grinned. "I do want to film it, actually. Can you say it again?" She set up her phone on the bench and began filming under the night sky.

I told her the same story again. By the time I'd finished, it was nearly seven, so I suggested we start heading home. We walked to the station, still holding hands, and passed through the ticket gate.

We lived in opposite directions. My train was set to leave before hers, as if alluding to what was to come. Minami wanted to see me off, so she came with me to my platform. After a while, there was an announcement; my train had arrived. Passengers spilled out of the doors.

I got on by myself, then turned around to face Minami, who was still on the platform.

I hope you live a long life. I hope you fall in love a lot. I hope the little bit of bad luck I had brings you a lifetime of happiness. I hope your life will be full of joy and that you'll never stop smiling.

"See you," I said finally.

"Yup. See you," Minami replied.

The door shut between us, and the train rolled out of the platform, leaving her behind.

I did it—I'd managed to keep from crying right up until the end. I hadn't cried in front of Minami. Looking at my own tear-streaked face reflected in the window of the train door, I wished for her happiness with every fiber of my being.

4

The week after, I began staying at the hospital full-time. December had arrived, and almost nine months had passed since I'd first been given my diagnosis. Unfortunately, my disease was advancing at a steady rate. I hadn't entered the terminal stage yet, but I would know the end was near when I stayed in a coma for several weeks.

Even so, I had nothing more to worry about. I hadn't left things too late; I'd managed to say good-bye to everyone before my sickness got too serious. And if I was lucky, I might even be able to see them at their Christmas Eve party. I knew it was a slim hope, but I clung onto it as my final wish.

Many people came to see me in the hospital. It was a rare disease, so naturally, it attracted a lot of attention from researchers. I met with all kinds of doctors—young, old, even specialists who'd flown in from overseas. It wasn't just medical people who came to visit, though. There was one person I knew well who paid me regular visits.

"How's it going, Tsukishima?" Hayami asked on one such occasion. It was nice that she always talked to me casually, as if I were perfectly healthy. We chatted about all sorts of things, and I asked her what was happening in the club and how Minami was doing. "Ena and Ichika are the same as always. And Tsubasa's doing things at her own pace."

"That's good. It sounds like nothing's changed," I said.

"And the new film's going well. I'll bring you a DVD once it's finished," Hayami offered. However, the ward I was staying in was for patients in palliative care, intended as a quiet space for them to spend their remaining days. It was probably hospital policy, but neither my room nor the public lounge had a TV.

"Don't you get bored?" Hayami asked.

"Well, I have my phone, at least. And I can chat with Minami while I'm awake."

"Whatever floats your boat, I guess. Here, I brought a DVD player you can attach to your phone, so you can watch stuff on that. I'll even throw in some DVDs for you—my top picks."

Back when I'd first met Hayami, I never imagined we'd become such good friends. I took her up on her offer and borrowed the player along with the movies. And just like that, one more thing was added to my daily routine: watching films.

Hayami asked for my phone, and she downloaded an app that linked to the player. I'd forgotten about one thing, though, and her eyes went wide when she saw my home screen.

"Whoa. What's going on? You've only got a messaging app and a calendar on your phone."

She was right—there was hardly anything on my phone now. I used to have apps for games, social media, and the news, but I'd wiped it clean at some point.

"Well...I don't really need it anymore."

"But..."

"I don't mean to sound bitter, but I just don't want to see any of it. What's happening in the world, what's ahead in the future..." *Because it's all going to leave me behind.* I finished the sentence in my head, unable even to say it out loud.

It was probably the same reason why there wasn't a single TV in this ward. Here, the patients were in a different world, set apart from the rest of society. The hustle and bustle of the outside world was irrelevant to us now, and being exposed to it would only torture us.

Hayami was silent. I realized I shouldn't have said that and tried to twist it into a joke. "So, that's my life now. I feel like a grandpa. Though grandpas these days might get offended by that."

She saw what I was trying to do and let out a chuckle, a wry smile on her face. "Don't go senile on me," she said.

"Wait, did I have lunch today?"

"You're in the hospital, Tsukishima. No way they'd forget about feeding you."

We talked some more after that, and she reassured me that I had nothing to worry about with Minami. I wasn't worried, though; whenever I was out cold, Hayami would step in for me, replying to Minami without a hitch. I could count on her to pull it off even after I was gone. Hayami would let the relationship fizzle out—little by little, my replies would get more sporadic, and eventually we'd stop messaging altogether.

My heart ached to imagine how sad and lonely Minami might feel when that happened, but it *had* to be less shocking than an abrupt ending. Thinking that brought me some comfort.

Before we knew it, it was already sunset. I suggested Hayami head home before it got too dark, so she got up to leave. Just before she walked out the door, she turned around.

"Uh, hey," she said.

I looked at her from the bed. It wasn't like Hayami to be hesitant about something.

"You know…if we told Tsubasa the whole truth, you might be able to spend more time with her. Don't you want that?"

Her question startled me. It was something I'd turned over in my head countless times: If I told Minami everything, we might be able to be together until my last breath…

"No," I said firmly, and Hayami looked taken aback. "Our plan is working—I'll fade out of her life in the least painful way possible. I don't want to drag her into my death and make her mourn for me."

Hayami stared at me wordlessly. Eventually, she looked down at her feet. "Stop it… It's almost like you actually love her," she murmured.

I thought about it for a little while, then said, "It's nothing that dramatic. She's just precious to me."

Alone in my room again, I gazed out the window, still sitting up on my bed. I found myself thinking about death and other ideas that used to feel so vague and distant to me. Once the sun went down, the dark sky glimmered before my eyes, like that night Minami and I had sat together in the park.

The light from the past was glittering in the sky.

5

Time seemed to go in circles rather than straight lines. I woke up, I killed time, I went to sleep. My days basically followed that pattern—the only difference was that on some days, I lost consciousness instead of actually falling asleep.

When I was awake, I exchanged messages with Minami. In the world of those messages, I was just a high schooler getting ready to fly overseas, my life untouched by the shadow of illness.

I watched the movies I'd borrowed from Hayami, too, and they often moved me to tears. My emotions hadn't dried up at all—I could still sense the beauty in things.

Sometimes I got sentimental and went back through old photos and videos I'd taken. I set my favorites as wallpapers on my phone, but Hayami teased me when she caught sight of it. Neither of us brought up the serious conversation from before. We just chatted about other things, like what we thought of the movies she'd brought.

It was finally the week before Christmas. My condition hadn't improved, but I did get one piece of news that cheered me up: My doctor gave me permission to go out on Christmas Eve, as long as there were no warning signs of a blackout. When I gave Hayami the verdict, she got excited for me, too.

The days went by as I slipped in and out of consciousness, and eventually, December 20 rolled around. I took my temperature that morning, feeling nervous. I'd figured out a certain pattern to my blackouts—so far, the longest blackout I'd had was three days, and after each blackout, I wouldn't pass out again for at least another two days. Which meant that if I lost consciousness on the twentieth or the twenty-first, there was a good chance that I'd be awake on Christmas Eve.

The thermometer beeped. For the first time in my life, I prayed for the number to be low. Normally, I was disappointed whenever it was, but right now…

Aware of my own throbbing pulse, I timidly checked the display. Colder than normal.

I spent the rest of the morning filled with a growing hope. It was past noon when I felt the onset of a blackout. Except… something was off. It felt a bit different from all the times before. My whole body went limp, and I felt groggy—but I didn't pass out immediately. The world kept swaying around me. I wasn't sweating, either. In my muddled thoughts, I wondered what was going on and what these strange new symptoms might mean. I forced my sagging body to move just enough to press the call button to alert the nurses. Like a thread snapping, I lost consciousness.

When I came to, I was lying in darkness.

It felt like some sort of bad joke. I thought I must've died.

But no, it was just dark in the room. I was alive, lying in my bed in the hospital. I should still have a few more months left in me. I wasn't going to die so easily.

I suddenly remembered to check the date on my phone. Although I shouldn't have had any idea of how much time had passed while I was unconscious, I somehow had the feeling that it'd been a long time. My fingers nearly trembled as I touched my phone screen.

December 24, 3:50 AM

I stared at the date, forgetting to breathe. For a split second, I thought I'd slept through the party—but I hadn't. I checked the time and date again and again, waiting for my brain to catch up.

"I...I did it. I really did it." My hoarse voice forced its way out. The tiny spark of recognition gradually spread all over my body, wrapping me in a warm joy.

I couldn't believe it at first, but it wasn't a mistake: Today really was the twenty-fourth. I'd managed to wake up right on Christmas Eve. Now I could create one final memory with Minami and the others.

I felt bad about bothering the nurses so early in the morning, but I pressed the call button to let them know I was awake. They called my parents, who came to see me right away. Since it was the first time I'd stayed unconscious for almost four days, they must've been worried; Mom seemed overcome with emotion as she gazed at me.

"Oh, Makoto... You really do sleep a lot, don't you?" she said tearfully.

As I was trying to come up with a jokey reply, Dad walked over to me with a grin and ruffled my hair with one big hand.

"Well done, Makoto—you woke up right on time. Don't you have that thing tonight? You promised your friends you'd be at their party."

"I mean, it wasn't like I said I'd *definitely* show up…but I guess it counts as a promise."

"I'm sure the doctor will let you go out today, no problem. Perfect timing! Like father, like son."

"What did you time perfectly, Dad?" I asked.

"I met my true love and have the best son a man could wish for—everything in my life was timed to perfection."

"That's stretching it a tiny bit." I laughed, but I was almost tearing up, feeling grateful to have them both there. After chatting with Mom and Dad, I opened the messaging app on my phone to send Minami a text before it was too late.

I saw that Hayami had been replying to her for me while I'd been unconscious, and I scrolled through the chat to catch up. There weren't any special notes from Hayami. Feeling nervous, I sent Minami a text:

"Turns out I can come to the party tonight."

She saw the message instantly, and her reply popped up.

"Amazing!"

"I might get a bit shy."

"I'm so happy, I'm totally gonna ditch my makeup classes."

"Not sure if that's a good idea…," I wrote back.

"Don't worry, I'm kidding. Can't wait to see you!"

"Same. Oh btw, I haven't had a chance to get you a present. Sorry about that."

"Just having you there is the best present I could've wished for!"

Staring at Minami's last message, I let it all sink in. I felt like crying just a little bit. That's how happy I was to have woken up for this special day. Tears welled in my eyes—not tears of sadness, but of joy. I'd cried for all kinds of reasons in my life, but this was by far the most cathartic.

I couldn't just give myself up to my emotions, though. I had things to do: filling in Hayami, getting through my medical examinations, the list went on. I jumped into action to get ready to spend the last Christmas Eve of my life with my friends.

Since I'd been unconscious for almost four days—the longest of any of my spells so far—the doctors gave me a whole battery of tests over the course of the morning.

It didn't stress me out, though; my doctor was a comforting presence, guiding me through every step of the process. When she asked me how I felt, I told her about how croaky my voice was and how my muscles felt kind of sore. Smiling, she said it was natural to feel that way after sleeping for four days straight. But the human body can work wonders. Soon my body got used to being awake again, and the stiffness gradually faded away.

After lunch, I had to go through more examinations. These ones were on a slightly bigger scale than the ones in the morning, but I had free time in between the tests. I'm sure Mom was busy, but she took time off from work to bring me some clothes to choose from for the party that night. My parents helped me pick out my outfit, as excited about my night out as if they were going to the party themselves.

Right around the time we were settling on the outfit, Hayami came to see me. When I'd texted her in the morning, she'd offered to come visit during the day. She chuckled fondly when she saw the clothes scattered around my room and greeted my parents. They'd already met before, and I got the sense that my parents trusted her.

"How about we give you two some space to chat?" Dad suggested. "Your mother and I can go to a café or something." My parents left the room, leaving the two of us alone.

Even though it had only been a few days since I'd last seen Hayami, it felt so good to talk to her again. We chatted about all sorts of random stuff as usual and joked around—nothing heavy.

But at some point, I found myself saying, "It feels like a miracle."

"Wow, dramatic." Hayami laughed quietly.

"That's how it really feels to me, though. After everything that's happened, my final wish actually came true—I can keep my promise."

"Well...miracles don't just happen."

"Yeah, I guess."

"And people don't wake up unless someone shakes them awake."

I looked at her in surprise; I hadn't expected Hayami to say something like that. She averted her eyes and let out an awkward laugh.

"You probably woke yourself up, Tsukishima. It's *you* who made it happen."

That was an out of character thing for her to say, and I was touched. "You don't sound like yourself," I said honestly. She glared at me and swiped at my arm without saying another word.

Though there were more tests in the afternoon, my body temperature never dipped below average. Dad was going to drive me to the party in the evening. When I got back to my room from the last examination of the day, my parents and Hayami were waiting for me there. I offered to give Hayami a ride, and we headed to Ena's house together.

The radio was on when we climbed into the car. Unlike other days, it didn't hurt to hear the goings-on of the world outside. The DJ put on some Christmassy music, and Dad kept up a lively conversation peppered with laughter. I thought Hayami might prefer a quieter ride, but she seemed to be enjoying herself.

"Here we are. Have fun, Makoto." Dad pulled up at Ena's house exactly on time. We thanked him for the ride, then turned to look up at the building.

For the first time that evening, I noticed just how much my heart was pounding. I was more nervous than I thought.

"Hey, don't just stand there, Tsukishima. Come on." Hayami prodded me and rang the doorbell. I hadn't heard Ena's voice in so long, but she answered over the intercom and unlocked the gate. We walked up the path, making our way to the front door. All the while, I thought about what to talk about with Minami, what to say first when I saw her.

"The door's heavy, so you open it," Hayami said.

I took hold of the handle and gently opened the door.

"Merry Christmas!"

Party crackers popped, making me jump. I had no idea they'd been waiting behind the door. Ena, Ichika, and Minami gathered around me, all wearing Santa hats and holding up crackers.

"Merry Christmas, Makoto." Minami smiled warmly when our eyes met, and a tingling sensation rushed through my body, all the way to the pit of my stomach. The sheer happiness that blazed in me almost took my breath away. But I pulled myself together and said the words that I'd longed to tell her in person.

"Merry Christmas, Minami."

My last Christmas Eve was about to begin, surrounded by the people I loved the most.

Scene 5.

I Don't Know How Much Time You Have Left to Live

9. INT. ENA'S ROOM – NIGHT

MAKOTO enters the room, ENA and ICHIKA pulling him by his hands. ENA and ICHIKA chatter excitedly. A Christmas feast complete with roast turkey is laid out on the table.

MAKOTO

Where did all this food come from?

ENA and ICHIKA proudly reveal that they worked together to make everything from scratch. MAKOTO is impressed. ICHIKA says that there's even a homemade Christmas cake waiting in the kitchen for dessert. AOI grumbles about the ridiculous amount of butter it must have in it, but she looks happy.

TSUBASA

Well, Makoto's here, so we're all set. Let's have a toast.

ICHIKA

We have a bottle of Chanmery, too, if anyone wants a fizzy drink.

ENA

Ooh, but I've got something better.

ENA whips out a bottle of champagne. AOI jumps in.

AOI

Hey, not so fast. That's definitely off-limits.

ENA pouts in disappointment while ICHIKA and TSUBASA crack up at AOI's flustered reaction. MAKOTO watches over them with a tender smile.

(N.B. This is just one possible scenario. Don't feel you have to follow the script word for word. Act natural and go with the flow.)

1

December 24, 6:00 PM

Makoto arrived at Ena's place, and for the first time in weeks, all five of us from the filmmaking club were in the same place. Ena's family was out, so we were alone in the house. Ena and Ichika swept Makoto along through the house to Ena's room, where a feast crowded the table, and our party was off to a lively start.

Ichika doled out plates for everyone. Ena was about to take advantage of the occasion to pull out a bottle of champagne she'd found in the house, but Aoi did everything she could to stop her.

Makoto was looking around at everyone with an affectionate smile. When our gazes met, there was a happy gleam deep in his eyes.

Before I knew it, I was leaning close to him and whispering in his ear, "It looks like it's going to be a fun Christmas Eve."

"Yeah," he said, gazing at me. I could tell that he was getting emotional.

Relieved to see that he wasn't anxious about anything, I said, "I'm just going to pop to the bathroom—back in a minute," and left the room. I took out my phone in the hallway to message Makoto's mom.

The screen lit up, displaying the date and time:

January 18, 6:21 PM

Makoto seemed to have no doubt that it was Christmas Eve, and I felt a wave of relief wash over me. I sent a brief message to Makoto's mom to let her know how things were going, put away my phone, then went back into Ena's room as my thoughts turned back to that autumn day I'd found Makoto in his hospital room.

"What's...going on?" I'd blurted out.

There was Makoto, asleep in a hospital bed when he should

have been home getting ready for his move. Aoi had been pretending to be Makoto, replying to my texts for him.

My head was spinning with questions. I didn't understand why Makoto was in the hospital. He wasn't in a normal ward for minor injuries or illnesses, either, but a private ward with special facilities.

"I thought Makoto just had insomnia," I said.

Aoi looked back at me in silence. After a long pause, she reluctantly replied, "Sorry. That's not exactly true."

"Then, what...?"

"Ever heard of narcolepsy? It pops up in movies sometimes. That's actually what Tsukishima has. He spontaneously falls asleep...but he's working hard to get it cured."

"Aoi!" I stepped closer. My childhood friend was trying to explain calmly, but I had my doubts. "You're hiding something, aren't you?"

"What do you mean?"

"That's not what he has, is it?" Without thinking, I grabbed the sleeve of her school uniform. "It *can't* be. Tell me, Aoi. What's happening to Makoto?"

Aoi looked away. "I'm not lying. He's been suffering from a disease that makes him suddenly fall asleep—"

"Then you could've told me that a long time ago. Why were you keeping it a secret? So I wouldn't worry about him? You've even been messaging me as him to make it look like he's really there..."

If Makoto had an illness that simply made him fall asleep, they wouldn't have gone so far to hide it from me. They could have told me everything; I would've been surprised, but that wouldn't have made me worry excessively or hate him. Instead,

Makoto and Aoi had gone out of their way to keep his condition hidden—which could mean only one thing.

"Makoto's sickness… Is it really bad?" I asked quietly, letting go of her sleeve.

Aoi looked at me. "Not particularly."

"Liar."

"I'm not lying."

"Then…why do you look like you're about to cry?"

Startled, Aoi wiped her eyes and looked away again.

Aoi was a more compassionate person than even she realized. But it was because of that empathy that she could pick up on subtle hints of cruelty and malice in the world. That was why she pretended to be more indifferent than she really was—to make herself appear invulnerable. She'd always been kind at heart, ever since we were back in elementary school. She'd adored her father, and when he disappeared, I'd found her crying in secret in a park.

"The air's too dry in here," she'd told me. "My eyes got dehydrated. That's all."

Thinking back, that was the moment I swore to always stay by her side. I would be there for this girl, who was so kind and generous, but who never gave away her weakness in front of others.

"Aoi…"

"What?"

"You've always looked after us. You protected us from weird grown-ups and creeps who approached us with bad intentions… I'm guessing you're doing the same thing now, covering up Makoto's illness. You're shielding us from something, right? But I want to know the truth—please."

Aoi didn't back down so quickly. She kept avoiding my gaze, staring down at the floor in silence. But she had to crack at some point. It couldn't have been easy for her to carry the burden of Makoto's secret by herself.

Eventually, something glimmered in the corners of her eyes and fell down her cheeks. It had been a long time since I'd seen her cry so openly. Without bothering to wipe the tears away, she told me what was going on.

I stared at the movement of her lips. Rain continued to pour outside.

When Aoi finished speaking, I could only stand, stock-still, in a daze. "What...?"

She'd told me that Tsukishima was sick, but I knew that already—he was suffering from some type of disease. And then she'd told me more.

"His doctor told him back in March that he only had one year left to live..."

Makoto...only had a year to live?

I was completely bewildered. Aoi turned to look at me, her tears dry now. She seemed to have made up her mind to tell me everything.

She told me again that the doctor had given him this diagnosis in March. She explained how his symptoms of losing consciousness had started to appear around summer break, how she'd noticed it, and how they'd worked together since then to do everything they could to keep it a secret. All their efforts had been for the single purpose of not making me grieve for him.

I was shaken. Denying the truth was the only way I could keep from breaking down.

"That *can't* be true," I exclaimed desperately. "Makoto didn't show any signs—"

"He's been doing all he can to hide it from you, Tsubasa. People's views of the world are shaped by their own perceptions. As long as you don't notice Tsukishima's illness, it doesn't exist in your world," she said in an unwavering tone.

The moments I'd spent with Makoto whirled around my head in mute succession—when he'd confessed his feelings for me, when we'd started making movies together, when we became something more than friends…

Through all those months, Makoto had been suffering from this illness. He had been keeping it hidden from everyone, just like the protagonist of our movie, so that he wouldn't make me sad. That was why he'd even come up with that lie about moving overseas…

Once Aoi's story had sunk in, I looked over at Makoto, who was still asleep in the bed. Before I knew it, I was reaching out to touch his hand. It was warm. He was breathing, his chest slowly rising and falling. He was alive.

But in a few months, he'd be gone.

It felt too unreal to me. An invisible weight pressed down on my body.

What kind of scene would this be if it were a film? I wished so badly that this all could have just been a movie. But it was the truth: an all-too-painful, suffocating reality.

"So, that time…when I found Makoto asleep in the clubroom, it wasn't insomnia."

"Sorry for lying to you. It was a symptom of his disease; the nurse and I hid it from you."

Realizing just how much Aoi had been protecting me, I didn't even know what to think anymore.

"So, what are you going to do, Tsubasa?"

The world kept moving forward, whether my brain was at a standstill or not. The clock kept ticking relentlessly; the sand kept trickling down the hourglass.

"What do you mean?" I asked back, my eyes glued to the floor.

"It's my fault you found out…but now that you know what Tsukishima's really going through, you have to make a choice."

"A choice…?"

"Are you going to tell Tsukishima that you know his secret? Or…are you going to pretend not to know? We'll have to figure out how to handle this from here on out, so you better decide soon, before he wakes up."

I could feel myself getting pulled into their secret; I wasn't a bystander anymore. I was too confused to make up my mind at first. I asked Aoi if I could have some time to think about it here in the room, but she said we should go somewhere else, since we didn't know when Makoto would stir. I told her I wanted to have Makoto in front of me as I made my decision so I could see his current condition with my own two eyes.

"Okay. I'll give you my visitor's pass, so keep it on you. If Tsukishima wakes up while you're still here…what happens next is up to you."

Aoi left, leaving me alone with Makoto. I sat down in the chair by the bed and gazed at him.

It was still raining—both outside and inside the room. The drops fell on my hands, which lay clasped in my lap.

It still felt unreal that Makoto was going to die, but I couldn't deny the proof all around me: the patient's ward; Makoto's sleeping form; the tears of my childhood friend; the dark shadow I'd sensed in Makoto, even though he should have been just another high schooler living a normal, peaceful life.

Makoto must have been suffering more than anyone else, but he had gone so far as to lie just so I wouldn't be sad. By pretending to move abroad, he was trying to fade out of my life and become a part of my past.

But now, I'd discovered his secret. If I told him that, he wouldn't have to keep up his lies anymore. He wouldn't have to disappear from my life so soon. That way, we could be together till the very end. I thought that was the best choice.

Except...it was only the best choice from *my* perspective. Aoi's words echoed in my mind and weighed me down like stones: *"People's views of the world are shaped by their own perceptions. As long as you don't notice Tsukishima's illness, it doesn't exist in your world."* Aoi had touched on the subtle difference between the truth and the reality you perceive.

How would Makoto feel if I told him I'd found out about his sickness?

All this time, Makoto had been doing whatever he could to protect our little world—the world in which I didn't know about his condition. Even now, when he was blacking out more often, he was still trying desperately to maintain it.

Would telling him the truth really be the right thing to do? Was it right for me to destroy that world he was trying so hard to protect, just because I wanted to be with him until the very end? Just because of my selfish idea that deep down, *he* must be wishing for the same thing?

It's probably when you accept that you're about to die that you reveal your true nature.

In Makoto's case, he always put me first, even when he was the one in pain; that was just the kind of person he was. He was someone who could care about others around him until his last breath. It was the essential truth of his life—the life he'd lived as Makoto Tsukishima.

I clenched my fists tight and gazed at Makoto.

The world was full of uncertainties, ambiguities, innumerable right answers. I wanted to live like Makoto in this world of ours—to become someone who could care about others even on the brink of death.

I wanted to ease Makoto's suffering. It was clear which path I had to choose—I had to prioritize Makoto's wishes, not mine. I wouldn't let him be the only one burdened by lies, but I would carry my own with me everywhere I went. Instead of letting him protect me all the time, I'd be the one to protect his world.

I decided to pretend not to have found out about Makoto's secret. I was sure that was the right answer for me. Once I'd made up my mind, the rest was easy. I just had to put it into action and make sure the truth never came out. With fresh resolve, I gazed at Makoto again.

But my feelings were trying to trick me—my field of vision started misting over. Protecting Makoto's lies meant I couldn't be with him up to the very end of his life. I wondered if I could be forgiven for showing my true feelings just in this moment, when Makoto was still asleep. Promising myself that this would be the first and last time, I stood up and went closer to the bed. I laid my head on Makoto's chest.

Sobs racked my body from deep within my throat, and I

couldn't control myself anymore. Before I knew it, I was weeping violently.

Even now, I couldn't be selfless like Makoto—deep down I wished that Makoto would wake up from the sound of my crying. If he opened his eyes now, he'd be startled to find me here, but he would realize what had happened and wrap me in his arms. If he embraced me like that, I would tell him that I wanted to be with him to the very end, even if that meant going back on what I'd already decided.

But Makoto wasn't asleep. He didn't wake up no matter how much I wept. He didn't give me his shy smile no matter how many times I told him I loved him and that I needed him.

I gasped between sobs like a little child, my chest shuddering—but eventually, my tears dried up, and I left the room to tell Aoi my decision.

2

The next day, Makoto showed up at the clubroom after school as if nothing had happened. And I talked to him just as I always did. I teased him, laughed with him, and we went about filming together. When it was time to go home, I suppressed the urge to follow him and didn't confuse him by asking to stay with him longer.

Aoi knew my decision already. When I'd told her, she simply said, "Got it." With her answering from Makoto's account, we exchanged a few texts so he wouldn't get suspicious. Even when he was unconscious, we kept messaging each other as we'd done before so he would feel at ease when he woke up.

Whenever Makoto and I had the chance to be together, we spent our time laughing and having as much fun as possible. Every second, every moment I spent with him was precious. The more I thought about the end, the more I cherished the time we had now.

Then, one day just before December, Makoto came to the clubroom after a long absence and made his announcement.

"My parents had to reschedule our move, so we'll be leaving Japan before the end of the year." He explained that he wouldn't be able to come to school anymore—that this would be his last day at the club.

Aoi had warned me about this in advance, and we'd already gone over how we'd react to the news. Ena and Ichika, who didn't know the whole story, were genuinely disappointed. Makoto looked at everyone, one at a time, as if he didn't want to leave. Finally, he turned to me.

"You've done so much for us, Makoto. Thank you." I managed to say what I had to. I forced myself to say good-bye with a smile to protect Makoto's world. I was a bit awkward and felt myself tensing up a bit—unlike the natural performances that I demanded from my actors—but Aoi helped me out, and once everyone laughed, things were back to normal.

Makoto seemed relieved to see my reaction. His last club meeting went by without a hitch—except for one thing that neither Aoi nor I had predicted. Ena invited Makoto to our Christmas Eve party. Since Makoto couldn't make any promises, I thought he would decline, but he said he'd let us know on the day if he thought he could make it.

We took a group photo and parted ways at the school gate. Makoto and I walked to the park together, hand in hand.

We didn't let go of each other the whole time we were sitting on the park bench. I couldn't help but think about how he would be gone soon and keep squeezing his hand. I felt the warmth of his hand as he squeezed mine back.

"The stars we see in the sky are actually light from the past," he told me, gazing up at the sky. He sounded a bit sentimental, which was unusual for him. He told me that the starlight we could see had been emitted eons ago, reaching out through time toward us.

Though it made me sad to hear him talk about the past, I held back my tears. I didn't cry in front of Makoto—neither at the park nor at the train station. But as I watched his train go, I broke down. Standing alone on the platform, I was overcome by my own feelings. I wept noiselessly, biting back sobs.

Makoto never came to school again. His homeroom teacher had apparently announced that he had to move away earlier than expected, and I overheard some people in my class talking about it, too.

People started to move on after a few days, though. I started skipping classes, going up to the rooftop to gaze at the sky. All I could think about was whether Makoto had been happy.

Aoi visited Makoto often to let me know how he was doing. She told me he was living a quiet life in a hospital ward cut off from the rest of society. But he hadn't forgotten about his promise to see us on Christmas Eve. She told me that he was holding on to it as his final wish.

It was my wish, too—that I might get a chance to see Makoto again one last time while I kept his lie a secret.

* * *

It was three days before Christmas Eve when Makoto went into a long coma.

With end-of-term exams out of the way, I was editing the film we were going to submit to the Eiga Koushien Competition. I'd been counting down the days to Christmas Eve, hoping against hope that our wish would come true. But three days before the party, when the term's closing ceremony was just around the corner, Aoi brought me the news.

"Tsukishima...might not make it to the party." She told me he was unconscious.

I had an idea, though. "Wait—we don't *have* to have the party on Christmas Eve, do we? We could do it on Christmas Day, or the day after that."

We could just talk to Ena and Ichika to move the party to a day when Makoto could make it—it was as simple as that. As for Makoto, we could let him know that we'd pushed back the date because I needed more time for postproduction on the film. That way, he'd definitely be able to make the party. We could be together one last time.

I thought Aoi would agree, but her face clouded over. "I talked to his parents… They told me he might be in the terminal stage of his illness now. So he might not wake up again for a while."

I stared at Aoi, my eyes widening in surprise.

"There's a chance that he might be out for a month or so. He might not wake up until January," she said.

That day, after school, Aoi and I went to Makoto's room in the hospital. Aoi had told his parents beforehand that we were coming, so they were waiting for us in the lounge of the ward. It was the first time I'd met them.

They'd already heard the whole story from Aoi. His mother and father both bowed to me gratefully, thanking me for going along with Makoto's lie.

I immediately bowed back to them. I introduced myself and asked them for more details about how he was doing now.

Since it was a rare disease, there was very little data to go off, but even so, it was almost certain that Makoto had entered the terminal phase. Just as Aoi had said, he wouldn't regain consciousness during December.

"Our son was really looking forward to the party, too. But… something tells me he knew it would be difficult for him to make it," Makoto's dad said with a hesitant grin. The way he smiled reminded me of Makoto. "Both of you have been doing so much to support him, and we're incredibly grateful for that. If you could send him some messages when he's awake again, just as you normally would, I'm sure he'd be content with that."

Aoi nodded in response. "When he's awake, I'll tell him about the party and how everyone was sorry he couldn't come. And maybe the four of us could write messages for him in a Christmas card. He'd love it, I bet."

His parents were happy to hear Aoi's suggestion. Aoi started going into the details of her plan. I listened to the discussion without saying anything.

Aoi was right—Makoto would probably be really happy to get a card from everyone. He'd known from the beginning that he might not be able to come to the party himself. He must've been prepared for that.

But still…that ending was unbearably sad to me. I was racking my brain for something more we could do for Makoto, but I couldn't think of anything.

After our talk with his parents, Aoi and I went to see Makoto, asleep in his hospital bed. The room he'd been in before was nice, too, but this room felt different. The interior had a calming effect, and soft light streamed in through the window. Choosing her words carefully, Aoi explained to me that this was a special ward where patients who had no chance of recovery could spend their remaining days in peace. The ward seemed to be fulfilling its purpose; it felt cocooned in a sort of restful tranquility.

I noticed there were no TVs anywhere in the ward. Since phones were allowed, Makoto could still message me when he was awake, and I could see his phone lying near his bedside. Aoi saw me looking at it and picked it up.

"You owe me big-time, so I'm sure you won't mind if I borrow this for a sec," she said to Makoto, who was still asleep. She held up the phone to show me his lock screen.

It was a group photo of our club that we'd taken before autumn had set in. It hit me just how much Makoto cared about us, and my eyes misted over.

That wasn't the only photo Aoi wanted to show me. She put in the passcode to unlock his phone. I was shocked to see she knew the code, but I was even more surprised by what was on his home screen.

It was a photo of me. And not just any photo—but one where I looked like a total weirdo. It was from our first date. I had on a pair of party shades with a big nose and bushy mustache attached, and I was grinning at the person taking the photo. I remembered asking him to take that one.

Did he really have to choose this *one, out of all our photos?* was the first thought that went through my head, but maybe it really was the best one. It was a picture of an ordinary, peaceful day. There was no hint of death's shadow, no illness, no lies or truths or realities. Nothing to worry about. Just a chill, stress-free day.

I felt the prick of tears in my eyes. I wasn't sure, but I had the feeling that photo hadn't been on his home screen before. He must've changed it after started living in the hospital full-time.

There were only a few apps on the screen, maybe to make the photo easier to see. No, even that was an understatement—he hardly had *any* apps left on his phone.

"Tsukishima said he doesn't want to see what's going on outside," Aoi said, noticing my confusion.

I turned toward her. "How come?"

"Well…maybe because he feels it's not relevant to him anymore. I guess it's painful for him to know what's happening in the world—since he doesn't have a future anymore."

I was stunned by Aoi's words. I felt bitter anger toward the world that had hurt Makoto so much, but there was nothing anyone could do about that. So he had cut nearly all ties to the outside world…

As I stood there frozen, Aoi gave a humorless laugh, as if she was trying to dispel our helpless frustration. "Still, I think we've got to give our all to do what we can do," she said. "Maybe we should head back to the clubroom—Ena and Ichika are helping with the editing. If we go back now, we'd still have time to make a bit of progress. Tsukishima made the movie with us, after all—imagine if we missed the deadline for Eiga Koushien. We wouldn't be able to look him in the face."

Aoi was trying her best to brighten up the mood. I cracked a smile in response. Since Makoto's parents had given us permission to visit him whenever we liked, all we had to do was sign in at reception to come and see him. I told Makoto I'd be back soon, and we walked through the silence of the hallway.

"Oh, look, an airplane trail," Aoi said, peering up through the window. I followed her gaze.

A single vapor trail drew a lonely line across the sky. We took in the quiet scene, surrounded by silence. This ward was protected from all kinds of noise—not just literal noise, but information. Nothing was brought in from the world outside, to shield patients from any source of pain. Without a phone, you might even lose track of what day it was.

I felt a rush as something whipped through my body. It was one of those sensations you'd call a flash of inspiration or a gut feeling. I stopped in my tracks as if I were pinned to the spot by my idea.

Aoi turned around, puzzled. "What's up, Tsubasa?"

I didn't even answer her as I chased that little spark deeper into my mind. What did I just think of? What fleeting idea had I brushed up against? I urgently traced back my thoughts, desperate not to let it slip from my grasp. It was a feeling I'd experienced many times before while making films.

Makoto. Phone. Christmas Eve. Something we can do for Makoto. Apps. A place cut off from the rest of the world. Losing track of days.

I was intensely focused going over my train of thought when something clicked.

That's it. I'd pinned down just where that inspiration had come from. Next, I started unraveling it in logical steps.

Was it even feasible? I couldn't tell. But it had to be worth a try. Even if it would be impossible to pull off by myself, with everyone's help, it might just be doable. Maybe there was something more we could do for Makoto after all.

"How about we turn whatever day Makoto wakes up into Christmas Eve?"

"Uh...what?" Aoi looked at me dubiously. "What are you talking about, Tsubasa?"

My heart was racing wildly. I was concentrating so hard that my head was throbbing. I didn't want to let this idea go—I *couldn't* let it go. This might be the whole reason I'd kept creating films all my life.

"There's no TV in Makoto's ward—not even in the lounge. And there's practically no apps on Makoto's phone because he doesn't want to see what's happening in the world. Right?"

"Yeah...," Aoi said carefully, processing my words and trying to figure out where I was going with them. This kind of back-and-forth was familiar to us; it was like those times when I would suddenly suggest an alternative idea just as we were about to finish a film.

"And...remember what Ichika said before, when we were brainstorming ideas for our next movie? About time stamps on the messaging app being linked to the device itself?"

Aoi nodded. Though we'd have to double-check, it should be possible to purposely adjust the dates on messages by setting the phone to a different date. That meant we could trick Makoto into thinking the date was December 24, regardless of when he actually woke up. I was trying to figure out a realistic way to pull that off.

It didn't matter whether it was January for everyone else. As long as Makoto believed it, that day would turn into Christmas Eve. Once again, it was the difference between the reality someone believed and the truth.

There were a number of obstacles we had to overcome, but it was by no means impossible to coordinate everything. We just had to change back the date of the phone to the correct one the next time Makoto lost consciousness. As I rattled off my ideas, Aoi listened closely.

"So, Tsubasa. What you're suggesting is..."

I thought Aoi would reject my idea, but she calmly backed me up with helpful comments. When something was unclear, she asked questions; she was breaking down my scheme in her own terms.

To talk about it in more depth, we headed to the café inside the hospital. There were a number of things we had to check, including whether it was really possible to adjust the time stamps. Putting our heads together, we refined our ideas and came up with a feasible plan. Since Aoi knew Makoto's passcode already, that wasn't a problem. When everything lined up, and we were sure it could work, our eyes met with excitement.

Trying to stay calm, we went through the steps we would have to take to put our plan into action. Though there were more problems to smooth over, none of them were insurmountable; as long as we dealt with them ahead of time, they were manageable.

For our plan to work, though, we'd need outside help. We had to ask for the hospital to go along with it, and we would also have no choice but to tell Ena and Ichika about Makoto's condition. Most important of all, we needed Makoto's parents to lend us a hand.

We decided to give ourselves some time to mull it over, so we each went back home to gather our thoughts.

Aoi texted me at around nine o'clock that night:

"This just might work."

It bolstered my confidence to know that Aoi was on board, too.

She arranged for us to meet with Makoto's parents, and we visited their house the following day in the early evening to tell them about our idea. With Aoi's help, I somehow managed to stay calm and collected as I told his parents the whole plan. Though my explanation might have been missing some pieces, his parents understood what we were trying to do. But they were hesitant.

"Are you sure you want to do this? It must be hard on you both," his mom said with a pained smile. "Don't worry about us. We'd gladly lie to our son if it's in his best interest. I'd do anything for him as long as it doesn't harm other people. I'd happily throw myself on the ground and beg. But...you don't have to make those same sorts of sacrifices. Even if you're used to acting in movies, I'm afraid you'd only be hurting yourselves this way."

I listened patiently for her to finish, then said my piece. I told her that we were willing to prioritize Makoto over ourselves. It was Makoto who had shown me how to live like that—to put others first. If I told Ena and Ichika about everything Makoto had done for us all this whole time, I was sure they would feel the same. When I shared those thoughts with her, Makoto's mom seemed to drift somewhere else, her eyes fixed on a single point on the table. I guessed she was thinking about her son, who was lying unconscious in the hospital as we spoke.

Makoto's dad, meanwhile, had been silent the whole time, deep in thought. Eventually, he said, "My son...used to get sick often when he was young, so it was hard for him to connect with the other kids." He looked straight at us. "I'd always hoped that he'd find good friends. But now I see I didn't have to worry about that at all. I can't tell you how happy it makes me to know that he's surrounded by friends and a girlfriend who care so much about him."

Makoto had once told me that I reminded him of his dad because I was so innocent and full of life. But in that moment, I realized that had probably been a front his dad had been keeping up on purpose. The man sitting in front of me now seemed gentle, thoughtful, and loving; he cared for his son more than anyone else.

In the end, his parents agreed to our plan on two conditions: first, that we should never push ourselves too hard, and second, that if any one of us felt like it was too much to bear, she should feel free to call off the plan.

Once that was settled, everything else went quickly. The next day was the closing ceremony of second term, and we asked Ena and Ichika to meet us in the clubroom first thing in the morning. Aoi and I told them about Makoto. We went over everything—not only his illness, his present condition, and how much time he had left, but also what we were planning to do despite that reality.

They were both shaken by the news and struggled to take it in. But once they'd been able to process it and accept the facts, they were eager to support us. They wanted to see Makoto right away, so as soon as the closing ceremony was over, we all went to the hospital together.

Ichika was shocked to see Makoto in his sickbed, and she burst into tears.

Ena stared at him, too emotional to react. "So *Makoto* was the protagonist," she murmured.

It wasn't just for my sake that Makoto had been hiding his condition; he'd been thinking about everyone he'd come in contact with, including Ena and Ichika.

After letting the two of them in on our scheme, we had to ask the hospital for help, too. For that side of things, Makoto's parents and doctor backed us up. It helped that Makoto was in a ward where special emphasis was placed on psychological care, limiting patients' contact with the outside world as much as possible. The hospital agreed to cooperate with us so that when Makoto woke up, he wouldn't accidentally see the real date on wall calendars or documents.

Of course, the best-case scenario was for Makoto to wake up on Christmas Eve or Christmas Day. There was still a slim chance of that.

I spent the afternoon of Christmas Eve in Makoto's room. If he woke up to find me sitting next to him, he might be rattled, but I had an excuse ready. I was still determined to protect his lies. As I gazed at him, I kept imagining him opening his eyes. I'd let everyone know and take Makoto out of the hospital so we could all meet up for our party. So we could laugh together again.

But Makoto didn't open his eyes. He lay as still as ever, oblivious to my presence. He slept through Christmas Eve and Christmas Day. And the day after that, and the day after that, too. I waited until the night of the twenty-eighth, and when he still showed no sign of stirring, I made up my mind.

I picked up his phone, quietly apologizing to him for using it without his permission. I changed the date of the device and turned off automatic updates. His phone now displayed the date:

December 23.

From that day on, changing the date on Makoto's phone to December 23 became a daily routine for me. I helped the nurses give him regular massages so Makoto would be strong enough to walk when he woke up. Ena and Ichika also pitched in, as did Aoi, though not without complaint.

By then, we had somehow managed to submit our latest film to the Eiga Koushien Competition. It was all thanks to Aoi, who told me to leave the rest to her this time and holed up in the clubroom as soon as winter break started to wrap up editing.

As the end of the year approached and the festive mood swept over the world, I visited Makoto every day. Each night, before I left, I set the date on his phone to December 23.

I thought about the day Makoto would wake up and made a flowchart of the how it might go. I wrote it out like a screenplay and showed it to Aoi. We talked it over with Ena and Ichika, too, perfecting our scheme.

On New Year's Eve, we stopped by Makoto's room, then went to a temple to strike the bell at midnight. In the morning, we met up again to visit a shrine for the first time in the new year. We made offerings and put our hands in prayer, and though none of us talked about what we'd wished for, I think we were all praying for Makoto.

Still, he didn't wake up.

The New Year holidays were over, and soon after winter break also came to an end. Yet Makoto remained in his coma.

We were waiting with bated breath for Makoto to come back, so each day seemed to drag on. Despite this, it was easy to lose track of how long it had been.

The first two weeks of January had already gone, and we were currently in the third. I had to come up with an idea for our next film, but all I could think about was Makoto.

I wasn't the only one distracted—all of us in the filmmaking club were. Even when we had our club meetings, our minds wandered elsewhere. We just killed time looking at our phones, reading books, or staring out at the sky.

Was Makoto really going to wake up? His disease was incredibly rare, and only a few people had ever suffered from it before, so it was hard to say anything definitive. There was even the possibility that he might never wake up.

It was right around the time those fears started gnawing at me that I got a message from Makoto's mom.

3

I'd woken up early that day and was sitting with a cup of coffee in my room, gazing absentmindedly out the window. I enjoyed watching the morning take shape—shafts of light streamed into the quiet, blue world, cars and motorbikes started making their way down roads, and the azure sky gradually paled to white. It was the beginning of a new day.

I'd already switched off sleep mode on my phone, and it pinged with a new message. I picked it up, guessing it was from Aoi, but it wasn't—it was from Makoto's mom.

"Makoto is awake."

Just three simple words, but I had never wanted to hear something more in my whole life. For a split second, I couldn't move—but I replied immediately. She told me that Makoto didn't suspect anything; he fully believed that he had woken up on December 24.

I hurriedly texted everyone in the club to spread the news. Every time my phone buzzed, I saw how excited they were.

Makoto messaged me, too: *"Turns out I can come to the party tonight."*

He had been asleep for almost a month, but he wrote to me as if nothing out of the ordinary had happened. Well, this was true enough for Makoto—for him, his latest blackout wasn't so different from all the others he'd had. Our wish to be with him one last time had caused that. I replied, matching his casual tone, then hurried to start putting everything together for that night.

I'd already told my parents about Makoto and our plan. It was an ordinary weekday, but I headed to Ena's house instead of going to school. I'd reminded everyone to speak out if they felt like it was too much of a burden on them—but Ena and even Ichika took the day off to get ready for the party. We decked out Ena's room and cooked up a Christmas feast.

Meanwhile, Makoto's parents and doctor kept him company. Aoi went to see him in the afternoon, too. She stayed by his side as much as possible, and she reported back to us that there seemed to be no doubt in his mind that it was actually Christmas Eve.

The sun set, and time ticked down to Makoto's arrival. His dad was supposed to drive him to Ena's house. We'd given him a recording we made from the radio on Christmas Eve, and he played it during the ride. We'd even planned out the route he would take, avoiding busy main streets so Makoto wouldn't be confused by the lack of Christmas lights, and made sure he wouldn't see the real date anywhere, including on billboards.

Aoi sent us regular updates that everything was going according to plan. And finally, Makoto was here, standing just outside Ena's house.

There was no reason to be nervous. We just had to have fun. That was the natural thing to do.

The doorbell rang, and Ena answered it. We huddled around the front door, waiting for it to open. I was trying to calm my nerves when I heard Ena call my name.

"Hey, Tsubasa."

"What's up, Ena?"

"Wanna say what you always say before we start rolling? Once we hear that, we can do anything."

I was puzzled at first, but I soon caught on. "Sure," I said with a grin. I took a deep breath. "All righty, here we go. Roll camera. Roll sound… Action!"

A few seconds later, the door opened, and we popped our crackers. A startled boy stared out at us from the other side of the door. It felt surreal to see him right there in front of us—Makoto, wide-awake.

"Merry Christmas, Makoto," I said, smiling at him, and his face filled with joy.

"Merry Christmas, Minami," he said back, flashing that smile I'd missed so much.

The night was as lively as one of our wrap parties. Makoto was the only one who didn't know the real date, but that wasn't a problem; Ena and Ichika's acting that today really *was* Christmas Eve was incredibly convincing, and they happily chatted with Makoto even more than usual. To Makoto, that frenetic energy must've seemed like a desire to make the most of their time together before he moved away.

Aoi, on the other hand, was her usual self. Sometimes she made sarcastic comments at Makoto, making him smile sheepishly, but that was just the way they were. As for me, I think I managed to stay calm, interacting with him as I normally would.

The party was supposed to double as a celebration for the completion of our latest project, so we had a screening for the film we'd submitted to the Eiga Koushien. When the movie ended, we deconstructed it together, going over every detail. We already knew the results of the competition—we found out at the beginning of the year that we hadn't been chosen for an award—but we were careful not to give that away to Makoto.

After that, we ate Ichika's homemade Christmas cake and had fun playing Ena's favorite board game. As always, Ena brought out the *amazake* at some point. Aoi tried to resist her at first, but in the end, she caved, and they roped Ichika in as well. The three of them ended up conked out on the sofa.

Just like that first party we had at Ena's, Makoto and I were the only ones left awake. It was chilly outside, but I invited Makoto out onto the balcony, like last time. We stood side by side, gazing at the starry night sky.

Our hands found each other. We didn't need to say anything; we were perfectly content simply being together in this serene pocket of time.

I felt that if I said something like "I had a lot of fun tonight," then that would signal our time was up. Makoto probably felt the same. So we both stayed silent.

As I felt the warmth of his hand, I thought about death. What did it mean to die? What did it mean to disappear from the world? For me, in that moment, it meant that I wouldn't be able to hold hands with the person I loved. That even if I squeezed his hand, he wouldn't squeeze mine back. That we would never be able to look into each other's eyes again.

"I'll never forget about you, Makoto. I promise." The words slipped out of me before I could stop myself, even though it might give too much away. Still, I could've been talking about our separation for all Makoto knew—not his death.

Makoto had been gazing at the stars, but now he turned to look at me. After a long pause, he said, "It's okay if you forget about me." He gave me a gentle, melancholy smile. "You have so much ahead of you, Minami. Anything can happen. I'm sure you'll meet lots of people, and you'll be able to share your movies even more. I'll always be wishing for your happiness, for your bright future—no matter how far away I am. Always."

I looked back at him, speechless.

"Oh, sorry. It sounds like I'm saying good-bye," he added. "We'll make movies together again once we're in college, right?"

He put on a cheerful voice, a faint smile crossing his lips. "You know, I actually didn't think I'd make it today, with all the stuff going on. So I'm really glad I could. I'm glad I have this one last memory…of Japan to take with me. Thank you, Minami."

The expression on Makoto's face was free of anxiety and regret. He was letting go of his own life, leaving the world behind, with nothing to hold him back.

I gave the answer I had to give: "Me too. I hope you take care of yourself overseas." I had to live his lie to the very end to protect his world. It was the only thing I could do for him…

"What's wrong, Minami?"

I thought I'd locked away that self-centered part of me, but here it was, interfering at the moment of truth. My vision blurred, and my eyes filled with tears. I couldn't stop them from pouring down my face.

Stop that, I berated myself. *Don't be selfish.* Crying would only serve to make myself feel better. If I could just get a grip on my emotions, I could say what I had to—to respect his wishes. *I can do it. I can say good-bye to him. So stop crying. Don't be such a crybaby.*

"I love you, Makoto."

I didn't know what love meant yet. Yet I heard myself say those words as tears streamed down my face. Even if it was nothing more than a word to me—or maybe *because* it was nothing more than that—I had to tell him, here and now. *Love* was the only word I had to offer him, the only one I could find in my short life. I wanted to put my feelings into words without holding anything back, no matter how embarrassed I felt to say it or how melodramatic it might sound.

Makoto looked surprised. Soon his expression softened into that gentle smile I loved best.

I pressed on; I stumbled on some words, and others got stuck in my throat, but I told him how I really felt. I'd had no idea what I was going to say beforehand—it all just came out of me in the moment.

"I'll probably never love anyone as much as I love you, Makoto." I told him that he was the one who'd taught me how it felt to fall in love, that he was the first person I'd wanted to confess my love to from the bottom of my heart. I told him that he was so kind and gentle and strong, even though he didn't look it. I told him there was a dark side to him, just like a protagonist in a movie—in fact, he *was* a protagonist in a movie—and that there were so many things I loved about him that I couldn't even list them all, even if I made an entire movie about it.

I told him that because I loved him so much, I didn't want to be the one to limit his future.

"Let's break up," I murmured. I told him that he didn't have to come back to Japan for college. He could find what he wanted to do anywhere in the world. Both of us could go wherever the world might take us and follow our own paths. "You deserve all the happiness in the world," I told him. "I hope you have a wonderful future waiting for you."

I might have sounded cruel to Makoto—but I fought through my tears and wrenched the words out of myself. No matter what, I would protect Makoto's world.

Makoto listened quietly, emotion swirling in his eyes, and with a glimmer, something slid down his cheek. It was the first time I'd seen him cry. A few more streaked down, but he nodded slightly a few times. Somehow he managed to give me a smile.

"You mean so much to me, too, so I agree—I think we should break up."

"Yeah," I whispered through quivering lips.

"Thank you for everything, Minami. I'm so lucky I met you."

I wished I could throw everything else aside and choose to be with him for as long as possible, but I desperately fought down that impulse. "Me too," I murmured. We were almost there: the ending that Makoto wished for.

"I'll be hoping for the best for you, too. That you'll find all the happiness you deserve and a wonderful future ahead. Minami… No, Tsubasa, I love you with all my heart."

For the two of us, this moment was our whole world. We felt free to say all the things we would've been too shy to say otherwise.

"You finally called me *Tsubasa*."

"I always wanted to."

"Call me that whenever you remember me. But never forget—you can go make your own world, Makoto."

"You too, Tsubasa. I hope you'll move on soon and find someone you love more than me."

"Can't."

"Just try."

And with that, we gave each other a tearful smile. With the stars watching over us, we broke up in the very spot I'd first asked him out.

Countless times in the past, I'd made last-minute changes to our movies, and this time was no exception. In the script that

Aoi had written, Makoto and I were supposed to drift apart over time, letting our long-distance relationship slowly fade away.

Maybe somewhere in the back of my mind, I'd thought this would leave Makoto with a guilty conscience, so I found myself rewriting the script on the spot. Aoi and the others would have to judge whether I'd made the right decision.

Wiping away our tears, Makoto and I went back inside to wake up the others. Instead of steady, sleeping breaths, we heard muffled sobs. Ena was turned into the back of the sofa, Ichika had covered her face with her hands, and Aoi's head was buried in a cushion. Their shoulders were quivering as they choked back sobs.

Eventually, Ena and Ichika got to their feet and threw their arms around Makoto, tears streaming down their faces.

"Good luck out there," Ena said.

"I'll never forget you, Makoto," Ichika promised.

Unlike them, Aoi never showed her tears. The only thing she said was "Who do you think you are, flying off like this?" Her face was turned away, and she cried noiselessly.

Before we knew it, it was time for Makoto to go back to the hospital, and his dad came to pick him up.

We all stood outside the front gate to see Makoto off. He rolled down the passenger's-seat window to give us one final good-bye. "Thank you so much for today. Bye, everyone."

"Take care, Makoto. Good luck," I said.

"You idiot," Aoi muttered.

"Don't get suckered in by some blond babe," joked Ena.

"Best of luck, Makoto," called out Ichika.

We all looked on as the car drove off into the distance.

And just like that, our story was over. We'd pulled off our plan.

"Hey, your makeup's running all over the place," Aoi told me, and when I took a second to check, it really was a hot mess.

"Well, not as much as mine, though," Ena said. She was right—her face was covered in smears of black. Up until then, we'd been too wrapped up in the moment to notice, but we finally got a good look at each other and burst out laughing. There was something to smile about waiting at the end of the story, after all.

Two months later, during spring vacation, we heard that Makoto had passed away. His mom got in touch with us to share how it had happened; it had been painless, and he'd taken his last breath as if he were just drifting off to sleep.

The four of us went together to the wake and the funeral. None of the other students from our school were there—everyone thought Makoto had simply moved away—but the school nurse came to offer her respects.

We talked to Makoto's parents there, too. They told us that Makoto had never stopped believing in our act; he'd never suspected that it had actually been January when we'd had the party or that all of us had known about his illness. Before he lost consciousness for the last time, he'd smiled and told them that he had no regrets whatsoever.

It felt wrong to think of someone's life and death as being cathartic—but I had no regrets. Of course, I wished Makoto never had to die, however, I decided to think that if Makoto had been able to live out his life the way he'd wanted to and pass away without too much suffering, then that was a good thing.

That spring, I'd lost the love of my life.

Yet even in a world like that, I still felt a desire to keep making films.

One day during spring break, I went to the park where Makoto and I had had our first date to capture the world as I saw it from there. I pointed my camera at the sky, the greenery, the leaves rustling in the breeze, the people, the cars passing by, the light, the clouds, the earth, everything.

But when I realized that there was one thing I could never catch on film, I couldn't hold back my tears.

I'd been able to protect Makoto's world, but something had been forever lost from mine. I wept for the loss, tears stinging my eyes.

One day, I might get used to this sadness. But at least for now, I wanted to let it all out.

As the world blurred around me, I stared at the video I'd just taken, not making a sound.

There, on the screen, was a world without Makoto—a world that, despite his absence, was so clear and beautiful.

Scene 6.

A Light from the Past

Stories I wanted to tell, perspectives I wanted to capture, ideas I wanted to leave behind—I had always filled my films with all of those things. And at the end of every film, there came the black screen and credits. No matter what the characters in the story had achieved or left unrealized, no matter what they had overcome or succumbed to, the credits marked the end of the movie.

But life was different. Sometimes, you live through something that makes you think, *If this were a movie, maybe the credits would roll here*—but life goes on.

It's been almost ten years since Makoto disappeared from the world. So many things have happened in those years that it would be impossible to talk about all of them.

At the end of the year he left us, we entered the Eiga Koushien Competition again and won the award for best screenplay, best actress, and best picture. It was like a parting gift for Makoto, if a little late.

Determined to win an award, we'd thrown ourselves into the creative process with more enthusiasm than ever before, devising a thorough, well-thought-out plan before launching into the filming. When we found out we'd won not one, but three awards, we were over the moon. I wished we could have celebrated with Makoto.

I got into a college in Tokyo where I could study film, through a special recommendation from my high school. Aoi did, too. We kept making movies throughout college, and in our third year, we even won a big award.

People around me said I was well on my way to becoming a professional director, and in time, that turned into my own dream. I thought that might make Makoto happy, too, as he watched me from heaven.

But the reality wasn't so simple. There was always someone more talented in the world. Still, I plunged ahead—because making films was my whole life.

I wanted to stay in the filmmaking industry after graduating from college, so I got a job at a mid-level production company. As a third assistant director—the bottom of the ladder—I spent my days and nights on filming locations.

The road to becoming a film director was a constant uphill battle. After one year, most of my fellow aspiring directors who'd joined the company around the same time as me had already dropped out of the race.

I didn't give up, though. Whenever there was a call for submissions for project pitches, I feverishly wrote proposals and screenplays in what little time I had in between work.

Three years slipped by like that. While my former colleagues and friends from college had their feet on the ground working as productive members of society, I was the only one who still had my head in the clouds, chasing dreams.

Though I could see the state of my life better than anyone, I still wasn't ready to give up. I kept pushing forward. But the future I sought eluded me. Of all the talented people out there, only a small handful could become directors, and eventually, my body broke down from overwork.

I still wanted to keep trying—I *thought* I wasn't done yet. But it turned out that I'd run out of steam. I was twenty-six then. I quit the company and found a normal office job.

You did your best, I told myself. *You worked hard enough. Remember all those awards you won when you were a student.*

Thankfully, all my new co-workers were nice people, and I got the hang of the job in no time. I didn't have many difficult tasks to do. Every day, I would wake up, go to work, do the same old tasks, go home, and sleep. Day after day after day.

After a year or so had passed by, I suddenly noticed something: There was a conveyor belt running beneath my feet. Each day slipped by as it carried me forward.

I'd changed in these last ten years, and so had the people around me.

Aoi, for example, started directing movies, too, once we started college. When she'd told me she wanted to try her hand at being a director, I encouraged her. During our undergrad, she would sometimes ask me for advice on her own films; at other times, we worked together as co-directors, or she joined my production team as an assistant director like in high school.

Once Aoi started directing, her talents came into full bloom. After all, it was Aoi who'd introduced me to movies in the first place. Only a couple of years into directing, her films gradually began to garner attention, praised for their screenplays, among other things. She often won awards in competitions.

The strength of her films lay in the script. And sure enough, when she was in her fourth year of college, she won a big prize in a screenwriting contest hosted by a TV station. Her script was turned into a TV movie, and a few years after that, she debuted as a director of commercial films.

"Maybe I wanted to make my dad's dream come true. You only get one shot at life, after all… Tsukishima taught me that." Aoi had told me that once.

Ena went through a transformation of her own as well. Sometime after Makoto passed away, she became serious about pursuing a career in acting. Back then, she told us that she wanted to give it her all, more than she ever had before. Although it took a lot to convince her parents, she managed to put her words into action. By the time she started college in Tokyo, she had already passed the audition for a theater troupe led by a famous director.

She actively took part in all kinds of activities to broaden the breadth of her acting. I didn't think she'd be the type to do something like that, but she also kept up a regular training routine to build up her physical strength.

Once she started focusing all her efforts on acting, it didn't take long for her to get noticed. In her second year at college, she landed a starring role in a play for the first time, and her performance turned heads. She kept working hard in the theater company, and eventually, a scout for a talent agency approached her, and she became a screen actor. She started acting in films while she was still in university.

Ichika ended up being more drawn to literature than films. She got into a university near our hometown, and after graduating, she became an editor at a publisher.

When I was in high school, I believed, naively, that the four of us in the filmmaking club would keep on making movies together, just as we'd always done. But in reality, the only time we managed to shoot a film together after Aoi and I left high school was when we went back home for summer break during our first year at college. And now I wasn't even making movies anymore.

At my current workplace, everyone's aim was to keep everything running the same; if something veered off course, we worked together to nudge it back on track. And so we went through the same old routine day after day.

At work, one of my colleagues ended up asking me out. I turned him down, but I found myself thinking that that kind of life—dating, getting married, having kids—didn't sound too bad.

It was right around that time that I received something in the mail.

It was the beginning of April, and I'd gotten back to my apartment after work to find a mysterious little package waiting for me in my mailbox. I wasn't expecting any mail, and it looked different than normal packages. The address was written in English; it looked like it had been posted from abroad. There was no return address, but when I saw the name written in the corner, I was startled.

Makoto Tsukishima

I thought it might be some kind of prank, but I couldn't think of anyone who would use Makoto's name like that. Perplexed, I took the padded envelope to my room and opened it carefully.

Inside was a smaller envelope and a memory card in a thin, clear case. I took out the envelope and removed the letter. In a familiar style of handwriting that still lived on deep within my memory were the words *Dear Tsubasa Minami.*

I knew the shape of those lines; Makoto's handwriting had always been incredibly neat. I remembered how I'd admired it back then, and I was convinced that this letter was from Makoto. But how was that possible when he'd passed away ten years ago?

My head was buzzing with questions, but I took a deep breath and read the letter.

Dear Tsubasa Minami,

It's been a while. How are you?

This is Makoto Tsukishima. You let me join your film-making club when we were second-years in senior high school. I was also your boyfriend until I moved overseas. I can't thank you enough for everything you did for me back then.

Ten years have gone by, and I think both of us are well on track following our own paths, so I thought now would be a good time to write to you.

I've been through a lot ever since I moved overseas, but I'm hanging in there. Whenever I was feeling sad, miserable, or overwhelmed, I'd look back on the days I spent with you in the club. That was the most fun I've ever had. Even now, those memories come back to me like it was only yesterday.

You might not remember much of it anymore, but the Christmas Eve party where I got to spend time with everyone just before moving away is one of my fondest memories.

Thank you so much for welcoming me in as a member of the filmmaking club.

I wanted to avoid looking backward, so I haven't tried to find out what you've been up to, but I'm certain you're letting your talent shine. Even if you're not in an environment where you can't make use of your skills now, I want you to know that you were the best director. You were the best leader of the club and the best partner.

I hope you'll forgive me for writing to you from so far away, but I will always be wishing for your success, health, and happiness.

There was more to the letter, but that was as much as I could read for the moment.

At first, I was surprised. *When did Makoto write this? How did he feel putting all this to paper?* I felt a pang of nostalgia at his kindness. My eyes grew damp, and I couldn't make out the words anymore.

It struck me that this letter had been written by someone who was about to die. Even though he was dying, he'd still thought about me in the future and left these words for me.

Tears fell from my eyes. I tried to steady my breathing, then washed my face and sat back down to read the rest of the letter. It wasn't long, but it was impossible to get through in one sitting. My vision blurred and tears poured from my eyes, but I took my time to read it all the way through.

There was another sheet of paper inside the envelope with an explanation about the memory card. The card looked new; it must have been bought recently. I started up my laptop and put it in. A single video was stored on the memory card.

Makoto's explanation was that he'd stumbled across some

videos from high school while organizing some old data on his phone, and he'd made a film out of it—although he'd hardly known what he was doing, he said.

I imagined Makoto editing the videos in that room in the hospital. I'd taught him the basics of editing—a fond memory of mine from those days.

In his note, he wrote that it was up to me to choose whether to watch it or not. I looked at the data of the file; the time stamp had apparently been tweaked, since it showed a date from several weeks ago. *He thought of everything.* I chuckled a little and played the video.

If I were to give a harsh critique, I would say that it wasn't really a film. It was more like a mishmash of videos, many of them blurry or wobbly, without anything resembling a script. The scenes changed abruptly, so that only the people who'd been present when the videos were shot would be able to follow the story.

And yet, I couldn't stop my tears from flowing.

I saw myself as a high schooler in the movie. There I was, going on a date with Makoto for the very first time, walking beside the railway tracks in the orange glow of sunset, getting excited at the zoo, laughing in a café on our way home from school, smiling under the bright summer sun.

That wasn't all. There were also videos of me filming with everyone, looking so happy—Makoto had probably shot them in secret in between takes. I saw myself as I was back then, when I was having so much fun making films that that was all I wanted to do.

Makoto's movie was coming to an end. I could see how little

time was left in the bar under the video. I gazed at the last scene, wishing it didn't have to end.

On the screen, I was sleeping at the desk in the clubroom. The room was dyed the color of sunset. It had probably been sometime during summer break, when Makoto and I had found ourselves alone after filming. The whiteboard on the side was crammed with ideas for the movie we were shooting. I vaguely remembered nodding off after getting tired from all the brainstorming.

Makoto, who was taking the video, called out to me.

"Minami."

I lifted my head from the desk and looked at the camera with drowsy eyes. "Oh, you're filming?"

"You told me that if you fell asleep, I should take a video of how you react when I wake you up," he explained sheepishly.

"Oh yeah, I remember now." I laughed.

"Do you enjoy making movies?" he asked. I could hear the smile in his voice.

"Yeah. A lot," I said without a moment's hesitation, beaming.

Then the movie ended.

I was pulled back to reality. The video player on my screen had gone black, and I saw my tear-streaked face reflected there. Just a moment ago, I had been the laughing girl in the movie—but the dark screen showed me as I was now, ten years older.

A flood of feelings rushed over me, and I broke down in tears. I wasn't sure why I was crying so much. Was it because I missed Makoto and his kindness? Or because I felt overwhelmed by the love I still felt for him? Was it because I felt ashamed of who I'd become, or frustrated at myself? Was it because I knew that the person who'd made this movie for me was no longer here, that he was lost forever? Or was it all of those things hitting me at once?

Some things you lose never come back—it's painful, but true. That time flew by, cold and swift, waiting for no one. But those weren't the only feelings the movie left me with.

For a while after, I sat there and cried my heart out.

I cried until I ran out of tears, and afterward, I felt lighter somehow. When I thought back, I realized that my heart had been dried up; I couldn't remember shedding a single tear over anything in the last few years. I felt like a weight had been lifted off my chest. I started wondering who it could have been that delivered this package to me. But of course, the answer was obvious. There were so few people who could have done it—it had to have been Aoi.

I was still good friends with her. The same went for Ena and Ichika. Our relationship hadn't changed since school, but since we worked in different fields, we hadn't been able to meet up recently. Not to mention the fact that Ena and Aoi were incredibly busy.

I messaged Aoi, asking if we could meet for a chat. She replied a few hours later, saying that she could free up an hour in the early evening on Saturday, so we decided to meet at a café in Tokyo.

"Aoi, you were the one who delivered that thing to me, right?" I interrogated her as soon as we sat down and ordered.

Aoi looked surprised, but she let out a chuckle.

"You got me. Didn't you even suspect Tsukishima's parents?"

"Not many people can pull off such a painstaking setup.

Besides, I thought Makoto might feel a bit bad asking his parents to do something like that. So that leaves you, Aoi." I thought about Makoto's parents as I answered. I had been going to see them until around the three-year anniversary of his death. They'd watched the film Makoto had left behind, *The Girl Who Dies from a Rare Disease*, and they'd encouraged me about my film projects at college.

"Fair enough," Aoi laughed. Our coffee came, and she took a sip. "Just to make it clear, though, I haven't looked at any of it—not the letter, and not the video, either. Tsukishima just asked me to pass it on to you in ten years' time, so all I did with the file he gave me was move it to a memory card."

"In ten years' time, huh…? Did Makoto say anything else?"

Aoi's expression shifted a little to something more solemn. She put her cup back down on the table. "Not when he gave it to me. After that last party, he was unconscious a lot of the time, and I was giving him more space, since I didn't want to tire him out by visiting too often. He called me up out of the blue to give me that letter for you. But…I did talk to him a bit sometime before that, and he told me he wondered whether you'd become a film director one day." Aoi sounded reluctant, even though there was no need for her to feel sorry or guilty about it.

"Really? He said that…?"

"I told him it wasn't that easy, so who knew. I didn't know if that was even a goal of yours, and besides, it's not the sort of profession you can just choose for yourself. Luck plays a big part in it, too. And then there are directors like me, who get by purely on luck and good scripts without any real talent."

Aoi gave a self-deprecating laugh, but I knew that if you looked up her name online, she'd come up as one of the leading young directors of her generation. There was no trace of jealousy or frustration in me; I honestly felt proud of her as a friend.

"That's not true. You do have the talent and the skills, and it's really impressive what you've achieved. You went pro through sheer hard work. You should be proud of that."

"I...only made it because I'm not picky. I know what kind of movies the general public likes, so that's what I aim for. I can't make something truly beautiful like you can, Tsubasa."

"I don't believe a word you're saying. You're just tired, aren't you?"

"Maybe. Sorry."

When I asked what she'd been up to lately, Aoi told me that she was working on a few projects as director while also subbing in as a scriptwriter on a commercial film. Ena had also been cast in one of her projects. I felt really happy for the opportunities they were getting, so I made sure to show her how excited I was. Aoi grinned back at me, and we chatted and joked like we were back in high school.

When it was time to go, we promised to meet up again soon. Just as we were about to go our separate ways outside the café, Aoi asked me a question.

"By the way, Tsubasa—do you ever think about making films again?"

I didn't answer at first. After a while, I said, "I don't know... I'm not even sure why I used to make movies anymore. What's the point?" A fake smile was plastered on my face, though I knew I didn't need to put on any sort of act in front of Aoi. I couldn't meet her eyes.

"There's no point to anything. Meaning is what you make it," she said calmly.

"What?" I looked at her, startled. Her steady gaze was fixed on me.

"A film director I like used to say that. When I heard those words, I thought, 'Wow, I'll never be as good as her. And that feeling hasn't changed, even now.'"

That was something I'd told Ena in my second year at junior high—Aoi was quoting my own words back at me. It's not like I had my own philosophy or anything, but I'd simply said what came into my head. When I was still directing movies, I used to believe that those spontaneous things—things that came out of someone by chance, without planning and forethought—could tell you everything there was to know about that person.

Each day slipped by as if I was being carried along by a conveyor belt. It was Monday again, and I went back to my usual routine. As I went about my ordinary days, a few snippets of conversation kept echoing in my head:

"He was wondering whether you'd become a film director one day."

"Do you ever think about making films again?"

I *thought* I'd put enough distance between my current self and my old aspirations. I shouldn't have felt any yearning to go back to the film industry, nor any need to turn my back on it. I even watched commercial blockbusters.

Yet deep down I still had it—that desire to live in the world of cinema.

At the same time, my mind kept turning back to Makoto's words. Did he want me to become a director, too?

As if in search of the answer, I watched Makoto's movie over and over again. It was a collage, lovingly assembled, of playful, ordinary scenes of a couple's time together. At first that was all I saw in it, but the more I watched it, the more I began to notice something else.

Back then, my head had been chock-full of movies. They were all I talked about.

"*What kind of movies do you like, Makoto?*" I asked in one clip.

"*With movies, there's intention and meaning to every single shot. That's what I love about it,*" I said in another scene.

And then there was the last line of the movie: "*Yeah. A lot.*"

One day, it dawned on me—I thought I had an inkling of the message that Makoto had breathed into his movie. It came together with Makoto's words that Aoi had conveyed, and the meaning of his film began to unfold within me.

Could it be that this movie was meant to spur me on? To give me an encouraging push in case I'd tried to become a film director but couldn't make it? In case I'd given up on cinema? To remind me of my love for the art, ten years ago?

I left that day and took advantage of the weekend to go back to my hometown for the first time in a while. It had been several years since I last visited Makoto's grave.

I stared at the stone, asking, "What are you really trying to tell me?" But, of course, he didn't reply. The living couldn't speak to the dead, and the dead couldn't speak to the living.

After that, I went to Makoto's house, taking his letter with me. I'd gotten in touch with his parents beforehand, and they welcomed me with open arms. The main reason I'd come back was to show them what Makoto had written.

Once we were all sitting in the living room, I handed them the letter. They leaned closer, reading it together with rapt attention. His mom teared up, and when she'd finished reading it, she dabbed at her eyes and said with a gentle smile, "I was surprised to hear from you at first—I'm so grateful you came all this way to share this with us. Thank you so much. It must've been a bother for Hayami, too."

I slowly shook my head. I knew Aoi well; she would never think anything she did for her friends or clubmates was a bother.

I'd also brought the memory card with Makoto's movie. But when his parents found out that it was something he'd made especially for me, they told me it wasn't for them to see and that they would be content if I kept it to myself as a special memory.

Then Makoto's mom got up and left the room. She came back with two notebooks left behind by Makoto.

"Please take them with you, if you'd like—maybe they'll be useful for your movies." She held them out to me. She must have thought I'd come to pick them up, just like Makoto had written in his letter.

I was about to say, "Actually, I don't make movies anymore," but when I saw their warm smiles, the words got stuck in my throat. I didn't want to burden them by staying too long, so I thanked them again and excused myself before teatime.

I'd promised my parents I'd have dinner with them at home. I thought of going straight there, but since I still had some time, I decided to wander around town for a bit. I hadn't done that in years.

I walked to the park where I'd had my first date with Makoto and through the familiar streets where we'd walked together. The general feel of the place was still the same, but in fact, a lot of things had changed since those days. Ten years was a long time.

I toyed with the idea of going to the zoo—the one that had come up in Makoto's movie—but the train line near my parents' house wouldn't take me there, and I didn't have that much time. So I visited our old school instead.

Though it was a Saturday, the people at the school kindly let me in when they found out that I was an alum, and I was allowed to walk around the school building as I liked. Memories came flooding back to me from every nook and cranny. *Teenage me would've whipped out my phone and started filming everything*, I thought as I walked past the nurse's office and the roofed walkway that led to the gym. When the sun began to set, I thanked the school staff and left.

The last thing I did was walk to the park near the school. The bench where Makoto and I had sat side by side that winter evening so long ago—it was still there, unchanged. I sat down on it and, after some hesitation, took out Makoto's notebooks from my bag.

There was a Post-it note taped to the cover: *"If Tsubasa Minami comes to visit with a letter, please give these notebooks to her. I'd appreciate it if no one looks inside until then."*

I carefully opened the first notebook.

In it, I found a record of Makoto's struggles in a kind of diary—how he'd spent his days since he discovered his terminal illness, how he'd felt, things couldn't reveal even to his parents, including his darkest thoughts. At times his writing was neat and delicate. At other times, he seemed to be spilling out his thoughts in a frenzy.

The diary entries became less frequent after a certain point, probably when he started coming to the filmmaking club. But the regular entries began again in August.

8/9

My temperature was low again today. It scared me, so I thought I'd try to write about it here.

I'm back in my room at the hospital. I hate it here. I don't want to be here anymore.

I want to see Minami. I want to go back to our clubroom.

It's really scary just waiting to black out.

I tell myself over and over that I know the drill by now, but I can't fool myself. I really hope I'll get used to it soon.

Apparently, Makoto had written this on one of the days when he'd worried about losing consciousness. He was venting all of his anxieties on the page. When I came across my name in his writing, tears pricked my eyes.

On another day, I saw Aoi's name, too.

8/21

Hayami said she'd help me. I used to think she was scary, but turns out I was wrong.

Everyone's kind. We're all kind at heart.

The world is so full of kind people, and I don't want to leave. I want to keep living.

I want to meet more people. I want to be a part of their lives and let them be a part of mine.

To this disease of mine: Please don't get in my way.

Please let my heart stay kind, too. Always.

I didn't know about all the inner turmoil that Makoto must have been fighting against. But one thing I can say with certainty is that Makoto was always kind, whatever the circumstances. His illness never took that away from him.

Don't worry—in my eyes, you were the kindest person in the world.

A shiver ran through me, even though it wasn't cold. It was hard to keep reading. With a heavy heart, I turned to another page.

9/14

I can't stand it anymore, so I'm going to vomit everything out here.

I hate this disease.

There's no use hating it. It's fate. Just accept it.

But there's no way I can just let everything go like that.

I want to talk with Minami about the future.

I want to laugh with her over all kinds of dumb things.

I want to waste time without a care in the world.

The zoo was fun. I want to go on a weekend date again. I wish I could make promises.

10/23

I'm an idiot. I'm fed up with myself. Even though I'd promised Minami I'd be there, I passed out this morning. I ended up causing a lot of people trouble.

I'm sorry, Hayami. I'm sorry, Hayami's mom.

Mom, Dad, I'm sorry. I don't want to make you sad, so I'm only apologizing here, but I hope you'll forgive me.

11/29

I quit the club today. I said good-bye to everyone.

I said good-bye to Minami.

I wanted to hug her tight. I felt like crying, being selfish, and screaming, "I want to stay with you right up until the end."

I'm such an idiot. I should've just done that.

Hayami told me not to give up on my happiness. She was right.

I should've done what I wanted.

I'm going to die, so what does it matter? I should've said that to fate, to God. I should've looked them all in the eye and said, "What do I care about what happens after I'm dead? That's not my problem."

I'm such an idiot. I can't believe how stupid I am.

But it's OK. Even if I can't hold her. Even if I can't stay with her till the end.

That's OK. That's how it should be.

I hope Minami will be happy in the future. I hope her dreams come true.

And then, up in heaven, I'll walk over to this cruel God and say: "See how amazing my girlfriend is?"

I'll never let you take her, though. I won't let you bring her up here until she's old and gray.

2/15

No pain, no bitterness, no regrets.

I feel light.

I haven't had to scribble in this dark notebook as much since I started spending time with Minami.

But having this notebook helped me for sure. Thank you.

That was the final entry of Makoto's diary. February 15—it was several weeks after the "Christmas Eve" party, the night we saw each other for the last time. The next time he lost consciousness after that, Makoto's parents had adjusted the date on his phone back, so the date on this entry must be the real one.

I was so glad to read, in his own words, that he'd really had no regrets at the end.

There was more in the notebook, though—a message addressed to me after the last diary entry:

Dear Tsubasa Minami,

I was actually going to throw out this notebook. But when I look back at it now, it's a record of the truth about my life and an account of how one person really felt after finding out he was dying.

I thought that maybe, in ten years, when you've moved on and I've become just a memory from your past, I might pass this on to you so you can make use of it. So I've decided to leave it behind.

I guess you know by now that I'm dead.

I'm sorry I lied to you. And more than anything else, thank you. Thank you for everything.

I used to think I'd be alone until I died. That I was just going to live out my life in quiet isolation.

But right now, I'm not alone. I'm surrounded by photos, videos, and memories.

This would never have happened if not for you, Tsubasa. Thank you with all my heart.

I better wrap this up—I shouldn't keep rambling on forever.

I've been thinking for a long time about what would be good to leave behind as my last words. I haven't come up with anything yet, though, so I'll think of something and write it down before I die.

I hope you won't laugh, even if it's not such a great message.

I couldn't move for a moment—his last words were here, in this notebook.

My feelings were so fragile now that a tiny nudge would have sent me bursting into tears. But I steadied my breathing and looked down at the last sentence on the page.

A nostalgic breeze swept through my heart—gentle, warm, and somehow ephemeral…

I am, and always will be, your biggest fan.

At some point, the sun had gone down, and the light from the street lamp was falling across the page. Not for the first time in this spot, raindrops pattered down. I wiped away my tears so that the notebook wouldn't get wet. But the rain wouldn't stop; it kept pouring from my eyes.

I waited until I calmed down. I dried my face and hands with a handkerchief, sniffling. Then, I picked up the other notebook Makoto's mom had given me.

Apparently, this one had been for writing down things Makoto wanted to do before he died. I opened the notebook filled with his wishes.

Tell Tsubasa Minami how I feel

* * *

I found my name on the page. This was probably the starting point of everything between us. Closing my eyes and listening, I felt as if I could hear Makoto's gentle voice. His face from that particular day came back to me, how he looked nervous as he told me, "*To tell you the truth, I like you, Minami. Uh, but it's not like I want to go out with you—more like I'm a fan...*"

Feelings welled up inside me, and tears once again traced my cheeks. When I opened my eyes, stars were glimmering above me across the deep night sky. If someone who knew more about stars than I did looked up at them, the constellations would have told silent stories.

The past drew me in. I remembered what Makoto had told me that day, right in the same spot I sat now.

How the stars we see in the sky are the light from the past.

Gazing at the glittering night sky, I thought long and hard about the meaning behind Makoto's movie. What had he meant with it? What message did he want to give me?

I thought I would know for sure if I read his letter and notebooks, but I still had no definite answer.

Maybe it wasn't meant to have a specific meaning in the first place. But if that was true...was I allowed to find my own meaning, in the way of a true cinephile? Could I think of his movie as Makoto cheering me on to light that fire in me?

If the light from the stars shone on us from all those years in the past, could I think of Makoto's movie as a glimmering star just for me—a light that reached me after ten years—as his final gift? So that I wouldn't forget the part of myself that was in love with cinema and forget about the past...?

Before I knew it, tears were streaming down my face again.

It was the first time I'd cried so much. It felt so cathartic. These were tears I could shed only because I'd burned out before I could fulfill my dream—and because now I knew that even if I'd failed once, I could always try again, however many times I wanted.

Sometimes, you live through something that makes you think, *If this were a movie, maybe the credits would roll here*—but life goes on. After all these years, I still see life that way.

For me, that climactic scene was the last night I spent with Makoto. We added splashes of color to the end of Makoto's life. If it had been a movie, the four of us would've watched his car drive off into the distance, and then the credits would've appeared.

Makoto Tsukishima	MAKOTO TSUKISHIMA
Tsubasa Minami	TSUBASA MINAMI
Aoi Hayami	AOI HAYAMI
Ena Toosaki	ENA TOOSAKI
Ichika Nagase	ICHIKA NAGASE
Written by	TSUBASA MINAMI, AOI HAYAMI
Directed by	TSUBASA MINAMI

Fade to black.

After that, people had to go back to reality. They might take something away from the film, but no matter how much they felt like lingering, they had to get up from their seats and return to their daily lives.

I wiped my tears and stood up—it was time I returned to my daily life as well. It was time I started running again toward my dream. With everything I'd been through already, I had nothing to fear. What kept me going, more than anything else, was that when I looked up, there was always a light shining above me—a guiding star that illuminated the way for people who were lost or who'd broken down before achieving their dreams.

But I wasn't lost anymore.

I lived my life in a world in which the credits had already rolled. I began to weave a new story: the story of a woman who strives to fulfill her dream of becoming a professional film director. It went without saying, but the path ahead would be challenging. No life left you unscathed.

I went back into the film industry. I threw myself into working as an assistant director at my old company. Though the people in my life worried about me, I chased after my dream. Over and over again, I stumbled and fell flat on my face. There were times when I couldn't take another step forward, weighed down by fatigue, times I wavered, not knowing what lay beyond.

Despite everything, I kept going. And as long as you keep walking, you'll get somewhere eventually.

My chance came when I was twenty-nine.

The film project that I'd been preparing over several years got picked up, and now I had the funds to make it happen. I shot it with professional actors. Though the distribution was limited to tiny hole-in-the-wall theaters, and it didn't keep running for very long, I was able to bring out my film as a commercial piece.

It wasn't as though my professional directorial debut was met with critical acclaim, but it was still received pretty well. It wasn't a major hit, but people heard about it by word of mouth and came to see it. That was enough for me.

On the last day of the film's run in theaters, I went to a mini theater in Tokyo around sunset and watched the whole story as a member of the audience. I gazed up at the screen as the credits rolled.

A LIGHT FROM THE PAST

Cast and Staff

Makoto Tsukishima	TAKU IIJIMA
Tsubasa Minami	CHIHIRO HAZUKI
Aoi Hayami	SAKI NARUSE
Ena Toosaki	SHIHO NOMURA
Ichika Nagase	HINATA SASAKI
School Nurse	ENA TOOSAKI (special guest appearance)
Screenplay by	TSUBASA MINAMI, AOI HAYAMI
Directed by	TSUBASA MINAMI

I had turned Makoto's life into a movie. It was a project I'd developed, with permission from Makoto's parents, when I'd seen a call for submissions for films based on true stories.

It was Makoto who motivated me to take another shot at filmmaking. So naturally, I wanted my first professional piece as a director to be a film about him. This was my way of thanking him for turning *me* into a movie all those years ago, my way of turning Makoto's words in his letter into reality.

Even if you're not in an environment where you can make use of your talent now, I want you to know that you were the best director. You were the best leader of the club and the best partner.

I hope you'll forgive me for writing to you from so far away, but I will always be wishing for your success, health, and happiness.

I'd read that letter so many times by now. I cast my mind back to the rest of Makoto's message, in which he'd left me a gift—the gift of his own life and his secret.

I wasn't sure whether I should write the rest of this letter, but I've made up my mind to tell you now.

When we were in senior high, there was something I was hiding from you.

If you're still making movies now, and if you ever find yourself in need of ideas or a story, please feel free to use my secret.

If you take this letter to my parents, they should tell you the whole story.

I'm embarrassed to show you, but there's also a notebook where I used to write down how I felt in my darkest moments. The contents might be pretty banal, but if it's useful to you in some way, even just a little, that would make me happy.

Even though I could only be a part of the club for about half a year, and I was away a lot of that time, I loved seeing how excited you got when you were making films. I will always treasure those times with you when we made movies together.

Thank you from the bottom of my heart for making my life feel so full.

For me, you were light itself. The light of life and the light of hope.

Be well. I wish you the very best for the future. Good-bye.

Makoto Tsukishima

The credits came to an end, and the lights went on in the theater. I stayed in my seat until I was the last one in the room.

Eventually, I got up. Just before I stepped out of the theater, I turned around to face the screen and bowed deeply.

Night had fallen outside. The sky stretched overhead with a depth that reminded me of that night so long ago.

A small group was waiting for me in front of the theater: Ena, who'd made a cameo appearance as the school nurse in my movie; Ichika, who'd often brought snacks and refreshments for us while we were filming and also appeared as an extra; and Aoi, who'd written the screenplay with me.

"Welcome back," Aoi said, grinning. "You're my hero."

"They say a hero always arrives late… Is this you trying to tell me I'm late?" I joked, trying to hide the fact that I was tearing up.

"Well, you've got a point. You did take a hell of a long time to get here," Aoi replied, catching my drift. I grinned back at her.

"Tell me about it. I was getting tired of waiting," Ena chimed in, lightening the mood. "You know I've been waiting for ages to get cast in your movie, Tsubasa."

But Ena had never been good at holding back her tears. She

was honest with her own feelings; she had wept openly when she'd reunited with her mom all those years ago, as well as at Makoto's funeral. Even now, there was the faint gleam of tears in her eyes.

"I'm really glad, though," Ichika said. She had grown up into a calm, compassionate woman. "You look full of life these days. Back when you quit your job and switched careers, you looked pretty worn out."

I gazed at my friend, as small and caring as ever. "You haven't changed a bit, Ichika—you've always been so kindhearted. And you're even great at cooking."

"Huh? What're you bringing that up for now, Tsubasa?" she asked.

"Oh, nothing. It's just a mystery why you're still single," I said casually.

"E-editors are super busy!" she protested, pouting like a child.

"Sorry, I know."

"Oh, burn!" Ena said with a laugh.

Aoi watched us all with a warm smile.

One story had come to an end, credits had rolled, the screen had faded to black. And after that, life had gone on.

But now, I knew it wasn't quite like that.

Life didn't just go on. Life began anew. It could be cruel at times, but we all had to start a new story even as we held on to our memories of the past.

What kind of story will I start now? I wondered as the four of us walked down the street. *What kind of film will I make?*

Since it was the last day of my film's run in theaters, the three of them had invited me out for dinner as a little celebration. On the way to the restaurant, I looked up at the stars glimmering across the sky. I gazed at the shimmering lights in silence.

I was sure that I would stumble a lot throughout the course of my life. There would be times when I hit a wall or shed tears of frustration. Even so, I could say with confidence that I would be all right, come what may.

Because the stars would always be there for me in the night sky. Because I had countless memories that I would always hold dear in my heart.

The light from the past would shine brightly in the sky and inside me, never to be extinguished.

Afterword

I first had the idea for this novel when I was invited to watch the filming process on the set of *Even If This Love Disappears from the World Tonight*. So many people were working together to shoot one scene, and you could cut the tension with a knife; everyone held their breath while the camera was rolling. Then, at the sound of the director's call to cut, the set would burst to life again. I was impressed by the whole operation, and I started thinking about writing a story related to movies.

Sometimes, you live through something that makes you think, *If this were a movie, maybe the credits would roll here—* but life goes on.

Having one of my novels adapted into a film had always been one of my goals. I'd imagined the credits rolling after it actually came true, and how I would live out the rest of my life. But then I realized that life doesn't simply go on—it starts anew. You have to keep starting over.

All sorts of things can happen in a person's life to make them lose their way in their own story—losing something, for instance, or giving up on something. Some people can start a new story straightaway—and of course, there are some who can't. However, I believe that everyone can begin afresh and embark on a new journey no matter how painful it is or how long it takes—to live a new chapter in their lives while treasuring all their past memories inside them.

Now for some words of thanks.

Life brings people together, just as it carries people apart. My editor changed while I was writing this novel. I am truly indebted to my old editor for guiding me ever since my debut as a writer. I am also incredibly grateful to my new editor for lending me their support and wisdom, even after they took over partway through. I look forward to our continued collaboration.

To Koichi, who created the cover art for this book—thank you, as always, for your beautiful work. We finally met at the premiere. I'll never forget that day, when I watched the finished film next to you, with Fukumoto in the seat in front of us. I look forward to our next meeting.

Finally, thank you to everyone who picked up this book.

I always thank my readers, and not once have I written these words of gratitude without actually bowing my head in thanks at my desk. This time is no exception.

Thank you very much for reading this novel. I would thank each and every one of you in person if I could, but since that's impossible, please accept this as my sincere gratitude.

I hope we meet again somewhere in the future.

Misaki Ichijo